HOLLY POINTE & MISTLETOE

CINDY KIRK

Copyright © Cynthia Rutledge 2018

All rights reserved.

No part of this book may be reproduced in any form or by any electronic or mechanical means, including information storage and retrieval systems, without written permission from the author, except for the use of brief quotations in a book review.

This is a work of fiction. Names, characters, places and incidents are products of the author's imagination or are used fictitiously. Any resemblance to actual events, locales, organizations, or persons, living or dead, is entirely coincidental.

CHAPTER ONE

Eight days ago Stella Carpenter swore off caffeine. This morning she instructed the barista to add a second shot of expresso to the grande coffee she ordered.

She'd quit because she didn't like being dependent on anything. Or anyone. Excluding, of course, her good friend Tasha, on whose couch she was currently crashing every night.

Shifting impatiently from one foot to the other, Stella pulled out her phone. She had time to wait. Being summoned to your former boss's office demanded a little liquid courage.

The middle-aged man behind the counter held up a cup and cast a glance in her direction. "Stella."

Until she'd been reduced in force from the *Miami Sun Times* three months ago, Stella had visited this particular freestanding kiosk daily. Eduardo had been a barista at this stand since she'd started her job two years earlier.

"It's good to see you again." His voice was as warm as the morning sun. "Are you working out of the office today?"

Her heart lurched as she lifted the cup from his hand. "Just came in for a meeting."

Stella stuffed a bill into the tip jar, then headed in the direction of the beautiful art deco building housing the *Miami Sun Times*.

Even though it was nine a.m. and almost Thanksgiving, heat already rose from the sidewalk, and the hairs on the back of her neck were moist. In southern Florida, there was no hoping for snow on Christmas. When her parents had relocated the family to Miami when she was in her teens, she'd quickly discovered that hot and sunny was the forecast no matter what the time of year.

Stella's heels clicked on the glittering sidewalk as she entered the building that housed the city's largest newspaper. For the past two years, she'd been a reporter and—in a pinch—a photographer and videographer.

Now her job and those of many she'd worked with were gone, replaced by freelancers.

Cool air rushed over her as she crossed the marble floor to the security station. Once cleared, she took the ornate bronze-decorated elevator to the office of Jane Myers, the newspaper's managing editor. The early-morning text from Jane had sent Stella's hopes soaring.

Freelancing had fallen short of paying her bills. It was at times like this that Stella wished her parents hadn't put her inheritance in a trust she couldn't touch until she turned thirty.

She'd been lucky her lease was up. Her first action had been to let her apartment go. The past three months, she'd been bunking on Tasha's couch.

Tasha's roommate had started to grumble about having another person in their small apartment. Last week Tasha had brought down the hammer, telling her she needed to be out by the first of the year. Stella understood, though she wasn't sure where she would go.

Thankfully, she had over a month to figure it out.

When the elevator doors opened onto the fifth floor, Stella stepped out and paused for a long drink of the steaming coffee.

Larissa, Jane's personal assistant, barely gave Stella time to push back her perspiration-dampened hair before ushering her into Jane's office.

Her boss's dark-brown hair was pulled back into a severe chignon. The pale-blue eyes Jane fixed on Stella were firm and direct. The red "cheaters" hanging by an eyeglass chain around her neck added a bit of whimsy, but there was nothing whimsical about Jane's no-nonsense gaze.

"Thank you for coming in on such short notice." Jane rounded the desk. Her stern expression softened infinitesimally.

Stella relaxed when Jane finally smiled but didn't let down her guard. "I was surprised to hear from you."

Jane leaned against her desk as if trying to ease the formal air of the meeting.

"It's been a while since we've talked." Jane inclined her head. "Do you have plans for Christmas?"

Whatever the reason for this unexpected meeting with the newspaper's managing editor, Stella knew it wasn't to discuss holiday plans. She found it odd that Jane was asking about Christmas when they'd yet to get through Thanksgiving. "No plans. I'm hoping to pick up a freelance job or two."

Something flickered in Jane's eyes, an emotion Stella couldn't interpret. Another woman might have launched into a speech about a balanced life. Those words would never make it past Jane's lips. No one was more of a workaholic than her former boss.

Stella inclined her head. "What about you?"

"I plan to have a few friends over. An eclectic group of Miami's movers and shakers. These men and women know where all the bodies are buried. Figuratively speaking, of course. I'm hoping to dig up some juicy kernels."

The comment didn't surprise Stella. Last year Jane had been brought in to shore up the *Sun Times*' bottom line. Immediately after her arrival, the paper began focusing on sensationalized news instead of serious, multisource journalism.

Stella hadn't liked the switch. She would always be grateful she'd been able to work for several newspapers that valued high-quality journalism.

To be fair, the *Miami Sun Times* wasn't the only paper doing what it could to set itself apart. Most were doing all they could to attract readers and increase sales.

"So, Stella. You said you're looking to pick up more freelance jobs before the holidays. Does that mean work has been slow?"

Her assessment caught Stella off guard, as did her expression, which struck Stella as something between concerned sibling and hungry wolf. "Well, no, not exactly—"

"Because I know how hard freelancing can be. Especially with *so many* journalists competing for work."

Hm, Stella thought, *wolf it is.*

"I have an assignment for you." Jane straightened, her tone all business. "It will involve travel and approximately six weeks away from Miami. All expenses will be covered."

Before Stella could comment or ask any questions, Jane continued. "If the end product meets with my satisfaction, there may be a staff position available for you starting the first of the year."

Stella kept her expression impassive despite the urge to jump up and do a happy dance. A chance to be back on staff was a dream come true. She'd spent the past three months sending out resumes all over the country but had yet to receive a single bite. "I'm intrigued. Tell me more."

Jane gestured to the guest chair before rounding the large modern desk to sit behind it, formalizing the interaction. Her boss folded her long, elegant fingers and rested them on the shiny onyx.

"Holly Pointe, Vermont, was recently recognized as the Christmas capital of the USA. Not just commercially, the people have been rated as the kindest in the country. The 'capital of Christmas kindness.'" Jane's sarcastic tone told Stella just what she thought of the honor. "I'm interested in doing a feature on the town."

Stella experienced a surge of excitement. This could be fun. Since her parents had passed away, holidays had been especially lonely times. Tasha was spending Christmas with her family in Jacksonville. She'd invited Stella to come along, but she'd gone the previous year and had felt like a fifth wheel. "I love heartwarming features, especially at holiday time."

"I don't believe you understand." Jane leaned forward, her eyes cool and assessing. "I'm not interested in heartwarming fluff. Positivity doesn't sell nearly as well as drama. I want an exposé of the town's underbelly. Whatever dirt there is, I wanted it dug up and in my inbox by December 24."

Stella hesitated. An infinitesimal second, but enough for Jane's eyes to turn to ice.

"I'm trying to help you, Stella, so I offered this to you first. But if this isn't your cup of tea, it's no problem. Juliet is also interested in coming back full time. I'm sure she'd be happy to take this on if you pass."

Though Jane offered no promises, Stella knew that if she delivered, she'd get her job back. Something told her that if she didn't—or if she turned down this assignment—she could also kiss any freelance work good-bye.

"I won't disappoint you." Stella met Jane's steady gaze. "When do I start?"

The day before Thanksgiving, Stella left for Holly Pointe. Instead of flying, she decided to drive the seventeen hundred miles to northern Vermont.

Traffic was heavy, but once Thanksgiving hit, the congestion eased significantly. Everyone had likely reached their destinations and were enjoying turkey and cranberry salad with their relatives.

That night, Stella ordered room service and researched Holly Pointe. She found numerous articles extolling the warmth and friendliness of the town's inhabitants as well as all its wonderful traditions.

She didn't have traditions. Not anymore.

Two years earlier, on a long holiday weekend just like this one, her parents had been killed by a drunk driver. Stella had been living in Gainesville at the time, working for the newspaper there, and her parents had driven up to celebrate Thanksgiving with her. They'd all been in high spirits because earlier that week she'd accepted a position with the *Sun Times*.

"We'll be able to celebrate Christmas in Miami," her mother had happily declared as she'd slipped into the car after another hug.

Stella could still see their smiles and her father's thumbs-up. By the time the sun had set that evening, they were dead.

It had been her work at the *Sun Times* that had gotten her through those hard days after the loss. Then she'd lost that, too.

Stella closed her laptop and flipped off the lights. Just like she had back then, she would focus on the work. Soon she would have her job and her life back.

The next morning, Stella completed her drive to Holly Pointe, arriving just before lunchtime. She snagged a parking space on Birch Road, which, according to Google Maps was the town's main street and the sight of last week's Snowman Parade. Stella stepped from her SUV. Her eyes were immediately drawn to the imposing courthouse at the far end of the roadway.

Built of brick and stone, the late nineteenth-century structure reminded Stella of a church more than a municipal building. It had rounded arches, endless gingerbread accents, and even a bell tower.

The buildings flanking both sides of the historic downtown district were equally impressive. Quaint storefronts boasted awnings and holiday lights. Brightly colored street-pole banners already touted the upcoming Christmas season.

Of course, for all Stella knew, those banners could be up year-round, considering that she was now in the Christmas capital of the USA. The thought made her smile as she reached the curb and turned in the direction of the coffee shop half a block away.

Once she had pulled into the parking space, she'd taken off her driving shoes and slipped on red heels. The way she saw it, there was no reason to be unfashionable simply because she was now in the boonies.

Stella strode quickly, eager for that first jolt of caffeine. She never saw the patch of ice. One second she was moving swiftly, enjoying the crisp air, the next her arms were whipping the air like windmills. Despite her excellent sense of balance, she could feel herself falling.

Please don't let me break anything, was her last thought before strong arms wrapped around her.

Once she was steady, the man immediately released his hold. But she'd been close in his arms long enough to catch the enticing aroma of his cologne. The woodsy, masculine scent of sandalwood and cedar fit this man to perfection.

At five foot ten, Stella considered herself tall, especially with three-inch heels. This guy topped her by a good two inches. Like her, he looked to be closing in on thirty. He wore a well-cut wool coat and had eyes the color of Venezuelan chocolate.

She realized she must have been staring when his gaze turned puzzled.

"Are you okay?" His voice held a hint of the New England accent she'd been prepared to hear.

"I am now, thanks to you." Stella extended her hand. "Stella Carpenter."

"Sam Johnson." He gave her hand a perfunctory shake.

This time it was his turn to stare, but not at her. His gaze dropped to the small patch of ice on the otherwise-clear sidewalk. Dark brows pulled together in a frown.

A man striding down the sidewalk stopped when Sam held up a hand and motioned him over.

"Something wrong, Sam?"

Stella noticed the man's name—Nathan—was stitched on his coat, just below the City of Holly Pointe logo.

Sam gestured with his head toward Stella then pointed to the ice. "Nate, this woman slipped and nearly fell. Can you please make sure this is taken care of right away?"

"I'll do it myself," Nate assured him.

"Thanks. I appreciate it." Sam's gaze returned to her, and Stella waited for him to continue the conversation. Perhaps ask where she was from and what she was doing in Holly Pointe.

Before he could say a word, his phone buzzed. He pulled it from his pocket and read the message.

"You're okay?" he asked again.

"I am."

He smiled. "Have a good day."

Puzzled, she watched him leave. He hadn't flirted, not one little bit. She hadn't noticed a wedding ring on his hand, not that the absence of the symbol guaranteed that the guy wasn't married. Stella thought of her ex-boyfriend Tony and others of his ilk who frequented the South Beach clubs.

She'd learned early on the necessity of "trust but verify."

Nate was now crouched low, scraping the last bit of ice from the concrete with what looked to be a putty knife. He, too, had obviously dismissed her.

After scanning the crowded sidewalk ahead for any other hidden dangers, Stella resumed her trek. On her way to the coffee shop, she passed Dough See Dough, a bakery that emitted the most amazing scents, and Memory Lane, an antique store that boasted a display of vintage Christmas toys for children.

Across the street sat Rosie's Diner, and since it was lunchtime, the place was packed.

Stella reached the Busy Bean just as a group of college-age men and women spilled out onto the sidewalk, laughing and talking. The last of the herd, a gangly boy in his early twenties, held the door open for her.

Smiling her thanks, Stella stepped into the beehive, savoring the warmth and the smell of cinnamon and coffee.

The place was already decorated for Christmas, with everything from coffee-bean wreaths and ornaments hanging from ribbons wrapped around a candy-cane rod in the window to a cookies-and-coffee-for-Santa display.

Stella spotted the man who'd saved her from a fall sitting with a gorgeous woman with a sleek mane of blonde hair. His total focus was on the blonde and their conversation.

At least, she thought, *he could smile.* She hadn't seen a hint of it when he'd been with her. Shoving Sam Johnson from her thoughts, Stella studied the board behind the counter.

When she reached the front of the line, she added a scone to her coffee order. Several minutes later, she carried the mug and the scone to an empty table in the middle of the dining area.

Her plan was to eat and drink slowly and listen to the conversations of those seated at nearby tables. To make it appear as if she weren't eavesdropping, Stella pretended to scroll through her email.

"I asked Dakota to come home with me for Thanksgiving." The young woman—she couldn't have been more than twenty—heaved a heavy sigh. "She turned me down."

"Her loss." The friend with the pierced eyebrow lifted her cup. "More men for us."

Or, "more boys," Stella thought with a smile. While she'd keep one ear open in case they started talking about something interesting, the girls appeared too young to give her the type of information she sought.

Instead, Stella tuned her ears to a nearby four-top where three women who appeared close to her own age chatted.

"It *is* a problem." The redhead sighed. "It's not like you can just pull a social media photographer out of thin air."

"Especially not at the last minute," the brunette with startling green eyes confirmed.

"Have you told Lucy yet?" The quiet, thoughtful way the woman with the soft-brown hair spoke reminded Stella of Tasha. That was where the similarity to her BFF ended.

Tasha was bold and vibrant, with a hint of the devil behind her impudent blue eyes. This woman wore glasses and very little makeup, and her hair lay coiled at her neck in an intricate braid.

Oddly, the understated look made Stella take a second glance. Or maybe it was the confidence that told everyone, including Stella, that this woman was in charge.

"I haven't mentioned any of this to Lucy. When she walked in, I was on the phone with Kinsley. She was calling from the ER." The brunette sighed. "How do you fall and break *both* elbows? I mean, one would be bad enough."

"I feel so sorry for her." The redhead's voice deepened with sympathy. "Not only because she's hurting, but she was really looking forward to tackling this job."

"We'll find someone else." The one Stella had dubbed the leader spoke with more confidence than she likely felt.

"Santa arrives tomorrow," the redhead announced.

"I know when he arrives, Melinda." The leader's tone held the merest hint of exasperation. "If I have to, I'll take the pictures myself."

The other two women's instant laughter was so contagious, Stella nearly laughed with them. She stuffed a piece of the lemon-ricotta scone into her mouth and fought the urge.

"Faith, you are a wonderful person but a horrible photographer." Melinda's eyes danced.

"I am n—"

"Remember last summer when you took the pictures of the HPBO picnic? You cut off everyone's heads." The brunette tossed her thick mane of sable hair and lifted her head. "While it's generous of you to volunteer, I'd vote for someone in the high school photography club before you."

Stella's blood began to hum. Social media photographer. The perfect job had just fallen—well, almost fallen—into her lap. All she had to do was be bold.

Not a problem for an investigative reporter.

She studied the table where the three women continued their discussion and patiently waited for a break in the conversation. After several minutes, she shifted in her seat.

They were finishing up their drinks but still chattering. She'd have to interrupt or risk losing the opportunity. And losing this opportunity could mean losing her chance at getting her old job back.

"Pardon me." Stella leaned forward, her body bridging the distance between her and the one called Melinda. "I didn't mean to listen, but I heard you say something about being in the market for a social media photographer."

Three heads swiveled in her direction, and conversation at the table abruptly ceased.

Keeping a bright smile on her lips, Stella continued. "Up until three months ago I was a staff reporter for the *Miami Sun Times*. I also filled in as a photographer and videographer when necessary."

The women exchanged glances. Finally, the brunette, whose name she still hadn't heard, spoke. "I don't believe I've seen you around town before. Are you here on vacation?"

Stella gestured with one hand to the empty chair at their table. "Would you mind if I join you?"

"No." The leader, Faith, spoke now. "Please do."

The scone was history, but there was still some coffee in her cup. Stella picked up the mug and changed tables. "Let me start with basics. My name is Stella Carpenter."

"I'm Faith Pierson." The woman pointed to the brunette, then the redhead. "Kate Sullivan and Melinda Kelly."

When no one said anything more, Stella realized that the bases were loaded. She was up at bat and needed to hit this one out of the park.

Out of the corner of her eye, she caught the dark-haired man eyeing her with a decidedly puzzled expression.

She ignored him. He didn't matter.

Stella was confident and primed to hit a home run.

CHAPTER TWO

"Before we discuss the position, tell me what brings you to Holly Pointe." Faith took charge of the conversation before Stella had a chance to launch into her "hire me" spiel.

On the long drive to northern Vermont, Stella had given much consideration to how she would explain her presence in the Christmas capital. As she preferred not to lie unless absolutely necessary, somewhere in Connecticut she'd decided to keep blatant falsehoods to a minimum.

"I lost my job with the *Miami Sun Times* in October. 'Reduced in force' is the technical term. The bottom line is I came to work one Friday and was told I no longer had a job."

Sympathy washed across Melinda's freckled face. "I had something similar happen to me a couple weeks ago at my job in Burlington. I only just got back to town."

"What have you been doing since?" This time it was Kate who directed the question at Stella.

"Freelancing. Waitressing. Sleeping on my friend's sofa." Stella's lips twisted in a wry smile. "Anything to pay the bills."

"What brought you to Holly Pointe?" Faith's brown eyes might remind Stella of a sweet Spaniel, but the look in those eyes were Pit Bull sharp. "When I'm short of money, travel isn't usually on my to-do list."

"I was an only child. Despite living in Florida, my parents loved to ski. As did I." Stella's lips curved for a second, caught up in the memories. "Each year we'd go somewhere new; Jackson Hole, Snowbird, Alta, Vail, we skied them all."

When Kate checked the time on her phone, Stella pulled her thoughts together and pushed ahead. "Our first ski trip to Vermont was to Jay Peak."

Stella had not only done her research on the resort just down the road from Holly Pointe, she'd actually skied there with her parents. "We came specifically for the backcountry skiing and enjoyed it so much we talked about returning. Then my parents were killed. They died in a car accident right after Thanksgiving two years ago."

"Oh." Melinda inhaled sharply, a hand moving to her throat.

"I'm so sorry for your loss." Faith's words were as smooth and comforting as the hand she briefly laid on Stella's.

"I can't imagine how hard that was for you." Kate's green eyes shimmered with sympathy.

Stella couldn't hide the tears that stung her eyes. "My friend wants me off her couch. There's nothing holding me in Miami, not anymore. I read about Holly Pointe being named the Christmas capital of the USA. If any place can cheer me up, it will be here."

Faith tilted her head. "How long will you be staying?"

"At least until the first of the year." Stella lifted one shoulder and let it drop. "Then I'll see."

"We'll need to check references." Faith gentled her tone. "With the rise in the importance of social media, we need to make sure you're as savvy as you say. Not to mention, in this position you'll have contact with not only adults but children as well."

"I understand." Stella rummaged through her bag. "I can give you the number of the paper's managing editor."

"Not necessary." After a few taps of her phone, Faith glanced up, a question in her eyes. "Jane Myers? Managing editor?"

"That's her." Faith's thoroughness made Stella extra glad she'd stuck close to the truth. Jane would give her a stellar reference. Not only that, the call would let Jane know that Stella had jumped into the assignment with both feet.

She could almost see the ball flying through the air on its way out of the park.

Stella glanced around the immaculate but simply furnished efficiency apartment. Located above the coffee shop, it boasted a tiny bathroom, a galley kitchen, and a living room with a Murphy bed.

In short, the place met her needs perfectly.

When she mentioned that she had just arrived and had yet to secure a place to live, Kate had waved over the bakery owner, Norma Douglas.

Norma was short and rotund with white hair, a round face, and a ready smile. She ran through the terms of the month-to-month rental with the efficiency of a teacher laying down the ground rules for a pupil on the first day of school.

She'd left out only one thing.

Stella reached into her purse. "How much of a deposit will you need?"

Norma waved an airy hand. "Katie vouched for you. That's good enough for me."

Kate, Stella had learned on the five-second tour of the apartment, was Norma's niece.

"I promise I'll take good care of the place," Stella assured Norma. "I'm long past the wild party stage."

Norma chuckled. "Oh, honey, you'll be lucky to find time to socialize. Handling the social media for this town is going to take most of your time. For the next month, most days you won't know if you're coming or going."

The image that brought to mind was exactly what Stella had wanted. She needed to be out and involved with the community in order to have something more to write about than Santa arriving on a reindeer-pulled sleigh—an event that was scheduled for tomorrow, along with ice-skating at a lake just outside of town.

A kick-off holiday party for the merchants was on tap this evening at the Bromley mansion. The large two-story Queen Anne home with its three-story central tower had caught Stella's eye when she'd driven into town.

She couldn't wait to do an internet search and find some pictures of the inside. The place was bound to be elegant. Thankfully, she'd included some party dresses in her suitcases. Though she hadn't been certain what to pack, her gut had told her that a holiday town would have an abundance of Christmas parties.

Her lips curved into a satisfied smile. Her new position as the social media photographer of Holly Pointe would give her entry into all the parties and events.

"—my husband."

Stella jerked her attention back to Norma and realized that while her mind had been wondering, the woman had continued to speak.

"Kenny is really looking forward to it."

When in doubt, smile and nod. Those words of wisdom had served Stella well over the years.

"Well, anyway, it's been lovely to meet you, Stella." The woman placed a hand on her arm. The kindness in the woman's eyes was so like her mother's that Stella's heart lurched.

With her other hand, Norma pressed an ornate copper key into her hand. "I hope you'll be happy here."

"I'm sure I will." Stella slipped the key into her pocket and followed the woman down the back steps. "I can't wait to get settled."

"Do you need any help with your bags?" Norma asked over her shoulder.

"I just have a couple of suitcases, so no, I'm good." They'd reached the bottom landing where the rich aroma of freshly roasted coffee teased her nostrils. "My car isn't far."

For a second, Norma's gaze dropped to her shoes, and Stella braced herself. But the older woman only smiled. She didn't say a word about the unsuitability of such footwear in this climate.

"Oh, I almost forgot." Norma gave a good-natured laugh and fluttered her hand in the air. "Sometimes I think I'd forget my head if it wasn't attached. You have a parking spot behind the building. Number four is yours."

"Thank you." Though Stella knew Jane wouldn't want to hear it, she'd been bowled over by everyone's kindness toward her.

Of course, it was still early days.

In her years of big-city reporting, Stella had come to realize that everyone had secrets. Most often, they were boring ones. It was juicy ones that Jane wanted her to ferret out during her stay in Holly Pointe.

Tonight Stella would pull out her red dress and take herself and her high heels to the Bromley house. She'd take loads of pictures and do plenty of listening.

She'd be back on staff at the newspaper before the New Year rolled around.

Standing on the sidewalk, Stella paused to take several shots. The lights on the Bromley mansion were understated and elegant. Hanging icicle and grand-cascade tube lights hung from the roofline while greenery interspersed with white lights and red ribbons decorated the porch rails. An evergreen wreath with a perfectly tied plaid bow hung next to the front door. Classic colorful bulbs twinkled from the snow-covered trees in the yard. The effect was one of warmth and elegance.

Unlatching the gate, Stella strode up the walk in her favorite Louboutin heels, intently scanning for stray patches of ice. Under her black boiled-wool coat, she wore a red-lace sheath dress. As she hadn't been sure how dressy—or casual—the party would be, she'd left the bling accessories in her suitcase.

Just as she reached the door, it opened, and the pretty blonde she'd seen with Sam waved her inside. The woman's smile might be warm and friendly, but her blue eyes remained watchful.

"You must be Stella." The woman extended her hand. "I'm Lucy Cummings, the caterer for this event. Faith told me all about you."

A young man appeared, dressed in dark pants with a white shirt and bowtie. "May I take your coat, ma'am?"

Inwardly, Stella cringed. Did pushing thirty automatically make you a ma'am?

"Thank you." She slipped off her coat and dropped the ticket he gave her into the clutch that held her iPhone.

Last year, Stella had scaled back from using various cameras with all the bells and whistles to simply using her iPhone for social media shoots. This still gave her the quality but was easy to use.

Once the dark-haired boy disappeared, Stella refocused on Lucy. "I appreciate Faith giving me this opportunity."

"She told me your former editor raved about you and your abilities."

"Yet I was still RIFed." Stella chuckled, but she didn't really feel like laughing.

She'd told herself that being let go was simply business and was no reflection on her abilities. Still, being discarded like yesterday's trash hurt. For two years Stella had lived and breathed the job. For what? To be kicked to the curb?

A look of sympathy filled Lucy's eyes. "Sometimes life just doesn't go our way."

Reminding herself that she'd been given another chance, which was more than most people got, Stella shrugged. "I believe everything happens for a reason."

"I've found people often say that when they want to comfort you. I'm not sure I believe it." Lucy's eyes took on a distant gleam before she gave a little laugh and appeared to shake herself out of her funk. "Well, I hope you enjoy living in Holly Pointe so much you'll want to stay on."

Stella only smiled. She glanced at the cherrywood staircase festooned with greenery and bows, admired the stained-glass window in the stairwell. "That's an Eastlake staircase."

Lucy's eyes widened. "How did you know that?"

"My father was an architect and a big fan of the British architect, Charles Eastlake." Stella stepped to the staircase and let her hand slide along the polished wood-carved acorn. "Dad loved the simplicity and geometric lines of the Eastlake style."

"I'm a fan, too." Lucy gestured. "Wait until you see the parlor."

They passed through what Stella recognized as a polychromatic painted archway into a room with a ceiling that had to be at least sixteen feet tall.

Stella didn't know where to look first. The large Christmas tree with the angel at the top nearly brushing the ceiling drew her attention the second she stepped into the room. Bows and gingerbread men as well as strands of popcorn and cranberries decorated the branches. Candies hung from paper chains and ribbons.

The tree had been positioned near a massive fireplace, the mantel decorated with small antique Christmas toys amid the greenery. Stella wondered whether the toys came from Memory Lane, the shop she'd seen on her trek to the coffee shop this morning.

Had she really only gotten into town today?

Stella pulled her attention back to the partygoers, relieved to see that she was dressed appropriately for the event.

Lucy gave her arm a squeeze. "Enjoy. Take lots of pictures."

It was a not-so-subtle reminder that while the others were here as invited guests, she was here to work. "Wait."

The blonde turned and raised a brow.

"I have a question." Stella lifted a hand and spoke quickly. "If you're not the one to ask, just let me know."

Lucy inclined her head. "First I need to hear the question."

"Do you have a shot list of photos you absolutely need? Also, if there are key attendees you want pictures of, could you point them out to me?"

"That's two questions, not one, but they're good ones." Lucy glanced around the room and made eye contact with Faith. Lifting her hand, she made a "come here" motion with her hand.

Faith appeared. The stretchy green-and-red-plaid long-sleeve pencil dress hugged her lithe figure and hit just above the knee. Cartoon Santas, snowmen, and penguins added an additional festive feel to the Christmas print.

The Santa hat that rested on Faith's braided hair made Stella smile. In the coffee shop, she'd gotten the feeling that this woman was one of a kind. The dress and Santa hat on Faith's head confirmed she'd been right.

"What's up?" Unlike Lucy, Faith's warm smile reached her eyes.

"Stella has some relevant questions, which need answers." Lucy's tone was businesslike as her gaze scanned the room. "Since you're president of the chamber of commerce, I believe you're in the best position to answer."

"I'm happy to do what I can." Faith exuded an energy, yes, but also a calm.

One that had Stella relaxing.

"I'll leave you two, then." Lucy's eyes narrowed on one of the servers, who was openly flirting with one of the guests. "I see a problem I need to address."

Stella watched as Lucy made a beeline straight to the man. She turned back to find Faith staring at her.

"Lucy takes her job as caterer seriously." Faith's voice deepened with approval. "She's a remarkable woman and a shining example of the saying that what doesn't kill you makes you stronger."

The intriguing comment had Stella wanting to know more. But she had a job to do. While talking with Lucy and Faith was important, she needed to prove herself first in order to gain their trust.

"What questions do you have?" Faith asked, as if sensing Stella's impatience.

Stella quickly relayed the questions she'd asked Lucy moments earlier.

Faith tapped her red lips. "In terms of shots we absolutely need, I'd like to see some of Lucy and Sam."

"Sam?" Stella's heart did a double flip.

"Sam Johnson is our city administrator." Faith pointed to where the man who'd saved her from a fall stood speaking with an older man with white hair and a beard.

As if sensing their eyes on him, he turned, and his eyes met Stella's. His lips curved then broadened into a full-blown smile when Faith waved.

"Sam is the tall one," Faith explained. "The man with him is Kenny Douglas. Kenny plays Santa when he's not brewing the most fabulous coffee in town."

"Norma's husband." Stella nodded as a couple more puzzle pieces fell into place.

"That's right." Faith's expression softened. "Would you like me to introduce you around? I know how difficult it can be to show up at an event where you don't know anyone."

"I appreciate the offer." Stella kept her eyes on Faith, wanting the woman to see just how much she really did appreciate her kindness. Even if she didn't need it. "But I think it'd be best if I just lurked, let people forget I was even around. I find I get the best pictures that way."

And the most information.

"Whatever you think best." Faith touched her arm. "If you change your mind or would like to know who someone is, I'll be circulating all night."

Suddenly confused, Stella cocked her head. "I thought Lucy was the hostess tonight."

"Her company is handling the catering," Faith clarified. "I'm the president of the chamber, and those in attendance are business owners in our community. These people who are here tonight are a huge part of what makes Holly Pointe special. I want to make sure they have an enjoyable evening and ensure they know just how important they are to Holly Pointe's success. Also, I'm here to address any of their questions or concerns about any of the activities and promotions we have scheduled for the next month."

By the time Faith stopped for breath, Stella's head was spinning. She nodded. "Got it."

Stella pulled out her phone and caught Faith's quizzical look. "Don't worry, I'm not going to spend the evening texting my friends. This is my camera."

Surprise skittered across Faith's face.

"Trust me. The pictures will be great."

Stella spent the next half-hour studying the guests, both in the main parlor and in a second parlor that was nearly as large as the first. The smaller room held high-top tables covered in white linen where guests could place their drinks and plates of hors d'oeuvres while they visited with friends. Chairs lining the walls afforded those who wanted to sit the opportunity to do so.

She noticed Kenny Douglas, a.k.a. Santa, had been frequenting the bars in both rooms. In the short time she'd been watching, he'd made three trips to the bars. No White Christmas Margarita or Cranberry Mojito for this Saint Nick. Whiskey neat appeared to be his drink of choice this evening.

She got a photo of him downing the amber liquid then plopping the glass back down for a refill. *Drunk Santa?* It had possibilities. Stella made a mental note to keep her eye on Kenny, not only tonight but in the upcoming weeks.

When Stella entered the second parlor, she'd immediately recognized recently retired NHL star Dustin Bellamy. He and his wife were reported to be in discussions for a network talk show. Ever since their marriage nearly ten years ago, Dustin and his wife, former supermodel, Krista Ankrom, had cultivated a wholesome family brand.

The two were always newsworthy. A shot of them together would add a nice touch to her article. Especially since Dustin was from this area. Hopefully, she'd eventually be able to get one that included their adorable twin boys.

Stella followed Dustin as he shook hands and chatted with the merchants. He seemed to have the ability to charm in spades.

Krista also seemed comfortable in this setting. For being the mother of two school-age boys, she looked as stunning as she had when she'd been at the top of her career.

The interesting thing was, Stella noticed when she looked closely, Krista and her husband were like two planets circling the same sun. Both made their way around the rooms, laughing and talking, but never intersecting.

Perhaps before arriving at the party they'd agreed on a strategy that involved seeing twice as many people with a divide-and-conquer method. Stella didn't think so.

There were no little smiles or sidelong glances. In fact, it almost felt as if they were avoiding looking in each other's direction.

Could there be trouble in paradise?

Stella didn't want to jump to any conclusions, but it could be that their ho-ho, oh-so-hearty Christmas cheer was faked.

Drunk Santa. Lying hockey player and supermodel. Both possibilities would have Jane salivating.

Stella wished she could feel happier about the way Jane was determined to spin the article. But she considered herself to be a serious journalist, and this smacked of tabloid sensationalism.

If I don't write the article, someone else will.

The thought should have brought her comfort, but it didn't. Still, Stella assured herself, she wouldn't include anything in the article that she hadn't verified. The fact that this town billed itself as the Christmas capital and the font of all human kindness, or something to that effect, well, it was only natural that people would try to prove differently.

Feeling better, she slipped into the hall and removed the ribbon that had been placed across the staircase cordoning it off. Standing a couple of steps higher should give her an interesting camera angle into the front parlor.

"Where do you think you're going?"

The familiar deep voice had her hand stilling on the banister.

Sam didn't even give her a chance to respond when he spoke again. "That area is off limits."

Stella turned and shot him her best smile. "I guess that makes me an off-limits kind of gal."

CHAPTER THREE

The woman's smile was so engaging, Sam had to smile back. From the second they met, he'd noticed that Stella Carpenter emitted a joie de vivre that drew people to her. His brother, Kevin, had been like that. The joke had been that a party started whenever Kevin arrived.

The thought of going through another Christmas without his little brother still stung, but after four years, it was more like a bee sting than a knife to the heart. Still, when he spoke, his voice was more curt than necessary. "Come back here, please. There's a reason that ribbon is blocking the steps."

Stella hesitated for a fraction of a second. Long enough to have Sam wondering just what he'd do if she continued up the steps. Run after her? And do what?

Instead of moving up or down, she crouched and brought up her phone, motioning for him to move to the side.

He moved slightly to the right, noticing the swell of her breasts and the way the dress hugged her curves. His body stirred. Completely understandable, Sam told himself. There was no denying that she was a beautiful woman.

Her hair was long and thick with a hint of a wave. The color ranged from a golden blonde to soft brown. Her eyes were hazel. Earlier today, in the outdoor light, they'd looked almost brown. Tonight, they were definitely green.

Sam couldn't take his eyes off her.

He watched as her gaze narrowed on the parlor he'd just left. The way she angled the phone told him she was taking advantage of the additional height of the steps for her photographs.

After a few seconds, Stella straightened and smoothed the front of her dress, the phone still in her hand. When she picked up the clutch she'd set on the steps, he expected her to drop the phone back inside.

Laughter rang from inside the parlor, and for a fraction of a second, the deeper, male part of the merriment sounded like Kevin's.

He turned back to Stella, the joy of the evening diminished by the memory, and found her taking pictures. This time not of the house or those in the parlor but of him.

Anger flashed, fueled by pain. "What are you doing?"

"You need to expand your repertoire of questions." Stella dropped the phone into her bag and offered him a cheeky smile. "You asked me that three minutes ago."

Without waiting for his answer, she sauntered down the steps, unhooked the ribbon, then replaced it once those high heels were back on level ground.

At six foot three, Sam was used to women hitting him midchest. Because of her heels, he was nearly eye-to-eye with Stella.

She gazed at him, challenge in her eyes.

He held on to his temper with both hands, wondering why he was suddenly seized with the overwhelming urge to kiss that insouciant smile from her lips.

In his family, Sam was known as being slow to anger, methodical, logical. Of course, in a family firmly entrenched in the arts scene, that wasn't saying much.

Keeping his voice conversational, Sam fought to keep his voice even. "Why did you take pictures of me?"

"Ask Faith."

Had the scent of her perfume, a sensual amber scent, addled his brain? Whatever the cause, he struggled to make sense of this strange conversation. "Faith Pierson?"

"Do you know more than one Faith?"

"You're saying she told you to take pictures of me."

"She did. I was instructed to get pictures of you and Lucy. That's Lucy Cummings in case there are more than one."

He couldn't help but smile. This woman was different from anyone he'd ever known.

Still, he was unprepared when she crossed the short distance that separated them to slip her arm through his. "I'd like to get better acquainted. Tell me about yourself, Sam."

While Stella understood that men usually preferred to make the first advance, as a reporter she didn't have the luxury of waiting. Even worse, she didn't have time to let Sam think he was the one actually doing the pursuing.

When the smile disappeared from his lips and he stepped back, she realized her mistake.

Being overeager was never a good thing. Stella told herself her attraction to him had nothing to do with him as a handsome male. It had everything to do with him being well connected in Holly Pointe. He likely knew where all the bodies were buried.

If the rationalization didn't entirely ring true, it consoled her. She couldn't let herself get involved with anyone in this town. Especially not this man. Once her story broke, anyone she'd come in contact with during her time here would feel betrayed.

A completely understandable response.

She thought of her father and how proud he'd been of her.

When she'd accepted the position at the *Sun Times*, he'd brought out his favorite Teddy Roosevelt quote, "Far and away the best prize that life offers is the chance to work hard at work worth doing."

In his mind—and in hers back then—she would continue to enact change by bringing the news—*the truth*—to the people. Only this time, her platform would be one of the largest newspapers in the state of Florida.

Stella knew exactly what her dad would think of the changes Jane had implemented. She shoved down the guilt, once again reminding herself that if she didn't do this article, someone else would. It wasn't a great argument, but it was the best she had at the moment.

It felt as if minutes, hours, had ticked by, but it was likely only a few seconds before Sam replied.

"Why?"

"Why do I want to get to know you?" Stella realized she hadn't expected the push back. "Ah, that should be obvious."

Shoving his hands into his pockets, Sam rocked back on his heels. "Humor me."

"Well, for starters, you seem like an interesting guy."

A mocking smile lifted the corners of his lips. "You've discerned that from a total of five minutes of contact?"

"It was actually closer to ten." Stella placed a hand on his arm. "I think you'll discover, as we get better acquainted, that I'm very intuitive."

"There you are. Faith asked me to find you. She thought she'd seen you headed in this direction." Kate came to an abrupt halt, her gaze settling on Stella's hand resting on Sam's bicep. "I'm sorry. I didn't mean to interrupt."

"You're not." With an aplomb that Stella might have admired given other circumstances, Sam stared pointedly at her hand.

Offering him a bright smile, she dropped it to her side.

Sam turned his attention to Kate. "Have you seen Lucy?"

"Last I saw her she was in the second parlor speaking with Kenny." Kate met Sam's gaze, and something seemed to pass between the two of them. "Dustin was also looking for you."

Sam smiled, and when he stepped past the brunette, he squeezed her shoulder. "Thanks, Kate."

Stella waited until Sam was out of earshot to speak. "He's an attractive man."

"He is." While the warmth remained in Kate's eyes, there was a warning there as well. "Sam's been through a lot the last few years. I wouldn't want to see him hurt."

The desire to ask what exactly this man had been through nearly overpowered Stella's good sense. But she'd made a mistake in moving too quickly on Sam. She wouldn't make another.

Besides, she had his name and enough information about him to start an internet search. By the time she went to bed tonight, she'd know nearly everything there was to know about Sam Johnson.

When the silence lengthened and she realized Kate expected an answer, Stella said truthfully, "I don't want to hurt anyone."

"It's just that we're protective of our own." The tense set to Kate's face appeared to ease. "I realize you need to get back to work, but Faith wanted me to quickly run through the upcoming schedule of events with you."

"Sure." Stella strolled with Kate into the second parlor, grabbing a glass of champagne off the tray of a passing waiter. She took a sip, found it delicious, then set the flute down on one of the tall tables and pulled out her phone. "Just give me a second to do a few more tweets."

"More?"

"Before the party, I scheduled several to post under the town's account, using the hashtag #christmastownusa. I posted to the blog on the town's website, touting the business community who embrace the Christmas spirit year round. I've also posted about the ice-skating event tomorrow at Star Lake and the arrival of

Santa Claus. Tonight I plan to do a mass email to those on the list reminding them of the upcoming week's events."

There was more to say, but Stella's throat was getting dry. She picked up the champagne and took a longer sip this time before once again setting down the glass.

Her thumbs flew over the phone's keyboard, and in a matter of seconds, the updates were done. When she looked up, she realized Kate was staring at her with a strange expression.

"What?" Stella touched a finger to her cheek. "Do I have something on my face?"

She reached for her bag, for the compact nestled inside. Before her fingers closed around it, Kate stopped her with a retraining hand.

"Your face is beautiful. Perfect, in fact." Kate's lips quirked up in a wry smile.

"Then why were you looking at me like that?"

"You're amazing." Kate shook her head. "You dropped into this position this morning and you've already got it under control."

"Thanks to Kinsley," she said, referring to the injured photographer. Credit where credit was due, Stella thought. "I met with her this afternoon, and she gave me the specifics on all the accounts as well as a list of December events."

Stella saw no need to mention that Kinsley, a lovely girl in her early twenties, had not formulated a marketing plan. Still, despite being obviously upset about not being able to do the job herself, Kinsley had graciously given Stella everything she needed to succeed.

Not everyone, Stella knew, would have been as gracious in that situation. In fact, she could think of any number of her former colleagues on the *Sun Times* staff who, given the same circumstances, would have done everything they could to torpedo her efforts.

Capital of Christmas kindness.

The phrase popped into her head, and Stella thought how funny it would be, and how sad for her, if the title turned out to be accurate.

"I know you said Kinsley gave you the list of upcoming events."

Stella nodded, picked up the glass of champagne for another sip.

"We added a couple more this afternoon, so the list she gave you isn't complete. I'll email you the updated one tonight."

"That'd be great." Stella rattled off her Gmail address. "Was anything added to this weekend's schedule?"

If there was, Stella thought, she'd need to get on it right away.

"No, most of the events we added relate to the Mistletoe Ball."

"I looked over the information on it and did a little web searching as well. Impressive." Stella had been amazed not only by the size of the event and the elaborate decorations in past years but also by its charitable bent. "I assume the money raised will be directed the same way as in the past."

Kate nodded. "Ninety percent of the profits will go to the University of Vermont Cancer Center in Burlington. It's a nonprofit comprehensive clinical and research cancer center. It's the only such organization in the state."

"The other ten percent stays in Holly Pointe."

"Yes, to address local health care needs."

Stella wondered whether the local money was really being directed where it was intended. She'd seen her share of small hospital administrators and doctors diverting money into their own pockets.

Another avenue to explore.

The way things were going, Stella would be too busy to think about the holidays.

Which was just the way she liked it.

As the sound of Christmas music being played on the lovely Steinway grand piano filled the air, Stella's gaze strayed to where

Sam stood, having an intense conversation with Dustin. Both men were attractive, but there was something about Sam that intrigued her.

Stella couldn't wait for the evening to end so she could dive into his background.

CHAPTER FOUR

Stella loved her Louboutin's dearly, but sliding them off and wiggling her toes in the privacy of her new apartment was a little piece of heaven. The party hadn't wound down until one. She'd added more pictures to the blog, Facebook page, and Instagram, then scheduled a few more tweets.

It would be naïve to think that most people only checked their social media accounts during working hours. The truth was, people were up and checking their phones and laptops at all hours of the day and night.

The ice-skating party, along with Santa's appearance, was scheduled for ten a.m. Reminders were needed so that parents and children didn't lose out on the chance to cheer Santa's arrival. Stella retrieved some pictures from last year's merriment and sent them out as a visual, illustrating this as a not-to-be-missed event.

Once Stella felt like she'd done everything necessary for her new job, she signed onto her account at the *Sun Times*. After a laptop disaster during a previous story had lost her a month's worth of research, Stella had gotten into the habit of keeping all her notes on the newspaper's secure server.

At Stella's request, Jane had reactivated her account when Stella accepted the Holly Pointe assignment. Now she could write without fear of losing anything important.

Stella keyed in her impressions, then paused. Until she was ready to submit the article, she preferred to keep these notes for her eyes only. Kenny Douglas might not be a drunk. Dustin Bellamy and Krista Ankrom might have a deliriously happy marriage. And the money raised from the Mistletoe Ball might flow through proper channels, just as it was intended.

She set her account to private, ensuring she was the only one with access to her thoughts and suppositions.

The last thing Stella wanted was for Jane to get all excited about the story going in a certain direction only to discover that Stella had been seeing things that weren't there.

Too revved to sleep, Stella let her fingers do the browsing she'd yearned to do all evening. She quickly discovered that Johnson was one of the top three surnames in Vermont. But she hit pay dirt when she narrowed the search to "Sam Johnson in Holly Pointe, Vermont."

Stella discovered that Sam was the son of Broadway producer Emily Danforth and playwright Geoff Johnson. It was quite an impressive pedigree. There were lots of pictures. Of him and his parents. Of him and his brother, Kevin. Of him with...

Stella's eyes widened in shock. *Britt Elliott.*

The Broadway actress, who'd won a Tony this year, was sizzling hot. Her star wasn't simply on the rise, it had shot straight into the stratosphere. Britt had gone from being a struggling and relatively unknown actress to being the darling of the stage.

She studied a picture of Britt and Sam taken two years ago at a New York City gala. Sam looked good in black tie. He and Britt looked amazing together. In every picture of the two of them together, he was smiling. Stella tapped her fingers against her lips and sat back. While Sam hadn't exactly been a grinch tonight, he also wasn't the man with the beaming smile in these photographs.

Stella flipped to the screen holding her notes. She keyed in what she'd discovered about Holly Pointe's city administrator. The data, while very basic, had endless possibilities because of Britt's star power and Sam's family lineage. A fact that made Stella feel just a little sick inside.

Still, she went back to browsing the web, wondering what Kate had meant with her comment about Sam going through a lot the past couple of years. Some sixth sense had told Stella that a woman was involved. She needed to find out whether that woman was Britt Elliott.

How did the brother factor in? There were pictures of him with Britt and Sam. Kevin was as blond as Sam was dark, taking after his mother in height and coloring. Sam was a clone of his playwright father.

Had Britt preferred the brother with the tousle of blond hair and laughing eyes? Was that why Kevin no longer lived in Holly Pointe? It didn't take her long to discover where Kevin was now.

Kevin now resided in the Holly Pointe Cemetery. According to the articles she read, Sam's fraternal twin had passed away at the age of twenty-six of Hodgkin's lymphoma.

When she googled Kevin, she found lots of pictures. Some with Lucy. Some at the graveside and of the family coming out of the church after the funeral service. Not many. But enough to make her blood boil. The paparazzi hadn't even had the decency to give his family time to grieve.

Even as the thought struck, Stella reminded herself that those photographers had simply been doing their jobs. She had friends who stalked celebrities in South Beach. They'd told her how much a good shot could bring in.

Still, a celebrity dancing the night away in a club seemed profoundly different from a parent or a brother grieving for a loved one. The expressions of grief on the faces of Sam and his parents brought back memories of her own parents' funeral.

She couldn't imagine people shoving a camera in her face or positioning themselves in the cemetery so they could zoom in and get a picture of her weeping.

There was right. There was wrong.

This had definitely been wrong.

Her heart ached for Sam, who'd lost a brother, and his parents, who'd lost a child. Though she normally tried to avoid thinking of those horrible days, memories flooded back. Family and friends spouting platitudes, saying her mom and dad were in a better place.

A few had patted her back and said that her mom and dad had lived long lives, even though they'd barely passed fifty.

Her mother hadn't had the chance to help her plan a wedding. Her dad would never walk her down the aisle. They wouldn't be there when she had a baby.

Her parents had done everything right. They'd been wearing their seatbelts. They'd driven a safe vehicle with five-star safety ratings. But there had been no way they could withstand the impact of a monster pickup that didn't even slow down, much less hit the brakes, when running a red light. Their killer, Mr. Three-Time Offender, had walked away with only minor injuries.

Stella glanced down at her hands, now bunched into fists on the keyboard. She took a shuddering breath and forced her fingers to unclench. She told herself she'd moved on, but could you ever really move on from such a loss?

She could still see the face of the man who'd gone to prison for motor vehicle homicide. One day he'd be free to start his life again, but her parents would still be dead, all their hopes and dreams snuffed out by his careless actions.

Work had been her salvation in the months following the

funeral. And now that was gone, too. Suddenly. Unexpectedly. Without warning.

There would be no second chances with her parents. But if she did this job to Jane's satisfaction, she had a chance to regain some of what she'd lost.

Stella refocused on the keyboard and entered in more notes.

She would get Jane the story she wanted. One way or the other.

Despite being up late, Stella woke at the crack of dawn, tossing out a few more tweets. She had passed Spring Lake on her way into Holly Pointe. Knowing she'd likely face potentially uneven terrain, she left her heels behind.

She stepped out of her vehicle and glanced down at the knee-high boots with rubber soles. If she'd been wearing this footwear yesterday, she might not have met Sam. Smiling at the thought, she lifted her gaze and widened her eyes.

Speak of the devil.

It was almost as if she had conjured him up. He stood at the edge of the ice-covered lake, wearing jeans, boots, and what she recognized as a Carhartt jacket. He was hauling big coolers from the bed of a pickup to the concession stand. Raising her phone, she snapped a few pictures.

Her favorite was a close-up of Sam bent over. The others were ones she might actually use for publicity.

Shifting her attention to the lake, Stella spotted Kate and Faith using short-handled brooms to sweep a dusting of snow off the backless benches that encircled the perimeter. The benches were obviously meant for putting skates on and taking them off. Stella glanced wistfully at the ice, wishing she could be out there today.

For several minutes she watched Nate, along with a couple of men she didn't recognize, clear snow from the ice.

After taking some shots, she strolled over to Kate and Faith. "Where's Melinda?"

Asking didn't seem strange since, in her brain, the three were linked. When she saw one, she expected to see three.

"Mel is getting the concession stand ready." Kate slanted a glance in Stella's direction and smiled. "You look ready to hit the ice."

This morning Stella had pulled on her ski coat and hat. She'd shoved her gloveless hands into her pocket. "I may look ready, but I'm missing one key ingredient. I don't have any skates."

"What size are you?" Faith raised her voice even though she stood not five feet away.

"Ten." Stella rolled her eyes, remembering Tasha's size-six feet. "I know, I know. I have Amazon-size feet."

Faith laughed. "Hardly. I'm a nine, and Mel is a ten. I bet she'd loan you hers. Just ask."

There it was again, Stella thought, the simple kindness this community appeared to have in abundance. "I'll think about it."

Kate must have been listening to their conversation because she paused in her sweeping and called out. "Don't just think about it, do it. You'll get some great pictures on the ice. Plus it'll give you a chance to embrace the experience."

Stella nodded. The woman made an excellent point. Still, it seemed that pointing a camera while trying to keep her balance might prove tricky.

Unless she was skating *with* someone...

She turned in the direction of the concession stand, where Mel stood laughing with Sam. Stella narrowed her gaze and felt something twist inside her.

Which was simply ridiculous. She barely knew the guy. Had only exchanged a handful of words with him. Of course, he had put his arms around her.

Only to keep her from falling ...

Stella pulled her attention back to Faith. Though this wasn't a business event like the party last night, to her, Faith remained the woman in charge. "In my notes it says the skating starts at ten."

"That's correct." Faith moved to the next bench, and Stella trailed behind.

Her gaze lingered on Faith's coat. It was a rosy flesh color, a midlength puffer coat capable of making even a thin person look as if she'd eaten her way through a box of Christmas cookies one too many times. Faith had paired the coat with a pair of red Ugg boots that sparkled and a red-and-white hat with a huge pom-pom.

On anyone else, the combination would have looked ridiculous, even laughable. Faith pulled it off.

Faith lifted the broom and paused. "Do you have questions about the start time?"

"Not about the skating, but about Santa Claus. It says he won't arrive until noon." Stella frowned. "It seems to me it'd make better sense if his arrival kicked off the event."

For a second, Faith hesitated. When she spoke, her tone was matter of fact. "Kenny isn't an early riser. He asked for a later start. We saw no harm in obliging him."

Was that because Kenny knew he'd be sleeping off too many shots of whiskey from the night before? The question hovered on the tip of Stella's tongue for half a heartbeat.

In the end, she remained silent. If she appeared too eager for details, she could raise suspicions. She would get more information by watching and listening.

"That was nice of you," Stella said when the silence lengthened.

But Faith's focus had returned to her task.

It felt to Stella as if she was the only slacker in the crowd. She sat on one of the recently cleaned-off benches and did her job. Overhead, the sky was a cloudless blue. Though the day was cold, there was little wind. Which meant that even Stella—used to the heat of Miami—was relatively comfortable.

She found herself smiling as she posted to Instagram, Twitter, and Facebook. The challenge of making a tantalizing tweet or a clever caption had her so engrossed that she didn't notice someone approaching.

A tap on her shoulder had her jerking. She swiveled and found herself gazing into Sam's warm brown eyes. In his hands were a pair of battered white skates.

"Mel wanted me to give these to you. Said something about you taking pictures from the ice."

Stella's heart pounded an erratic rhythm. From the shock, she told herself. She'd been so totally focused, she hadn't heard the crunch of his boots. "Faith and I were talking. I mentioned I wished I had some skates. Taking pictures while circling the lake would give me some interesting angles."

And she was rambling. She flushed, but thankfully her cheeks were already red from the cold.

"Well," he held out the skates. "Melinda say she'll be too busy handling the concession stand to skate. She said you could wear hers."

She lifted the skates from his hands and saw him frown.

His gaze lingered on her hands. "You aren't wearing gloves."

"It's easier for me to key." She held up a hand when she saw him open his mouth. "The gloves that are supposed to work with your phone never work as well as they say they do. Once I post this tweet, I'll—"

Once Stella finished the tweet, she slipped gloves from her pocket and pulled them on. "—do this."

"You're not used to this climate." His expression was one of concern. "Don't leave the gloves off for too long. No tweet or Instagram post is worth getting frostbite."

"Aye-aye, sir." Stella gave a mock salute and kept her tone

lighthearted. But she was touched both by his concern and by Mel's generosity.

Before she could say more, Sam turned to speak with Nate, and the quiet peacefulness of the lake was shattered by the arrival of families and more children than she could ever recall seeing together at one time. Granted, she never attended events specifically geared toward children in Miami, but this was a deluge.

Did all these kids know how to skate? The second her thoughts registered the question, she dismissed it. Her father had come from Minnesota, and he used to regale Stella and her mother with tales of snowshoeing, ice fishing, and cross-country skiing. And, yes, ice-skating.

She remembered him telling her that's why she had a knack for skiing. It came naturally, through her DNA. Then he'd given her a wink while her mother laughed.

Pain as sharp and hot as a lightning bolt ripped through her, stealing her breath. Stella had found herself thinking of her parents more in the past twenty-four hours than she had in the past six months. It couldn't be the climate. While they'd spent vacations skiing, they'd spent more time at the beach.

It had to have something with the people in these parts. They reminded her of her northern-born father. While he loved the weather of South Florida, Stella knew he would have liked the camaraderie of this community. As would her mother.

Stella sighed and shoved thoughts of her parents aside. Even happy memories could be distracting. If she was going to put together a Jane-worthy story, she had to stay focused.

The sight of Dustin and Krista's twin sons had Stella ripping off her gloves and pulling out her phone. They were an adorable twosome, dressed in identical ski jackets. Blond curls whipped around their cherubic faces as they ran toward the lake, holding their skate bags against their chests.

When Stella raised her phone to snap a picture, Sam's hand pulled her arm down.

"What?" She barely kept the annoyance from her voice.

"Dustin and Krista don't want the boys being photographed. It's a security thing." He spoke in a firm tone that brooked no argument. "We respect their privacy when they're in Holly Pointe."

The twins were now engulfed in a group of boys about their same age, making getting a good shot nearly impossible.

"What about paparazzi?" Stella asked.

A muscle in his jaw jumped. "They're not welcome here."

"How do you keep them away?" Stella asked, genuinely wanting to know. "The last I knew this was a free country."

The chill that filled the air between them had nothing to do with the temperature. For a long moment his gaze searched her face, as if looking for . . . something. She kept her expression impassive.

Everyone told her she had a great poker face. But something he saw, though she had no idea what it was, had the tense set to his shoulders easing. "We're a welcoming community, but we look out for each other and protect our own."

Stella nodded as if that made perfect sense. It did, at least as far as it went. But in her journalistic career, she'd seen far too many cases where protection and cover-up were entwined.

She wasn't sure whether that was the case in this town. But she was sure going to find out.

CHAPTER FIVE

From a high spot on the bank, Sam watched Stella circle the ice while talking nonstop to Kate. Both women were excellent skaters, and they seemed to have a lot to say to each other, though he noticed that Kate was doing most of the talking.

Sam took a sip of the hot cocoa he'd purchased—his contribution to the scouting fund—and thought back to each time he'd seen Stella in conversation with someone.

It struck him that she was always listening while the other person talked. That could be because she was new to Holly Pointe and listening was her way of getting better acquainted. Stella also needed information for the town blog and for all the other social media she had her fingers into.

She'd been a reporter. Likely still considered herself one at heart.

"Who's the woman with Katie?"

Sam didn't even turn. He knew that voice. Derek Kelly was a local contractor and a friend. "Her name is Stella Carpenter. When Kinsley was injured, she got the social media job."

Beside him, Sam could see Derek's gaze study the reporter as she skated around the lake. "She's a looker."

Sam nodded. No argument from him.

"Where'd she come from?"

"Florida."

"How'd she end up in Holly Pointe? Does she have family here?"

Derek had an inquisitive nature. Sam had always thought his friend would make a good detective. "She told Faith her family had once skied here. She lost her job and wanted to try somewhere different."

"She leaves sunny Florida to come to Vermont during the winter?" Derek's gloved hand rose to his chin. "I'm betting there's more to the story."

"She asks a lot of questions, but I think that's just her reporter background." Sam watched Stella throw back her head and laugh. Whatever story Kate was telling her was obviously entertaining. "She arrived in town yesterday."

"How'd she already get a job?"

"The story is she was having a cup of coffee in the Busy Bean and overheard Faith talking to Kate and Mel about Kinsley's accident."

"Quite a coincidence."

"Not really. Those tables are so close, it's almost impossible not to overhear other conversations." While something about the woman unsettled Sam, the notion of her having some hidden agenda in Holly Pointe seemed farfetched.

"I don't know." Derek narrowed his gaze. "Her coming here out of the blue seems odd. Sort of like when Jaycee returned to town after being gone for years."

"That experience has made you suspicious of all women. I get that. I'd feel the same if I were you." Sam still found it difficult to believe that their childhood friend, Jaycee Collingsworth, had deliberately tried to trap Derek into marriage. "But Stella isn't Jaycee. Other than the fact that she listens a lot more than she talks."

"Which means she knows a lot more about you than you do about her."

"You're right." Sam's sardonic smile had Derek grinning.

"You've got a plan."

Sam nodded. "I believe it's time I find out a little more about Ms. Stella Carpenter."

Stella wasn't sure how it happened. One moment she was circling the ice with Kate, the next she was with Sam. Though she was flattered that he wanted to skate with her, she was also a trifle annoyed.

She and Kate had spent ten minutes gliding across the ice discussing everything *but* the citizens of Holly Pointe. Kate was warmed up, and there had finally been an opportunity for her to bring up Santa, er, Kenny, when Sam skated up.

"I wouldn't think a southern girl would know how to ice-skate."

"My father was from Minnesota. When I was little, we would go back to visit relatives. Do you like to ski?"

"What part of Minnesota?"

The question came out of the blue. Hadn't he heard *her* question. "Pardon?"

With an arm around her waist, one hand resting on her hip while the other hand held hers, they glided across the ice as if they'd been skating together for years. Though she'd certainly been held by a man before, she'd never felt this comfortable so quickly.

"You said your father was from Minnesota. I was merely asking what part of the state."

"Oh, Minneapolis." She regrouped. "What about—"

"Do you still have family there?"

Stella wished he would stop asking questions. She was the one gathering information, not him.

"Yes. My grandparents live there." She decided to use this as a segue to discussing his family. "Does your—?"

"What about your parents?"

She blinked. He'd interrupted again.

"They died two years ago." Then, because she knew he would ask, she added. "It was a car accident. A drunk driver ran a red light and hit them."

"I'm sorry for your loss." His fingers tightened around hers. "I can't imagine losing both of my parents at once."

Focus on his family, not on yours, Stella told herself as grief surged. "Do your parents—"

"Faith said you used to work for a newspaper in Miami."

The guy was like a jack-in-the-box. Each time she opened her mouth, he popped up and asked another question. He'd blown right over her and squelched her question with such thoroughness that she couldn't raise it again, not right now anyway. Not without the inquiry appearing calculated.

"Yes." Stella resisted the urge to sigh. "I worked for the *Sun Times* before I was let go due to budget cuts in September."

"Yet you waited until now to come to Holly Pointe?"

She opened her mouth, determined to steer the conversation back to this community when he continued.

"Why now? Why not two or three months ago?" Sam slanted an assessing look in her direction. "I would think being in a strange town during the holiday season would prove difficult."

"Why would you think that?" She was well aware she hadn't answered his question, but heck, if he could ignore her questions, she could ignore his.

"Traditionally this time of year is about home and family." His voice took on a probing quality. "Why come to a place where you don't know anyone? Why not go to Minneapolis and spend Christmas with your grandparents?"

"I could have gone to Minnesota. My grandparents are still alive and living in a retirement community. But with losing the job, well, I felt like too much of a failure."

"Is that the only reason?" His dark eyes seemed to bore into her soul.

"It probably should give me comfort to be around family at this time of year, but it doesn't." Stella somehow managed to keep her tone matter of fact. "I look like my father, and I'm a reminder of what they've lost. I see the pain they try so hard to hide, and it makes me feel bad."

Sam nodded as if he understood. "Don't you have friends in Miami?"

"Most of my friends were people I worked with at the *Sun Times*. They're scattered across the country, wherever they could find a job." Stella gave a little laugh. "I envy them. I'm certainly willing to relocate. I've sent resumes far and wide, but not even a nibble."

When he closed the mouth he'd opened, she knew she'd addressed the question he'd been about to ask.

A tightness filled her chest. "Not one indication of interest."

That fact made the carrot Jane had dangled even more appealing.

The hand holding hers squeezed in an expression of comfort.

Lost in her thoughts, Stella barely noticed that they'd slowed or that the other skaters were whizzing by them. "My friend Tasha let me bunk on her sofa for a couple of months."

At his questioning look, she added. "I had to let my apartment go. It was too expensive, and my lease was up. I couldn't sign another one. Not only did I not have the money, I didn't know how long I'd be in Miami."

When Stella paused for breath, she realized with sudden horror that she'd been rambling. Instead of *him* telling *her* his secrets, *she'd* been the doing all the talking.

"I still don't understand why Holly Pointe. Just the trip here had to make a serious dent in your savings."

The man was like a dog with a bone. He should have been a reporter.

"Tasha, the friend I was bunking with, told me I had to move out. She has a small apartment, and her roommate was tired of having me on the couch." Stella paused as a parent stepped onto the ice to take a picture of his child. "Ohmigoodness."

Stella jerked from his grasp nearly sending the both of them toppling to the ice.

"What's wrong?" His gaze scanned the area around them as if searching for threats.

"The only reason I'm here today is to snap pictures." She slipped her hand into her pocket and pulled out her phone. "I haven't taken a single one since I've been skating."

"You're also here to enjoy yourself."

At her "get real" look, he grinned. "How can you report on the flavor of the town without allowing yourself to get a feel for all it has to offer?"

"Good point." She agreed with him. *If* her being here was as she'd said. The trouble was, Jane wanted a spin. And in order to get her old job back, Stella had to find a way to give Jane what she wanted.

Sam cocked his head. "Where's your camera?"

She lifted her red phone. She loved everything about her iPhone. "This is it."

"Your phone is your camera?"

The doubt in his eyes didn't surprise Stella. Several years ago, heck, even two years ago, she never have thought she'd see the day when a phone's camera would replace her Fuji. "If I was doing studio photography or high-end work, I'd use something else. But an increasing number of social media photographers use their phones exclusively. It's less intrusive and easier to lug around. The pictures look great online."

He didn't appear convinced. "If you say so."

"You'll say so, too, when you see the ones from today." She studied the crowd for subjects who would convey that this was a fun family event for kids of all ages. She pointed. "See that guy over there?"

He obediently followed the direction of her finger. "Coach Walters?"

As the man was the only adult in a sea of kids, she nodded. "I want to get a shot of him."

"Why?"

"He's got an interesting face, and you can see the kids adore him." She thought for a moment. "He's like a Pied Piper."

Sam snorted. "I don't think he'd appreciate the comparison."

Too busy setting up the shot in her head, Stella didn't respond. If she crouched down and caught him as he passed . . .

She took off, weaving through the crowd of skaters. She was nearly to the center of the lake when Sam caught up to her.

"What are you doing?"

Stella grimaced, remembering her manners. Or rather her lack of them. "I'm sorry. I should have said I needed to get to work."

"I thought you wanted a picture of Coach." He stared in puzzlement at three young girls intently working on spins.

"I want a low angle shot of him as he passes by." Stella gingerly squatted, but when she raised her phone and leaned over to check the angle, she nearly toppled.

Once again, she was saved by a pair of strong hands.

"Thanks." She grinned. "This is getting to be a habit."

"I don't mind." He returned her smile, and Stella went warm all over. "Why go low?"

"When you photograph from below eye level, it makes the person look powerful."

"Like a Pied Piper?"

"Exactly." Stella glanced at the ice and grimaced. "I'm going to have to sit. Would you mind standing in back of me while I do? Just so someone doesn't plow into me and hurt themselves."

"If you sit, you'll get wet." He pointed out the obvious. "And Santa will be here at noon, so you won't have time to go back to your apartment and change."

Darn if he wasn't right. "Got a better idea?"

To her surprise, he appeared to be giving the dilemma some thought. "Okay, you crouch down. I'll be directly behind you, hands on your shoulders, steadying you. It's not ideal, but it'll work. As long as you shoot quickly."

Out of the corner of her eye, Stella saw the coach and his entourage of adoring children headed their way. "Okay."

She scrunched down, and Sam did the same behind her. His hands on her shoulders gave her the stability she needed.

As the man passed, Stella did a burst of shots. When one of the children beside him said something and the man tossed back his head and laughed, Stella caught it.

She was ready to stand when she spotted two girls—who couldn't be more than twelve—skating slowly and acting as if they didn't notice a group of boys about the same age trying to get their attention.

The faces of the girls were reddened from the cold, but their smiles held an innocent happiness she wanted to capture.

Straightening just enough to be at eye level with them, Stella took several shots, then watched in horror as one of the boys skated backward right in front of them. With no time to react, they both tumbled to the ice.

She caught the fall, as well as the giggles that followed with her camera. And something more.

When the two started to lose their footing, Sam was already skating the short distance to them. His tall body protected them from other skaters while he pulled them to their feet. Only when the girls had resumed their circle around the lake did Sam skate off to speak with the boy.

She couldn't tell what he said, but the boy's cheeks turned even redder, and he hung his head. Then Sam slapped the boy on the back as if to say all was good, and he returned to Stella.

His kindness had a lump forming in Stella's throat. "That was nice of you."

"What?" As if noticing her gaze still on the girls he smiled. "They're good kids."

"You know them." That explained a lot.

"One is the daughter of a friend of mine. The other one, well, I don't know her, but I know the family."

"That's why you went to their rescue."

A puzzled look skittered across his face. "I would have helped them even if I didn't know them."

"That wouldn't happen in Miami." Stella knew she wasn't being fair to her home community, but it was how she felt. "If you don't know someone, you don't get involved."

"Then it's a good thing you don't live there anymore." He smiled and held out his hand. "C'mon, it's time to play."

~

It's time to play?

Sam nearly groaned aloud. If Kevin were here, he'd have laughed his ass off at such a comment. Seriously, could he have sounded anymore lame?

But Stella smiled and put her hand in his.

There was something about this woman that short-circuited his brain. She'd been stunning at the cocktail party in that short dress and high heels, with miles of long toned legs.

But today, in her ski coat, with her sun-streaked hair tumbling around her shoulders, he found her equally lovely. He liked that she was tall. And strong. He didn't know too many women who could—or would—crouch down on skates and twist their bodies into weird angles, all in hopes of getting just the right shot.

They skated in comfortable silence for several minutes. Sam liked that she wasn't a person who felt the need to fill every moment with aimless chatter.

While Sam found himself attracted to her, Derek was right. There was still so much about her he didn't know. He was still searching for the right question when she spoke.

"You're a good skater."

He smiled. "Thanks for the compliment."

She dipped her head. "I've been trying to do better."

"You lost me."

"I read a lot of self-help articles. I read somewhere recently that when you think something nice about a person, you should tell them." Stella offered an embarrassed laugh. "You know, instead of just thinking it."

"I like the concept." Sam studied her face, thought for a moment. "Tell me, Stella Carpenter, what's the best compliment you ever received?"

"I don't know," she said with a breathy laugh, waving away the question.

Sam wasn't about to let her off the hook this easily. He studied her, an expectant smile on her lips.

Several long seconds passed.

"Okay. Shortly after I started my first full-time job out of college, I did a series on teens making a difference in their communities." She smiled, and her eyes grew bright with memories. "What those boys and girls did sparked other communities to step up and institute some of the changes in their own backyard."

"You were recognized for your journalistic skill."

"Yes, but that wasn't the compliment." Pride filled Stella's voice. "My father told me he was proud I'd grown into someone who cared about others, that I'd become someone who strove to make the world a better place."

Tears formed in her eyes, but she quickly blinked them back. "What about you? What's the best compliment you ever received?"

He should have anticipated that she'd turn the tables on him. The woman could teach a master class in redirection. The thought made him smile.

Still, could he really expect her to share and then not reciprocate? He took her arm as an unsteady burly man holding the hand of a small child got a little too close.

"My brother once told me my greatest strength is that I don't give up on those I care about." Sam felt the familiar tightening in his chest. In the end, he'd had no choice but to give up, or rather accept that his smart, happy-go-lucky brother wasn't going to win his battle with cancer.

"Sometimes," Stella sighed, "even the best memories can be bittersweet."

Sam caught sight of a team of reindeer pulling a sleigh over the hill just as a cheer rose up from the crowd. "Here comes Santa Claus."

Stella shifted her gaze. Her eyes lit up. "Race you to the side."

She shot off like a rocket and had a start of several feet before he took off after her.

Sam never had been able to resist a challenge.

CHAPTER SIX

Stella stepped back and lowered her phone. There were only so many pictures of Santa, reindeer, and children that one woman could take in a day.

She'd tweeted, blogged, and done her utmost to show the fun everyone was having at Star Lake. Her work here was nearly done.

Tonight, she would begin again. While a soup supper, including a chili cookoff, might not sound like fun, after being out in the cold for hours, Stella was looking forward to being in a warm church basement and downing a bowl of spicy chili.

For now, she'd have to settle for a steaming cup of hot cocoa while waiting for Santa to leave the area. Stella increased her pace when she noticed there was no line at the concession stand.

She strode straight to the window. "Hey, Mel."

"Stella, hello. I was wondering if you were going to stop by to see me." Mel smiled. "You've come at a good time. For most, hot chocolate simply can't compete with petting a reindeer."

Stella waved an airy hand. "Once you've pet one, you've pet them all."

Mel laughed. "What can I get you?"

"Hot chocolate, of course." Stella set her money down on the weathered counter.

"Coming right up." Mel filled a disposable cup and handed it to Stella. "On the house."

"Thanks, but I can pay." She did, after all, have an expense account from the *Sun Times*. Though the thought of what she was expected to do for that money made her feel a little sick inside.

"After what you and Sam did for Camryn and her friend, the cocoa is on me."

"Camryn?" Stella took a sip and felt the warmth all the way down to her toes.

"The girl with the blonde hair who fell on the ice." Mel's expression softened. "She's my brother Derek's daughter."

Forget six degrees of separation, Stella thought. In this town, they were down to four. Or maybe two.

"I didn't do anything," Stella protested. "Except take her picture before she fell. Sam was the one who helped them up and gave the boy who caused the fall a scolding."

Mel pushed the money back toward Stella. "I've already thanked Sam. He told me he wouldn't have seen them go down if it hadn't been for you."

Sensing this was a battle she couldn't win, Stella scooped up the money and stuffed it into her pocket. She lifted the cup of steaming cocoa in a mock salute. "Well, thank you. Camryn is a cute girl."

"She's a doll. I always thought when I marry and have a daughter, I'd want her to be just like Cam." A bleak look filled Melinda's gaze.

There was a story here, Stella thought. But even if a group of teenagers hadn't arrived at the stand, Stella wasn't sure she'd have asked any questions.

"Thanks for the skates, Mel." Stella lifted a hand in a wave as she walked away.

The ding of her phone had her glancing down at the screen.

Call me.

The text was from Jane. A chill traveled up Stella's spine.

She'd only been in Holly Pointe for forty-eight hours. Jane couldn't be expecting a story already, could she?

～

Stella had never been to a soup supper at a church before. Not sure exactly where to go, after hanging her coat on one of several freestanding metal racks on the main floor, Stella simply followed the crowd.

The stairwell leading to the basement was wide, and there were people coming up as she went down. Which was to be expected, considering the supper started at five, and it was now nearly six.

She probably should have come promptly at five, or even a few minutes before, to get a few shots of the setup. But her conversation with Jane had been a downer.

Despite the fact that Stella had only arrived in town yesterday, Jane was already pushing for results. When Jane continued to press for *any* possibilities, Stella mentioned Santa might have a drinking problem.

"Be sure and include that in your article," Jane asserted even though Stella stressed she had no proof.

By the time Stella clicked off the call, she had a headache. Though much of the tension gripping her neck had to do with Jane, Stella knew her conversation with Sam had contributed.

Simply telling him what her father had said about her journalistic integrity had guilt rising like bile in her throat. Dan Carpenter wouldn't approve of this assignment. Heck, Stella wasn't all that thrilled with it herself.

But as she'd told Jane this afternoon, she would verify and confirm before putting any impressions in the article. The managing editor hadn't argued with her, hadn't said anything in response to the statement. But even with a thousand miles separating them, Jane's disapproval had come through loud and clear.

A short nap, two ibuprofen, and half a can of cola later, the headache was gone. Feeling better than she had in hours, Stella reached the bottom of the steps and squared her shoulders, reminding herself that the article wasn't due for nearly a month. That gave her plenty of time to gather information and verify any suspicions.

She let her gaze slide around the large fellowship hall, taking note of the lighting and picking a couple of good spots for pictures. Then Stella found herself searching for the three women she'd begun to think of as friends and the one man she couldn't seem to shake loose from her thoughts.

Coming up empty on all four, she pushed aside her disappointment and reminded herself that she was here to work, not socialize.

Despite the plan to ease into this evening's event, Stella took a couple of shots that she quickly posted. She updated the blog and Instagram with some amazing soup pictures before getting in the line.

An easel at the front of the line held a whiteboard with a list of available soups: chicken noodle, vegetable barley, fish chowder, and baked potato.

Stella frowned. The soup she'd looked forward to all day wasn't on the board. "What happened to the chili?"

The woman behind the makeshift counter was talking to another volunteer and obviously hadn't heard the question. A light touch on Stella's shoulder had her turning.

"You're looking for chili?" The man was about her height, with sandy hair and green eyes that twinkled. His flannel shirt, work boots, and scarred knuckles told Stella he was no stranger to hard work.

"I am." She returned his smile. "Do you know where I can find some?"

He jerked his head in the direction of a hallway. "That-a-way."

Stella had noticed several people entering the hall but had simply assumed the restrooms were in that direction.

"It's homemade bread and soup in this room." About her age, the guy had square shoulders and a broad chest. "Chili and cinnamon rolls are down the hall."

"Did you say cinnamon rolls?" Stella's mouth instantly began to water. Sweets, especially pastries, were her kryptonite.

"I realize pairing them with chili makes for an odd combin—"

"Not odd at all." She stopped him with a hand on his arm. "Honestly, I think it sounds amazing."

"Hey."

Stella swiveled her head, and there was Sam.

The blue in Sam's sweater provided a nice contrast to his dark eyes. His curious gaze settled on her hand, the one still resting on the stranger's arm.

"Sam. Hi." She smiled and let her hand casually drop as pleasure rippled through her. "I wondered if I'd see you here."

"I was telling Stella, if she's hoping for chili and cinnamon rolls, she's in the wrong line."

Stella cocked her head. "How do you know my name?"

"I told him." Sam grinned. "Derek and I are friends."

"You're Mel's brother." Stella studied the guy for several heartbeats. "You were one of the guys cleaning the ice off the lake."

"Derek Kelly." He flashed an engaging smile. "You're an observant woman."

"Guilty as charged," Stella lifted both hands. "I used to be a reporter. Curiosity and alertness are two necessary qualities."

"I bet."

Stella waited for him to say more, but Derek simply slanted a glance at his friend.

"Is Mel coming tonight?" she asked.

Derek shook his head. "She's working at the diner this evening."

At Stella's obvious confusion, he continued. "Our mother owns Rosie's Diner. Mom recently had knee surgery, so Mel and I have been filling in when needed."

"That's nice of both of you."

"We're family." He appeared startled by her comment. "Of course we'd help."

That was how it had been with Stella and her parents. They'd do anything to help each other out, to be there whenever needed. Once they were gone, she realized just how much she'd depended on their guidance, on their support.

For months, it had been a major effort to just get out of bed in the morning. Once her world began to settle, Stella had vowed that she would never become that dependent on anyone again.

She would stand on her own two feet.

"Are you going to check out the other room?" Sam asked, as if bored by the conversation.

"I am. Which means I better get out of this line and into another." Stella extended her hand to Derek. "It was nice meeting you."

Derek shook it. "The pleasure is mine."

"I'll come with you." To her surprise, Sam turned to Derek. "What about you? Don't you want chili?"

"Naw, I've got my heart set on baked potato soup and beer bread." Derek waved a hand in the air. "You kids go and have fun."

Stella chuckled.

Sam rolled his eyes. "If you change your mind, you know where to find us."

Us.

It was silly to get a buzz from a carelessly tossed word. But it had her relaxing as they strolled down the hallway, the freshly polished linoleum floor gleaming in the fluorescent lights.

"And here I thought the other room was crowded." Stella slipped out her phone and snapped a few photos as they fell into a line that extended into the hall.

An older woman with peppered hair pulled back in a low knot turned. "The cinnamon rolls are from Dough See Dough. They're absolutely amazing."

"Just the smell is making my mouth water," Stella admitted.

When they finally reached the front of the line, Stella discovered another fact about the delicious-smelling rolls. They were huge.

She slanted a pleading glance at Sam. "Want to split one with me?"

"Sure." He waved away the one about to be handed to him. "None for me, Darlene."

"If you change your mind, just let me know." Darlene reminded Stella of her mother, with brown hair cut in a bob and wide lips curved in a perpetual smile.

"Will do," Sam told the woman as they moved down the serving line.

"Welcome to the chili cookoff." It took Stella only a second to place the man. Santa, er, Kenny.

"We have three kinds of chili this evening. The Boilermaker Tailgate is spicy and includes Guinness beer. The Flatlander is both spicy and sweet. For those who prefer no legumes, we have a Texas no-beans option." Kenny handed Stella and Sam each a tray. "You'll get one small bowl of each, but feel free to come back for seconds. On your tray is a ballot, and we ask you to vote for your favorite of the bunch."

Stella had questions, but the line was pushing her forward. She waited until she and Sam were seated at the end of a large table with a bunch of high school kids to ask him.

"When do we pay?" She glanced down at her tray. At the three bowls of chili and the humongous cinnamon roll. At the glass of iced tea that Sam had picked up for her from the refreshment table along the wall.

Sam gestured with one hand to a large glass jar filled with bills. "Free-will offering."

"What if someone doesn't pay?"

Sam dipped his spoon into the Boilermaker chili. "Then, they don't pay."

"How is that fair?"

Sam gazed at her with eyes that reminded her of liquid chocolate. "This is a community event with a lot of volunteers. If someone can't afford to give—or chooses not to donate—that's okay."

The Christmas capital of kindness, Stella thought as she forked off a bite of the massive cinnamon roll and watched an elderly couple slowly make their way to a nearby table.

Two teenage boys followed, each carrying a full tray. They set the food on the table the couple had chosen. Seconds later, they returned with two cups of coffee from the refreshment table and set them in front of the couple.

"I don't want to get old," Stella mused, listening to the couples' effusive thanks. The woman even insisted on giving each boy a hug. "I don't want to be dependent on anyone."

She said it with such fierceness that Sam set down his spoon and raised a brow. "Is aging the issue? Or accepting help?"

"I don't want to be in the position of having to lean on anyone." Stella lifted her glass of tea and took a long drink. "Ever."

Sam dipped his spoon into the Boilermaker bowl even as his gaze remained firmly fixed on hers.

She steeled herself for what was to come. She'd mentioned the same to Tasha once and had gotten a lecture about everyone needing someone and that's what friends are for, blah, blah, blah.

Then Tasha's roommate had butted into the conversation and

asked, Wasn't leaning exactly what Stella had been doing by crashing on their sofa the past two months?

Stella had been struck dumb for several seconds. Then the roommate cast a pointed glance at Tasha, who then told Stella they'd decided it'd be best if she was out by the end of the year. Stella had been embarrassed.

Sam slanted another quick glance at the couple before his gaze returned to Stella. "In Holly Pointe, we take care of each other. I suppose you could say the couple leaned on the boys because they needed help with their trays. But they're also teaching those teenagers a valuable lesson."

When Stella said nothing, Sam continued.

"People love to help. It's a win-win for both parties." Sam reached across the table and surprised Stella by covering her hand with his. "You're one person, Stella. No matter how hard working you are—or how determined—you can't do it all. In Holly Pointe, there's no need for you to even try."

Stella met his eyes. When their gazes locked, she couldn't look away.

"I realize you have a big job to do, but while you're here, make time for yourself. Enjoy all this community has to offer."

Stella's heart skipped a beat when his fingers linked with hers.

"And know that if you need anything, all you have to do is ask."

CHAPTER SEVEN

When Stella awoke Monday morning, the first thing she did was pull back the curtains and glance out the window. She breathed a sigh of relief. It appeared that Sunday's snow storm, which had added an extra four inches of the white stuff to the ground, had moved out, leaving the day clear and sunny.

Yesterday, Stella had stayed inside, spending the day on her laptop. She'd begun by researching everyone she'd met and inputting copious amounts of notes into her Holly Pointe file. While no specific piece of information had jumped out at her, she felt more settled.

Knowing the backgrounds of those she'd met—and those she planned on meeting—gave her the basic blocks she needed to build on in the upcoming weeks.

She'd hoped to find more on Kenny and Norma but discovered the two didn't have much of an online presence. Speaking with them in person appeared to be her best strategy. She decided to spend a little time in the coffee shop before exploring the town.

As she reached the bottom of the steps, Stella inhaled deeply.

The rich aroma of coffee had her pushing through the door leading into the Busy Bean.

Kenny and Norma were at the counter while two young women in their early twenties acted as baristas. For nine o'clock on a Monday, the shop was surprisingly busy. Stella counted at least four groups playing cards as well as a handful of business types at other tables on their phones or laptops.

She didn't see Sam, but his friend stood near the pickup counter with a guy she didn't recognize.

Stella strode up and tapped Derek on the shoulder. "Shouldn't you be working?"

He turned. "Stella, hello."

Even as a smile lifted his lips, Derek glanced toward the doorway. "I didn't see you come in."

Stella gestured with one hand toward the back of the shop. "I live upstairs. I don't even have to go outside for my morning jolt of caffeine."

"Lucky you." Derek turned toward the other guy. "Zach Adamson, I'd like you to meet Stella Carpenter. Stella is new to Holly Pointe and is handling the social media for the holiday season."

"Pleased to meet you." Zach cocked his head. "You're the one who replaced Kinsley. She's still bummed over that."

"You know Kinsley?" Stella didn't know why she bothered to ask. Everyone in this town seemed to be either friends or relatives.

Zach pushed back a tousle of jet-black hair and nodded. "She's my cousin."

"Kinsley was very helpful in giving me all her notes so I could hit the ground running."

"Stella is from Miami," Derek said to Zach, then reached around to grab the two large cups that Kenny had set on the counter. "Thanks, Kenny."

"Coffee is hot." Kenny, his long hair pulled back into a low pony, should have looked ridiculous wearing a red apron with dancing reindeer.

Instead, he looked sweet, like a big panda bear that you couldn't help wanting to hug.

"Just the way I like it." Zach took the cup Derek handed him.

"I wish we could stay." Derek offered a regretful smile. "But we've got work."

"Me too. You guys have fun." Stella barely restrained herself from asking Derek whether he'd seen Sam.

"Take care." Zach offered her a friendly smile before heading out the door with Derek.

While Stella doubted that Zach had any deep dark secrets that Jane would find newsworthy, she would add him to her list. During her brief conversation with the two men, the line at the ordering counter had disappeared.

Norma looked up from the register. "Good morning, Stella. Just give me a minute. I need to replace the paper."

Stella watched for several seconds while the woman fumbled to insert a new roll in the register. Though Stella had no doubt that Norma had replaced the roll hundreds of times, this morning the older woman couldn't seem to get her fingers to cooperate.

"Kenny!" Norma's call pitched high.

Her husband was at her side in a second. He smiled at Stella then took the roll from his wife's frustrated fingers. "Let me do that."

"I can't seem to make them work." Her voice quivered.

"You haven't had any caffeine today." He patted her shoulder, his eyes as soft and comforting as his voice. "Have Adriana make you up a latte, then you can sit and relax a minute. We're not busy right now. I can handle the counter."

Even as Kenny quickly and efficiently replaced the paper tape, Norma opened her mouth as if to argue.

"I'd love some company," Stella offered. "Unless you'd prefer to relax alone. I totally get that, too."

Kenny shot her a grateful glance.

"Why, thank you. I'd love to join you." Norma's brow furrowed as she turned back to her husband. "Are you sure you can manage without me?"

A look passed across Kenny's face that Stella couldn't decipher. "For a few minutes, I'll be fine."

It wasn't long until Stella sat with Norma at one of the tables by the window. The café au lait she'd ordered sat in front of her, as well as a piece of coffee cake that Kenny had insisted she try.

"How do you like working with your husband?" Stella asked.

Norma's gaze shifted to where Kenny stood, laughing with a customer at the counter. Her lips curved in a smile.

"I love being with him." Her gaze met Stella's. "Kenny is the love of my life. I've known him since I was seventeen. We married when I was nineteen and he was twenty."

"Wow." Stella forked off a bite of coffee cake and brought it to her lips. "You've been married a long time."

"Fifty years next month."

"Was Kenny always so . . . jolly?"

Norma chuckled. "Kenny loves people. That's why, about ten years ago when Stan Phipps, who used to play Santa, moved away, Kenny took on the challenge. It's a perfect fit. He adores the little ones."

"Do you and Kenny have any children of your own?"

"We have three girls." Norma took a long sip of her latte and relaxed against the back of her chair. "They're scattered across the country."

"Will any of them make it back for Christmas?"

Norma's smile slipped just a little. "Not for Christmas. They'll all be back for our fiftieth celebration next month, though. That's when we'll have our Christmas with the little ones."

An image of Holly Pointe in January flashed before Stella. Cold and snowy. "You got married in January?"

Norma laughed. "We did. It was twelve degrees below zero that day, a record that held until several years ago when the entire state was in the deep freeze."

"Twelve degrees below zero sounds like a deep freeze to me." Stella gave a mock shiver. "Actually, twelve above sounds cold."

"You get used to it. In fact, I love snow days." Norma's lips curved, and Stella could see that she was thinking back. "There isn't anything like sitting on the sofa in front of a fire with your special man while snow falls outside."

The older woman painted a pretty picture of a life well lived with the one you loved. Stella fought a pang of envy.

"I can't imagine life without my Kenny." Norma set down her cup. "Not that we haven't had our ups and downs. I don't think you can be married for five decades and not experience hard times."

The comment had Stella realizing that she'd nearly squandered the perfect opportunity to discern whether Kenny really did have a drinking problem. She'd been so caught up in enjoying her time with Norma that she forgot why she was in Holly Pointe.

Stella took a bite of coffee cake and chewed thoughtfully. "When would you say was your most difficult time?"

"When Leslie, she's our oldest, was diagnosed with diabetes. She was nine." Norma closed her eyes briefly as if merely thinking of that time brought pain. "Oh, she's doing fine now, but at the time, it felt as if our familiar world was crumbling around us. Leah was seven and Laura was four. They needed their mom and their dad, too."

Something in the way Norma said *and their dad* had Stella pressing when she would otherwise have backed off. "I bet Kenny took it hard. If he's anything like my dad was, he'd do anything to protect his little girl."

"It was difficult," Norma admitted. "He was so sad and worried about Leslie. We'd just purchased the coffee shop, and there was a lot of pressure."

"Did he bury himself in work?" Stella kept her tone conversational.

"More like the bottle." The words slipped from Norma's lips. She blinked as if realizing what she'd just said. "I'm sorry, I don't why I'm telling you all this."

Stella reached across the table and covered Norma's hand with hers. "Sometimes we just need someone to talk to."

"I don't want you to think Kenny has a drinking problem. That was a long time ago and very short-lived. It didn't take him long to realize that alcohol wasn't the answer." Norma expelled a breath and appeared to settle. "The doctors got Leslie's insulin dose regulated, and we went on with our lives. I believe that Kenny and I emerged from that dark time even closer."

"Sounds as if you've got yourself a great guy."

"I do." Norma slanted a glance in her husband's direction and gave him a little wave before returning her attention to Stella. "If you decide to remain in Holly Pointe, I hope you'll come to our anniversary party. I'd love for you to meet our daughters."

"If I'm still here, I'd love to attend your party."

But as the conversation veered toward more inconsequential matters, Stella wondered whether she'd still be welcome once the article came out. Not that what she'd heard today proved that Santa had a drinking problem.

But the fact that Kenny had turned to alcohol before was a red flag and definitely something worth exploring further.

"Took you long enough to get here." Sam strode from the barn to the truck that had pulled up in the drive, which boasted reindeer antlers and a red nose on the front grill. "You guys working bankers' hours these days?"

Derek jumped out of the pickup's cab. "Yep. Me and Zach, we don't like to start our day much before ten."

Zach, who'd already exited the passenger side, called over the hood. "Then we have to get our scone and latte at the Busy Bean."

Sam snorted out a laugh. He knew that Derek had likely driven over to nearby Maple Grove on snow-packed roads for the lumber before heading out to his place. Sam was actually surprised they'd gotten here as early as they did. Because it was difficult to know exactly when they'd arrive, he'd decided to work from home today.

He moved to the back of the truck to check out the lumber. "These are some nice pieces of cedar."

"Only the best for you," Derek said with a grin. "Speaking of the best, we ran into Stella."

"She's a beauty." Zach appeared to warm toward the topic. "She seems nice, too. Real friendly."

Sam shot him a sharp look.

"Sam has his eye on Stella." Derek informed Zach with exaggerated patience. "Which means hands off."

Zach raised his hands. "I only looked, I didn't touch."

"I don't have my eye on her," Sam insisted.

"He's lying," Derek told Zach, his tone matter of fact.

Sam pretended to further inspect the cedar planks. "What was she doing?"

"Getting a coffee." Derek glanced at the barn. "That door looks worse every time I'm out here."

"That's why you're here," Sam reminded him.

"Wow. I never thought of that." Derek grinned and punched Zach in the arm. "Did you hear that, Zach? That's why we're here."

"I wondered why we were driving all the way out here." Zach

grinned. "Now that I know why we're here, I guess we better get to work."

"You two should do stand-up." Sam rolled his eyes.

"I'll keep that in my back pocket for when business is slow," Derek said with a straight face.

"You do that." Sam opened the rotting barn door the men would be replacing and stepped into the building.

It didn't take long for Derek and Zach to get down to business. While saws whined and tape measures snapped, Sam put out fresh water and fodder for the horses that had once been Kevin's pride and joy.

His brother had loved Icelandic horses and had stabled his three at Sam's farm. Kevin had fallen ill shortly before purchasing the horses, so the care of the hearty and spirited animals had fallen almost entirely on Sam.

He hadn't minded and had actually grown quite fond of the animals that his Christmas-loving brother had named Dasher, Dancer, and Vixen. Even when Kevin hadn't been feeling the best, he'd come out to ride.

Sam and his brother had taken many long rides. Known for their surefootedness and ability to cross uneven terrain, the horses had taken them across meadows to the neighbor's blueberry farm. Each time Sam looked at the horses, it comforted him to know that he was caring for something that had given his brother such pleasure in the last months of his life.

Once Sam finished with his chores, he stopped to check on the construction progress. To his surprise, he found that Derek and Zach had one door ready to be hung and the other nearing completion.

"You guys work fast. Next time I'll pay you by the hour."

"Next time," Derek responded without missing a beat, "we'll be slow as molasses."

Sam laughed. "Seriously, I appreciate you making time for this. I know it isn't a big job but—"

"Hey, big or small, we do 'em all." Derek flashed a smile.

That might be true, but Sam knew it was the big jobs that paid most of the bills.

"Have you had lunch?" Sam asked. "I've got some leftover pizza from last night."

"Thanks, but once we finish here, we're headed to Hank Nilsson's place. He called this morning. Apparently he discovered his toilet's been leaking for some time. When he pulled up the vinyl, he found the subfloor was rotten." Derek watched as Zach expertly measured a board and cut it. "Since he's just down the road, we thought we'd try to get you both done this afternoon."

"Makes sense." Sam paused. "Did you have any trouble getting out here?"

"If you're asking if the road was open, the answer is yes. Obviously, because we're here."

"But—" Sam prompted.

"I was glad for the four-wheel drive." Derek shook his head. "If we'd gotten another inch last night we wouldn't have gotten through. I could see the plow had gone through, but it had drifted pretty badly."

"That's what I thought." The farm where Sam lived had originally belonged to his parents. They'd purchased it as a retreat against city life.

The farm was located far enough from Holly Pointe to be private, but close enough that a drive into town normally took only fifteen minutes. Except for particularly snowy days when the wind blew the road shut.

That had only happened a handful of times and wasn't a big deal. He had a freezer full of food and kept a backup generator in case the power went out.

"Well, I'll let you guys get back to work. If there's anything you need, let me know." Sam leveled his gaze on Derek. "Stop by the house before you leave. I'll give you a check for your labor and the materials."

Derek waved a hand. "I can send a bill."

"You could, but you had to pay for the materials up front. And the work will be completed. I want you to have the money today."

"Sure." Derek nodded. "Thanks."

He'd just pushed open the side door when Derek called out. "Zach was right. She looked mighty pretty this morning."

Sam turned back. "Who?"

"Stella." A half-smile pulled at Derek's lips. "She had on these skinny jeans and heels. Very sexy."

Sam inclined his head. "Why are you telling me this?"

"You might want to invite her out to dinner sometime."

"Yeah," Zach concurred. "You've got all these Christmas lights up. Women go crazy for that kind of stuff."

Sam shrugged.

Derek grinned. "And when she's out here, if I were you, I'd pray for snow."

CHAPTER EIGHT

Stella left the Busy Bean determined to explore the downtown area. She'd barely gone a half a block when she returned to her apartment and exchanged her heels for a pair of wool socks and Ugg boots. While the sidewalks had been cleared and salted, the air held a crisp edge.

Crisp? Heck, who was she kidding? She could see her breath.

Minutes later, she stepped out into the cold air dressed for the season in a red ski parka with a striped scarf wound around her neck. A chunky knit hat with a faux-fur pom-pom kept her head warm. Stella felt positively festive in her winter attire.

She paused on the sidewalk, not to reevaluate her shoes as she had earlier but in amazement. In the midst of yesterday's snowstorm, Christmas had fully arrived in Holly Pointe.

The business district was decked out and ready for the upcoming holiday. Every storefront boasted lights, and each window held Christmas displays. She wondered whether there was an official directive prohibiting hawking Christmas goods until after the Thanksgiving weekend.

If so, Stella heartily concurred. But she was just as glad that the community had turned that corner.

Overhead, piped-in Christmas music filled the air, and Stella found herself humming along. There was just something cheery about Christmas songs.

"I love your hat." A young woman tossed the compliment over her shoulder, accompanied by a friendly smile as she and her friend hurried past Stella on the sidewalk.

"Thanks." Stella wondered if the woman had read the same article she had about the value of random compliments. Then again, this was a friendly community.

People looked you in the eye and smiled when they met you on the sidewalk. They spoke with you as if you were friends instead of complete strangers when you stood in line. The entire town seemed to subscribe to the notion that strangers were just friends you hadn't met.

When the woman with the compliment opened the door to Dough See Dough and the smell of sugar and yeast floated out, Stella was oh-so-tempted to follow her and her friend inside. But she kept walking, reminding herself she hadn't yet had a chance to work off the calories from the coffee cake.

Besides, she was on a mission to see the business district.

The antique store called to her, especially when she saw a Furby in the window. Stella adored the electronic pet she'd received for her eighth birthday. Her hand was on the shop's ornate brass door handle when she saw Melinda step inside Rosie's diner.

Stella hadn't spoken with Mel since Saturday at Star Lake. Now that she had more information on Kenny, she might be able to gather more details from Melinda. After looking both ways, Stella jaywalked across Birch Road, dodging a huge snow pile near the far curb.

Instead of rushing inside, Stella took a moment to appreciate the exterior of the diner. A green-and-white awning stretched out over a large plate glass window where the words "Rosie's Place" were etched into the glass. A white wooden bench sat in front of the building. Stella could almost see the bench flanked by bright pots of flowers during the spring and summer months.

Holly Pointe would be pretty in the spring, she thought with a sigh. Regardless of what she'd intimated about staying here, Stella knew she'd be gone long before the snow melted and flowers filled the pots.

Stella pulled open the door of the diner. Sounds of laughter and conversation immediately spilled onto the sidewalk along with the tempting aroma of fried meat and grilled onions. Stella's stomach gave one enthusiastic thumbs-up.

For a period of time in her early twenties, Stella had flirted with being a vegan, but being a carnivore came much more naturally, and she'd made the switch back without much of a fight.

Inside the toasty-warm eatery, Stella spotted the sign on a metal stand requesting that patrons seat themselves. After a second's deliberation, she chose a booth by the window. The seats were upholstered in burgundy with a V-shaped insert of white in the backs. The tabletop was gray Formica with silver edging.

Though nothing fancy, the place had a homey vibe that Stella found appealing.

Based on the people streaming in through the front door, it appeared the lunch rush had left the starting gate. The waitresses, both in their late teens or early twenties, appeared to have the dining area divided into two sections.

Wearing jeans and red shirts emblazoned with the Rosie's Place logo, the girls moved from table to table with well-oiled efficiency.

At the moment, Melinda was nowhere in sight.

"Hi. I'm Fauna. What can I get you?" The young woman with spiky blonde hair cocked her head, a pencil poised above her notepad.

"Shauna, do you have a menu?"

"It's Fauna, like Shauna only with an *f*." The girl, er woman, pulled the plastic-coated menu from the tabletop holder and handed it to Stella. "I'll give you a few minutes to—"

"No. I can decide." Stella flipped open the menu and scanned the items. "I'll take a Green River and a hamburger, hold the onions."

"Got it." Fauna spun on her heel.

"Wait."

The waitress turned and lifted a pierced brow. "Something else?"

"My name is Stella, and I'm a friend of Mel's. If you see her, tell her that if she has a minute, to stop out and say hello."

Curiosity filled the girl's gaze as she studied Stella. "Will do."

Stella had eaten most of her burger and drank half her Green River—which she discovered was a bright-green lime-flavored soft drink—before Melinda made an appearance.

The redhead's face brightened when she spotted Stella. She hurried across the shiny hardwood floor and took a seat opposite Stella.

"I was hoping you were still here." Mel absently brushed back a curl that had come loose from the hair pulled back in a severe knot. "I'm training a new cook, and he didn't understand that— Well, no matter, he's doing great now. How are you?"

There was such warmth and gladness in Mel's voice that Stella fought a wave of guilt. She reminded herself that she genuinely liked Melinda. She was not simply using their burgeoning friendship to get information for her article.

"I'm good. Just exploring the town this morning. Faith texted that there would likely be sledding on the big hill north of the high school this afternoon. I thought I'd head over there once school gets out and get a few pictures." Stella smiled. "Hopefully, there will be lots of colorful coats, hats, and sleds to make the scene appear festive and inviting."

"I have no doubt." Mel yawned, covering her mouth with the tips of her fingers. "Sorry. I'm exhausted."

"I have trouble with insomnia sometimes, too."

"The only trouble I'm having is that I could sleep all the time."

"Which means you must need the rest." Stella wondered if her friend's lack of sleep had to do with worry over her mother's recent surgery. "How's your mom coming along?"

"Doing better every day. Thanks for asking." Mel glanced around the diner. "It's driving her crazy not being here, but I told her that's why she had kids. We'll keep the place going until the doctor clears her to be back."

"How long has she had the business?"

Mel's gaze turned thoughtful. "She purchased it when I was three, so that means she's owned it for over twenty-five years."

Stella took a sip of her Green River and tried to recall what she knew about Mel's parents. Not much, she realized. "What about your father? Does he help out, too?"

"My dad died not long after I was born. A freak construction accident." Mel's gaze scanned the dining area, as if making sure the two servers had everything under control. Satisfied, she refocused on Stella. "Mom married my stepdad, Bruce, when I was six. That marriage lasted nearly ten years, but Mom was smart enough to get a prenup, so when they split, he didn't have any claim on the diner."

"Do you think he'd have tried to take half?" Stella kept her tone offhand.

"I don't think so." Mell shrugged. "But it wasn't a happy marriage."

"Ten years is a long time to stay when you're unhappy."

"I think Mom stuck it out for so long because she doesn't like to fail at anything." Mel shrugged. "The marriage wasn't horrible. They just weren't a good fit."

Stella nodded sympathetically. "Not happy like Kenny and Norma. Norma was telling me she and Kenny will be married fifty years in January."

"No, nothing like Kenny and Norma." Mel's smile lit up her

face, chasing away the signs of fatigue. "That marriage is a match made in heaven."

"Norma admitted they've had rough times. Something about a lot of stress when their eldest daughter was first diagnosed with diabetes." Stella kept it vague, hoping Mel would fill in.

"My mom mentioned something about Kenny having a rough go of it when Leslie was diagnosed. Apparently, Kenny's mom had diabetes and had a lot of issues because of it, so he was extra worried when Leslie got the diagnosis."

Before Stella could ask any questions, Mel continued.

"I wasn't even born then, so I don't really don't know what went on." Mel picked up the paper from the straw and folded it. "What I know is that I've never seen a happier couple than Kenny and Norma."

Stella decided there was no point in asking more questions. It was apparent if anyone had the information she sought it would be Rosie, not Mel.

"I almost forgot to mention, I saw your brother this morning." Stella switched topics. "He was with his friend, Zach."

"They're together a lot. Derek and Zach are business partners," Mel informed her. "As well as best friends. He was always over at our house. In fact, Zach and I dated in high school."

"That's interesting." Though her gaze remained fixed on Mel, Stella kept her tone casual, as she stirred the ice in her drink with the straw. "Now that you're back in town, do you think you'll pick up where you left off?"

Mel made a face. "It's too soon for me to think about dating again."

"Was there someone special in Burlington?"

"Yes, but it wasn't going anywhere." Mel straightened. "It's for the best we're no longer together."

"I've had a few relationships that time and distance assured me I was better off without." Stella hesitated for just a second. "My last error in judgement ended up being married."

The spoon Mel had been toying with slipped from her fingers and clattered to the table. "You dated someone who was married?"

"I didn't know he was married." Stella expelled a breath, feeling stupid all over again. "Tony said he was single. Looking back, I realize there were signs I ignored. Not necessarily flashing neon lights that said "This Guy Is Married," but indications that he was involved with someone else."

"I'm sorry." Reaching across the table, Mel covered Stella's hand with hers. "I can't imagine how betrayed you felt."

"It hurt," Stella admitted.

"You cared about him."

"At the time." Stella gave a little laugh. "But once I stepped back, I realized something. I liked Tony, but I didn't love him. I was using him to keep the loneliness at bay. If we'd ever made the mistake of getting married, we'd never have gone the distance. We'd have eventually broken up, like your mom and Bruce."

Stella paused for breath and realized with sudden horror that she'd been rambling. Worse, she'd been spilling her secrets to someone she'd just met. Though she had to admit, she felt closer to Melinda than she did to friends she'd had for years.

"I'm sorry, Mel." Stella could feel the heat on her cheeks. "You've got enough on your plate without listening to my stories of past mistakes."

"We're friends," Mel paused as if seeking confirmation of that fact.

Stella nodded.

"Well, friends listen and friends console." Mel's lips quirked upward. "Sometimes they even kick each other in the butt if one of them is acting particularly stupid."

"Which I was."

"You moved on." Mel's gaze grew distant. "I moved on. That makes us strong, brilliant women."

Mel must have seen the questions in Stella's eyes because she held up one hand. Two bright patches of color now prominent on her pale cheeks. "I'll save my big mistake story for another time when we have lots of wine and more privacy."

"Whenever." Stella told her.

"It may be a while. The episode is still fresh. I need some time to process."

"I'm not going anywhere. Take all the time you need."

Mel lifted a brow. "Do I take that to mean you've decided to remain in Holly Pointe?"

"Let's just say I'm giving it serious consideration." It was unfair to lead Mel on—and to lead herself on as well. While Stella had started to think how nice it would be to make a home here, she had to be realistic.

Her life was in Miami. Her job was in Miami.

And once the article came out, Stella would be persona non grata in this town.

Unless, she didn't turn in the story...

But that was crazy. She'd made a commitment to Jane, and she needed to complete the assignment.

"Are you okay?"

Stella blinked. "I'm fine. I was just wondering if you'd seen Faith."

"I believe she's working in her shop all day." Mel thought for a moment, then nodded. "Yes, she mentioned having some projects she needed to finish up and get out in the mail."

"Her shop?"

"Her business—Faith Original—is located a couple of blocks from here on Willow Street." Mel's expression relaxed, as if thinking of Faith brought comfort. "Christmas is her busiest season. I was actually surprised to see her at the lake on Saturday. But she takes her job as president of the chamber very seriously."

"What kind of business is Faith Original?" Stella asked.

Mel smiled. "Once you finish here, you need to stop over and see for yourself."

Like all the shops in the area, the frontage for Faith Original was dressed for Christmas. Someone with considerable talent had painted white birch trees on the window along with little snowflakes. Six or seven cardinals in flight accented the rows of tiny red lights edging the bottom and top of the window.

A black sign with white lettering proclaimed, "Faith Original." The black-and-white look was crisp and professional, and the swirly hand-lettered font added a touch of whimsy.

The whimsy had Stella smiling as she pushed open the door to the sound of tinkling silver bells. Like Mel, she always smiled when she thought of Faith.

The shop wasn't large, but somehow the showroom managed to hold every manner of signs without seeming cluttered. Stella saw all sizes; from small ones that could fit in her palm to ones that would fill a good-size space on any wall.

One large one held only words in a bold script that spoke of love. The first line had Stella's heart squeezing tight. "Don't just pretend to love others. Really love them."

Was that what she was doing? Pretending to love this town and the people in it while getting ready to put a knife in their back?

It was as if the sign was speaking directly to her. Stella shifted her gaze and reminded herself that there was nothing wrong with gathering and reporting factual information.

The door to the back room opened, and Faith hurried out. "I'm sorry to keep you waiting—"

Her smile widened when she saw Stella. Faith held out both hands as she crossed the room, easily dodging a display reading, "Smile. Sparkle. Shine."

On this table were signs with magic wands, some strewn with glitter, and a few with only words. Stella's favorite was the one proclaiming, "She leaves a little sparkle wherever she goes."

She wondered whether that's how the citizens of Holly Pointe would view her once they read her article. Or would they see her as someone who whipped up a storm, then left town?

Stella didn't have time to do more than wonder because her cold hands were caught up in Faith's warm ones. There was something about the woman that soothed and steadied her.

Perhaps it was the way Faith always looked you straight in the eyes with a friendliness that made you feel completely accepted. Or the slow way she had of speaking, with just the merest hint of southern accent. An accent that, Stella realized, hadn't registered until just this moment.

Stella had assumed that Faith had grown up in Holly Pointe. But she was obviously a transplant. The thought piqued Stella's curiosity.

"You have a lovely shop." Stella squeezed Faith's hands then stepped back.

"It's small but, because most of my business is online, it works." Faith picked up a rustic sign from the Christmas display that read "It's the Most Wonderful Time of the Year." "This is a huge seller, but surprisingly I also sell quite a few of 'Seas and Greetings.'"

Stella studied the blue crabs with the Santa hats. "I love the font and the crabs. I can see people in Florida going for this one."

"That's the state where most of those end up being shipped," Faith confirmed.

"Do you paint them all yourself?" Stella was amazed at the detail and the skill.

"I do." Faith smiled. "A labor of love."

"I'm impressed."

"I'm blessed to be able to do something that brings people joy and brings me a livable income." Setting down the Christmas sign, Faith moved to a display containing what Stella thought of as motivational sayings.

Faith picked up one that was striking in its simplicity. "Be Kind Be Bold Be Brave Be You."

The message had Stella's gut clenching.

"I'd like you to have this one. Consider it an early Christmas gift." Faith held it out. "This reminds me of you."

Stella saw no choice but to take the sign. "It's lovely, but how does it remind you of me?"

"Partially because you're a reporter."

"Former reporter," Stella clarified.

"I imagine being a reporter is as much who you are as what you do. Oh, forgive my lack of manners. Please, let me take your coat."

Stella took off her hat and slipped out of the coat.

After stuffing the knit cap into the coat sleeve, Faith hung the parka on a lovely antique coat tree with porcelain hooks. Then she gestured to Stella to have a seat in a wooden folding chair that was as ancient as the coat tree.

"What do you mean that being a reporter is as much who I am as what I do?"

"I believe to be a good reporter you have to be open-minded and compassionate. You have to possess a desire to tell the truth." Faith's soft brown eyes warmed. "Those characteristics are at the core of who you are, whether you're currently employed by a newspaper or not."

Stella's hands tightened around the sign she held in her lap. "A reporter sometimes offends. It's the nature of the beast."

"Of course," Faith concurred. "Bringing the truth to light takes courage. Exposing wrong takes being brave. But under it all is the knowledge that what you're doing, what you're writing, matters and is for the greater good."

CHAPTER NINE

An hour and two cups of herbal tea later, Stella left Faith's shop with her sign in a shopping bag and a heavy heart. Her cheery mood of the morning had taken a serious nosedive.

Faith's admiration and view of journalistic integrity was misplaced. *Naïve*, Stella told herself, latching on to the word. Yes, Faith's view of journalism was naïve and not at all in sync with life in the twenty-first century.

Stella tried not to think too hard about the fact that up until a year ago, she herself had viewed the industry in the same way as Faith. But things changed, and reporters had to change with them or go the way of the buggy whip.

Or stand in the unemployment line.

There was absolutely nothing wrong with writing a factual story about a small town in northern Vermont. Stella had already made it clear to Jane that she would not include any information she hadn't verified.

It was a weak argument for betraying her new friends. A story about a small Christmas town didn't need to include a drunken Santa or a couple's marital issues. If money was diverted to wrong sources, that would make sense to include. The other two smacked of sensationalized journalism.

Still, Stella reminded herself for the zillionth time, if she didn't write this story, someone else would. At least she would be factual. She had a couple of reporter friends who wouldn't care whether what they wrote was skewed.

Better her than them, she reassured herself.

Though school wouldn't get out for another hour, Stella decided to head to the hill on the high school's north side for some preliminary shots. Faith had said the school was within walking distance but had advised driving.

Stella decided the fresh air was what she needed to clear her head. Unfortunately, the wind had picked up, and she was walking right into it. She told herself that would only make the trek home more pleasant.

She tugged up the scarf with her gloved hands, making sure it covered her nose and mouth. The sidewalks were cleared, but the walk soon felt endless.

"Hey," a familiar deep voice called out. "Want a lift?"

Stella was no fool. She scurried—well, as much as you could scurry while wearing Ugg boots on snowy sidewalks—toward Sam's truck. Wrenching open the door, she slid inside. The warmth wrapped around her like a lover's caress.

"I'll take that as a yes."

Pushing down the scarf to expose her face, Stella shot him a rueful smile. "It's colder out there than it looks."

"The wind picked up."

"I noticed that." She leaned her head against the back of the seat and reveled in the air from the heater.

"Where were you headed?"

"The high school. Faith said it was a little over a mile from her shop. She told me I should drive." The warmth from the heated seat was heavenly. "I should have listened to her."

Sam made no move to put the truck into gear, but Stella

didn't care. She was out of the wind and warming up. That's all that mattered right now.

"It's closer to two miles from her shop to the school." Sam's concerned gaze swept over her.

"So I had another mile to go?"

"A little less, but close enough."

Stella made a face. "Then, I'm doubly glad you stopped to give me a ride."

"What's at the school?"

"Sledding. I wanted to get some pictures."

She didn't say more, didn't have to, as she could see the recognition in Sam's dark eyes even before he nodded.

"You planned to walk home in the dark?"

"What? No," she shook her head. "I wasn't going to stay that long. Just an hour or so."

"It's winter. The sun will set around four."

Stella cocked her head. "It doesn't set until around five thirty in Miami."

"You're farther north."

"I can tell." Stella took off her gloves and rubbed her hands together then stuck them under her legs, letting the warmth of the seat heat them up.

Sam's gaze turned sharp and assessing. "Your coat is adequate, and so is the hat. But you need better gloves. Mittens are warmer. Look for ones that are arctic rated."

Stella glanced down at the ones in her lap. "These were fine for skiing."

He shrugged. "They weren't keeping your hands warm today."

"You're right, they didn't."

Sam reached across her and opened the glove box. "Take the pair in there. You can use them until you get new ones that work."

Stella took the mittens. Even she could see they'd be too big. "But they're—"

"I realize they're big. But they're also warm."

Thanks to the air blowing on her and the heated seats, her fingers were warming up. But Stella knew once she stepped out of the truck, her hands would be cold again.

"Thank you." She sighed. "I'll have to take them off to snap pictures."

"Once you're done, put them on again."

"Did anyone ever tell you that you're bossy?" But her tone teased, and he grinned.

"Only you. Now put on your seatbelt, and I'll drive you to the high school."

Sam watched Stella put the mittens on then take them off during the short drive to the school.

She studied the inside. "All of this winter stuff is still new to me."

"You didn't grow up in this climate." Sam kept his tone light. "I'm sure you could teach me a thing or two about alligators and lizards."

She chuckled. "More than you probably want to know."

"Around here, there really isn't a lot to learn. When it's cold, you dress warmly. You don't go out in a blizzard if you can help it. You steer a car in the direction of a skid and you make sure your vehicle always has plenty of gas." He paused for a moment. "That's about it."

"You forgot one thing." She pinched the glove between her finger and thumb and dangled it in the air. "Mittens are warmer than gloves."

"You're a quick study, Ms. Carpenter." Sam kept his tone light. "If you decide to stay, by next winter you'll be a pro at this stuff."

She dropped the mitten to her lap. "I like it here."

Stella made the confession as if the thought surprised her.

"You didn't expect to?" He slowed the truck as he entered the lot used for evening sporting events and pulled into an empty spot next to a minivan.

"I knew I liked the area when my parents and I skied Jay's Peak. But that was vacation, and other than the staff at the resort, I had no contact with anyone who lived here."

"Now that you've got a few days under your belt, what do you think of us?" Sam found himself holding his breath. It was then that he realized that he cared a little too much what this woman thought of the area. And him.

"Everyone is nice. It's like you're a family." She flushed. "That probably sounds stupid."

"Not stupid at all." Sam made no move to open the door, reluctant to leave the truck and share her with the world. "I feel that way too. I think you appreciate the family feeling more when you don't have any of your own around."

Stella unfastened her seat belt then shifted in her seat to face him. "How long has it been since your parents lived here?"

Because of their celebrity, Sam didn't usually talk about his parents with strangers. But Stella wasn't a stranger. Not anymore.

"For as far back as I can remember, my parents had one foot in Holly Pointe and the other in the city."

"You're talking about New York City?"

"Yes." He smiled. "That's where their work is, and really, their hearts are there too."

"Then why even have a home in Holly Pointe?"

"My father grew up here. My mother came from a farm in Iowa."

"Seriously?"

"Why? You don't think small-town folk can succeed in New York City?"

To his surprise, Stella appeared to be mulling over the question. "I think it would be more difficult."

"Actually, I disagree." As she'd done only moments before, Sam relaxed back against his seat. "I firmly believe coming from a stable base with a strong work ethic is why you see so many people from communities like Holly Pointe and small-town Iowa succeed."

"It seems to me there's such a temptation to stay with the familiar. Or to head home when the going gets tough."

"It comes down to how much you want the dream. Whatever that dream may be." Out the windshield, Sam observed a steady stream of people heading to the hill. If Stella wanted pictures of the sledding, she wasn't going to get them sitting in the cab of his truck.

He pushed open the door and waited until Stella joined him on the sidewalk to continue the conversation. "People like me who enjoy this type of life and who can meet their goals in such an environment stay. Those like my parents leave to soar elsewhere."

"You were never tempted?" Stella hesitated. "Not even when you were dating an up-and-coming Broadway star?"

Sam slanted a sideways glance. "You're speaking about my friendship with Britt."

"The tabloids made it sound like more." Though Stella's tone remained offhand, he heard the question.

Sam considered carefully his next words. Now that Britt had made it big on Broadway, like his parents, he was careful what he revealed.

Not because he didn't trust the person he was speaking with but because they might say something to another who would say something to another. By the time someone posted on social media about what he'd supposedly said—because that would inevitably happen—it was so far from the truth as to be unrecognizable.

"Britt and I were good friends. We still are." And that was all he planned to say on the matter.

Stella inclined her head. "Do you ever go to New York to see her?"

It suddenly struck him that Stella might be concerned that he and Britt were still involved. "When the play that my father wrote and my mother produced opened, I went to see it. I saw Britt at the party afterward. We were all thrilled with the great reviews."

"That was the role that won her the Tony."

"You seem to know a lot about Br-Broadway." Sam almost said "Britt" but caught himself in time. Derek's warning flashed like a neon light in his head.

"I looked you up online." Stella studied him through lowered lashes. "When I'm interested in a guy, I like to know as much about him as I can. Have you done a search on me?"

Startled, Sam could only stare. "No."

"You may not have done it yet." Stella flashed a blinding smile. "But you will."

The snow-covered hill provided the perfect backdrop for the brightly colored coats and sleds. The sun hung low in the sky, and it was times like this that Stella longed for her Fuji.

Still, she was able to adjust the shutter speed and light sensitivity for better exposure.

While she moved around for better angles, Sam remained off to one side. He was talking with Derek, who'd brought his daughter and a couple of her friends then stayed to watch.

Stella posted to various social media sites, proclaiming that December fun in Holly Pointe didn't just happen at Christmas. Slipping her camera back in her coat pocket, she gratefully pulled on the mittens and strode to where Sam and Derek stood. "I'm ready to leave whenever you are."

"Did you get some good shots?" Derek asked.

Stella recognized his coat as a Carhartt. Instead of a stocking cap, Derek's head and ears were covered by a trapper hat with fur ear flaps. While not exactly in the height of style, Stella now understood and appreciated the value of warmth.

"I did." Stella glanced at the hill where Camryn and her friends were piling on a long toboggan for another run. "I took several of your daughter and her friends. "If you'd like them..."

"I'd love to have them." Derek glanced at Sam. "Give her my number and she can text them to me."

"Will do."

"Excuse me, Derek." Stella surprised Sam by taking his arm. "Sam and I have an appointment."

Sam cocked his head.

She flashed a smile. "You and me are going to slide down that big ole hill."

Sam lifted his hands. "I don't do sledding."

"You used to." Derek's comment earned him a scowl from Sam.

"C'mon, Sam, please. Do it for me."

What was it about her smile that he found so impossible to resist? "Okay."

Derek laughed and promised to take pictures as Stella took Sam's hand, and they started up the hill.

"Thank you. Sincerely." She cast a sideways glance and squeezed his arm. "I can't write about something I haven't experienced."

"Your parents were from Minnesota," he reminded her as they reached the top. "Do you really expect me to believe you never went down a hill on a sled?"

"I've gone down a hill or two in my day." There was that smile again. "But never with you."

∼

That night, after dropping Stella off at her car and heading home, Sam opened up his laptop and keyed in Stella's name.

He checked her educational background and her work history. She'd graduated from the University of Florida in Gainesville and had interned at the local newspaper. After graduating with a journalism degree focusing on reporting and online media, she'd been hired by the local paper.

It was during her time with the local paper that she'd been recognized for the series of articles on teens making a difference in their community. Sam studied the picture of her with the award. Though that couldn't have been more than three years ago, she looked younger somehow. A fresh-faced innocent.

That would have been before her parents had been killed. The kind of tragedy she'd experienced would destroy anyone's innocence.

Her LinkedIn page confirmed her education, her position in Gainesville, and the one at the *Miami Sun Times*. On one of her personal account pages he found a picture of her with four other reporters who'd been downsized the same September day from the *Sun Times*.

Everything she'd told him checked out.

Before closing his laptop, he did a search on her parents, then wished he hadn't. In the pictures with Stella, they all looked so happy. Stella had even posted several shots on that Thanksgiving weekend before they died, celebrating Stella's new job with the *Sun Times*.

Stella hadn't known that when they got into that car to drive home that she would never see them again. At least with Kevin there had been plenty of opportunities to say good-bye. To let him know how much of a difference he'd made and how much he'd be missed.

Stella had never had that chance.

Sam sat back.

When he'd dropped Stella off tonight, it had taken all his

willpower not to kiss her. The attraction that had been simmering since that first meeting on the sidewalk had only continued to increase.

Each time he was with her, he liked her more. And he had the feeling that interest went both ways. The only thing holding him back was the thought that she might be leaving.

But was that really a reason not to get involved? So what if she left in a month? By that time, whatever sizzle existed between them could be long over anyway.

Look at him and Britt. There had been potential there, but when she'd wanted more, he'd backed off. In the end, the bond they'd forged had been one of friendship.

It could be the same with him and Stella. There wasn't any reason, at least none he could think of, that should stop him from enjoying her company and getting to know her better during the time she was in Holly Pointe.

Sam steepled his fingers. Yes, there was so much more about Stella Carpenter to explore.

He couldn't wait to begin.

CHAPTER TEN

Stella uploaded the pictures of Dustin and Krista's twin boys sliding down the hill on a bright-red sled to her private account at the *Sun Times*. They were either with one parent or the other, even though there had been plenty of space on the big toboggan for both parents.

Which proved absolutely nothing.

Especially since, while one of the parents was with the kids going down the hill, the other one was taking pictures. The four were extremely photogenic and could be a poster for "Families Having Fun."

There might not be any trouble in the marriage, but Stella wished she could see more intimacy between the couple. They didn't need to hold hands; even a loving glance or two would have assuaged her suspicions.

Which meant she needed to continue to observe and document her observations.

That had become increasingly difficult this afternoon when she'd dragged Sam to the top of the hill. He'd gotten into the spirit by borrowing a sled from the daughter of a friend of a friend. The lime-green toboggan that had once held four children now only held her and Sam.

Stella sat in front with Sam's arms around her as the kids gave them a big push. The hill, which she'd labeled as "small" in her blog post, seemed somehow larger now that she was at the top and careening downward.

Stella couldn't remember when she'd laughed so much. They'd borrowed another sled, this one more of a classic, for their last trip together. Then each had gone down alone on a brightly colored saucer sled.

While the saucers were fun, except when she overturned near the bottom, Stella missed Sam's arms around her.

He'd come quickly to her assistance when she'd taken the spill. Pulling her up, he dusted off the snow, and for a second, just a second, she swore he was going to kiss her.

Her lips had begun to tingle, and her breath had come in short puffs.

Then he'd stepped back and handed the saucers to two middle-school-age boys and thanked them for the loan.

Just remembering that moment had Stella lifting her fingers to her mouth.

She'd wanted him to kiss her. Heck, it had taken all her willpower not to wrap her arms around his neck and kiss him first.

Only that stubborn willpower had stopped her and the knowledge that by the time New Year's Eve rolled around, she'd be back in Florida.

Oh, and the knowledge that by that time, he'd probably hate her.

Immediately after the thought surfaced, instead of accepting it as fact, Stella took a moment to dissect it.

While it was true that she'd be leaving Holly Pointe at the end of December, did that really prevent her from exchanging a few kisses with Sam?

While it was also true that she was committed to writing a story on Holly Pointe for Jane, she'd also stressed to the editor that her story would not be filled with innuendos or exaggerated facts. If there was something that could be corroborated and would appeal to the readers of the *Sun Times*, she would include that information.

Other than not informing Sam that she was doing the article, he shouldn't have a problem with her simply reporting the facts. As the city administrator, he should welcome the publicity.

Still, she wished she could be completely up front with him about why she was here. But she knew that if she was, he would tell the others, and the town would close ranks. Stella wouldn't get her story, and Jane would give the open staff position to someone else.

Not to mention that Holly Pointe would lose out on valuable publicity.

No, it was better if she kept her mouth shut.

Her fingers returned to her lips for another brief moment before she returned to inputting her notes on Dustin Bellamy and Krista Ankrom.

"Can you believe tomorrow officially marks the start of the holiday season?" Kate waved a forkful of roast beef in the air. "I know I'm going to sound like my grandmother, but seriously, where did the year go?"

After taking photos of several houses that had gone all out with Christmas lights and decorations, Stella had accepted Kate's offer to meet for lunch at Rosie's. Unfortunately, Mel was stuck in the kitchen today and couldn't join them.

Puzzled, Stella pulled her brows together. "What about the event at Star Lake? I thought that was the start? I mean, Santa already made an appearance."

"I realize that's a bit confusing." Kate offered a rueful smile. "I'll explain it all after another bite of this fabulous hot beef sandwich."

Kate took a moment to stab some beef, bread, and potato, all smothered in brown gravy, onto her fork.

Stella glanced down at her salad then back at Kate's plate. Next time, she'd forget about being good and get the hot beef.

"Ohmigosh, that is fabulous." She smiled at Stella. "Want to try a bite?"

"I'm tempted," Stella told her. "Seriously tempted. But I'm afraid I'd like it so much I might snatch your plate, and you'd be left with my salad."

"Good to know." Kate hunched over and pretended to be guarding her food. Then she sat back and laughed. "I love you, Stella. I'm so glad you came to Holly Pointe."

Her laugh was such a happy sound that the couple at a nearby table turned and smiled.

"I'm glad I came here, too."

Stella thought about what the holidays would have been like had she stayed in Miami.

Tasha would have left town to spend Christmas with her family. Since Tash and her roommate had made it clear they wanted her out, Stella would have felt compelled to quickly find somewhere affordable to live, not an easy task during prime tourist season.

She would have been stressed and probably very much in grinch mode. Instead, she was spending December in the Christmas capital of the USA.

Which reminded her . . .

"You still haven't told me why tomorrow's the kickoff of the season."

Kate wiped a spot of gravy from the corner of her lips. "The thing is, we used to have Santa's initial appearance be at the First Friday event, which has always been the week after the Thanksgiving weekend. But several years ago, residents wanted a change. Many of them had family in town over Thanksgiving, and they wanted the kids to be able to see Santa during that weekend, so we moved it back a week."

"You're telling me the town caved."

"Well, here's the thing. Having Santa show up Thanksgiving weekend has become really common across the country."

Stella thought of Santa's Enchanted Forest and how Santa was there for two months starting the first part of November. "You're right. Just like we now expect to see Christmas decorations up in October."

"Exactly." Kate pushed the plate back and heaved a satisfied sigh. "I'm full. But that was amazing."

As much as Stella understood that Kate loved food, she was done talking about roast beef. At least until she ordered her own plate of it next time she was in the diner. "Let me see if I've got this straight. You're saying Kenny, er, Santa, makes two first appearances."

Kate gave a decisive nod. "Right."

"And tomorrow is the true start of the holiday season in Holly Pointe."

Another nod. "Right."

"On the list of events Faith gave me to cover, it simply says, 'Lighting of town tree. Santa Claus arrives.'"

"That's true," Kate acknowledged, "but there's more to the night than those two things."

"I thought maybe there was."

Kate smiled. "It's really special. It's not only the lights on the tree; the courthouse explodes in lights. Everyone applauds and cheers. The high school band plays Christmas songs, and everyone sings."

Stella could practically see the crowds and lights and hear the tuba rendition of "We Wish You a Merry Christmas." She raised her fingers to her temples feeling a headache coming on.

Kate laughed. "Seriously, it's loads of fun. Some people dance while others sing. There are red-and-white-striped inflatable balls that look like pieces of holiday candy being batted around."

Feeling slightly shell-shocked, Stella only nodded. Last year, when she'd gone home with Tasha, any holiday events she'd attended had involved fine wine and china plates. This sounded a whole lot more . . . energetic.

Because Kate stared expectantly, Stella offered a weak smile. "Sounds exciting."

"Be sure to dress warmly." Kate gestured with one hand, though Stella's feet were safely tucked under the table. "Leave the heels, pull out your Uggs."

"Got it." Stella hoped she wouldn't regret asking, but it was best to be prepared. She forced some enthusiasm into her voice. "How long, ah, will this fabulous night of frivolity last?"

The twinkle in Kate's eyes told Stella she wasn't fooling anyone, least of all her friend. "About two hours."

"Then everyone just goes home?"

"Some do. Some go to the bakery, coffee shop, or one of the restaurants. Those with children can usually be found in the courthouse ballroom, which has been decorated for Christmas. On First Friday, the room is filled with Christmas-themed games for children."

Stella's head spun. "So many events, so little time."

Kate patted her hand sympathetically. "You'll get tons of great pictures. Do you know what else?"

Stella was almost afraid to ask. "What?"

"You'll have a whole lot of fun."

Dressed for an arctic apocalypse, Stella strolled down the street to the imposing courthouse. Even if she hadn't spoken with Kate or had the email from Faith indicating where tonight's even was being held, she'd have known exactly where to go.

The main street had been closed to vehicular traffic and there was a surge of bodies going in only one direction.

"Hey, little lady, it's good to see you again." The gray-haired man with the handlebar moustache offered her a smile. He had a little girl in each hand.

He must have caught her look because he grinned. "My two grands, Addie and Allison. Their mom and grandma are each working games inside the ballroom."

"There's a bazillion lights on the tree," Addie informed her.

"Once they turn on, Grandpa is going to take us to see Santa." Allison gazed up at the older man as if seeking confirmation.

"Yer darn tootin.'" The man shot his granddaughter a wink.

They were nearly to the courthouse when Stella placed the man. He'd been one of a foursome playing cards at the Busy Bean the day she arrived in town.

She recalled seeing Kenny walk over to the table and place a hand on the man's shoulder as if they were friends.

"I don't believe we've met. I'm Stella Carpenter. I'm handling the social media for the Christmas season." Stella smiled. "I remember seeing you at the Busy Bean the first day I arrived. You're a friend of Kenny's."

"And of Norma's too. Stood up for Kenny at their wedding." The man returned Stella's smile, showing a large gap between his front teeth. "Name's Larry Kotopka."

As the crowd neared the courthouse, Stella saw Larry's gaze searching the crowd. Searching for what? His son-in-law? A friend?

"I bet it's nice having," Stella paused, conscious of the closeness of little ears, "Santa Claus as a good friend."

Larry returned his attention to Stella. "Holly Pointe couldn't have picked a better man for the job."

"Agreed." Stella thought quickly, had to think quickly, because she knew in a second Larry would be gone. "It's got to be stressful."

She started to say more, then left it at that. At the beginning of her career, she'd discovered that creating a presumptive sentence got her more answers than a direct question.

Whoever she was speaking with usually assumed she already knew the information they were about to reveal.

"Yeah, Norma's diagnosis hit him hard." Larry made a sound between his teeth as he shook his head.

Norma's diagnosis?

Stella thought of the jovial woman with the white hair and ready smile. A knot formed in the pit of her stomach. Though Norma didn't look sick, that was no guarantee of good health.

"I hope she can beat . . . it."

"I told Kenny they'll have many more years together." Sadness passed like a shadow over Larry's face. "In time he'll come to believe me. Right now, he's struggling with all of it."

Had he turned to the bottle because of the stress? She wanted to ask but it didn't feel like the right time.

"I wish I could do something to help him and Norma." Stella meant every word. She'd grown fond of Kenny and Norma.

Apparently, Larry could hear her sincerity, because he stopped walking and turned to Stella. "There is something you can do."

"Tell me what it is. I'll do it."

"Pray for Norma. Pray for Kenny. That's what they need most right about now."

Stella stared for a minute, then slowly nodded. "I will."

"We'll see you around." Larry glanced down at his granddaughters. "Tell Stella Merry Christmas, girls."

"Merry Christmas, Stella," the girls said in a single sing-song tone.

"Merry Christmas, Stella." This time it was decidedly male voice, and a strong arm shot around her shoulders.

Sam pulled her to him, preventing a collision as three teenage boys wearing Santa hats, pushed through the crowd.

"Charlie." Sam gripped one of the boy's arms. "This isn't a football field."

The boy, broad shouldered and strong as a bull, turned and grinned. "Sorry, Sam."

The kid bellowed to his friends. "Slow down. You're not rushing the line."

"I didn't know if I'd see you tonight." Stella couldn't keep the gladness from her voice.

"I was hoping to run into you," he said.

"You were?" The words sounded oddly breathless even to her own ears.

"I thought to myself, Who would I like to spend First Friday with? And do you know what?"

Stella couldn't keep from smiling. "What?"

"Your name was at the top of the list."

CHAPTER ELEVEN

She fit right in. Like a piece of a puzzle that had been missing for so long you weren't sure of the last time you'd seen it. But once found, it slid in perfectly.

Sam watched Stella charm a couple of tourists from Quebec City. He listened as she conversed with them in flawless French and took their picture.

Stella spoke French?

He'd learned something new about her today.

She turned to Sam. "They want to know when we're going to light up the tree."

He liked the *we* part of that statement. Despite being here only a short time, she was quickly becoming part of the community and his life.

"I'll be throwing the switch in one minute." The words had barely left his lips when the countdown clock, temporarily installed on the side of the courthouse, started up.

A roar rose from the crowd as they noticed the movement in the digital clock. They began to count down each second. Fifty-six. Fifty-five.Fifty-four.

Stella leaned close to his ear to be heard. "You flip the switch?"

He nodded, knowing he couldn't be heard above the crowd. With every second, the crowd had grown louder. Pulling his phone from his pocket, Sam pointed to the app displayed, then to the tree.

Understanding shown in her eyes. There was no need to update the tourists. They were now counting down the numbers with everyone else.

Stella reached for the camera tucked into her bag, then made some adjustments to the settings.

Sam followed her with his eyes as she backed up and jostled for a better position on the steps leading up to the front of the courthouse. Though he understood she was hoping for a better angle, everyone was packed together like sardines with all eyes on the tree.

One glance at his phone's display confirmed that he had fifteen seconds. Of course, with the crowd counting down, he really didn't need to look.

Gesturing with his head toward a narrow concrete ledge that flanked both sides of the broad swath of steps, he shoved the phone in his pocket and cupped his hands.

Without hesitating, she put a boot into his hand and sat on the ledge, above the crowd. He kept a hand on her leg, steadying her. Sam wouldn't let her fall. He pulled the phone out of his pocket with no time to spare.

"One," the crowd roared.

Sam hit the button and a million LED lights flashed on.

A huge cheer rose from the crowd, but Sam's eyes weren't on the lights or the trees but on Stella who was intently snapping pictures. Of the tree. Of the crowds. Of the amazing lights.

When the music began and everyone started to sing, Sam realized that, just like the sledding, this was a part of the evening that Stella needed to experience, not observe through a camera lens.

"Stella." Despite the fact that he stood beside her, he yelled her name to be heard over the singing voices.

She continued to snap photos.

There seemed only one way to get her attention.

Sam moved the hand that had been steadying her a couple of inches up her thigh. Through her jeans he felt her muscles tighten, and his body reacted almost immediately.

Her head jerked to the side, and her eyes met his.

Without taking his eyes or his hand off her, he motioned with his free hand for her to come to him.

She shifted on the ledge, swung her leg over, then held out her arms to him. Because it was such close quarters, once back on the steps, she was pressed against him.

Sam leaned down, his lips brushing her ear as he told her, "You need to sing."

The melody shifted from "Silent Night" to "I'll be Home for Christmas." For those unsure of the words, the screen that had held the countdown clock now displayed the lyrics.

It took Stella until they reached the part about "please have snow and mistletoe" to fully join in, but when she sang the words, it felt as if she was singing them directly to him.

Three more songs, and the crowds began to disperse, with many headed into the courthouse, while others lined up for pictures with Santa, and still others made a beeline into various businesses.

Sam was sorry when the people around him stepped away, giving them room to breathe again. He'd liked the feel of her soft curves pressed up against him, the light scent of her perfume teasing his nostrils.

Stella cocked her head. "Why did you want me to stop taking pictures?"

As the sing-along had now concluded, she only had to raise her voice rather than shout to be heard.

"It didn't have a thing to do with taking pictures," he told her.

"Would you like to go inside the courthouse? We can check out the setup and activities. Not to mention thaw out a bit."

"Sounds . . . heavenly."

He chuckled. "Which part?"

"Thawing out, of course."

They climbed the steps and had stepped inside the warmth when she slanted a questioning glance in his direction. "You didn't answer my question."

Sam maneuvered her out of the foot traffic to an alcove by one of the many large windows on the main floor.

"Here's the deal." He took a second to collect his thoughts. "Your job is to utilize social media to allow those who aren't here, or even those who are, to see everything this community has to offer."

Stella gave a slow nod.

"Pictures tell only part of the story. The rest you convey with words. To do justice to the event, you need to experience it."

"I *was* experiencing it," Stella reminded him. "Taking pictures and experiencing it all firsthand."

He shook his head. "You were on the outside looking in through your camera lens."

The confusion on her face told Sam he needed to find another way to explain.

"Think about how you felt when you were singing, when your voice blended with hundreds of other voices." He expelled the breath he didn't realize he'd been holding when understanding dawned in her eyes.

"You would have never had that same feeling if you'd just kept taking pictures." He felt a rush of tenderness for her. "I want you to live and breathe life in Holly Pointe. Not only for the sake of your social media posts, but for yourself."

"Why?"

The question caught Sam off guard. Telling himself the question deserved a thoughtful response, he took a moment to consider.

"You've been through a lot in the past two years. You deserve to be fully immersed in the goodness that is this community. To have it wrap its arms around you and give you comfort." Sam realized too late just how lame that sounded. While true, he could have come up with a better way to say the same thing. "What I meant to say—"

Her hand on his arm stopped the words, and he realized she was standing close. Very close. As close as they'd been outside when there had been no choice.

She had a choice now.

As did he.

Sam remained firmly rooted to where he stood.

Placing the palms of her hands flat against his coat front, Stella gazed up at him. "I want that, too. Thank you for thinking of me."

He stared down at her beautiful face, his gaze drawn to her full, red lips. "I haven't been able to stop thinking of you since you arrived in Holly Pointe."

"I seem to have the same affliction." Those tempting lips quirked upward. "I guess we just have to decide where we go from here."

Though Stella hadn't been far from his thoughts the past week, he hadn't given much thought to the likely next step other than spending more time together.

But with his own desire reflected in her hazel depths and her mouth only inches from his, Sam knew exactly what the next step had to be.

He lowered his head and pressed his mouth to hers.

∽

Before Stella had a second to breathe, his lips were on hers, exquisitely gentle and achingly tender. She was quite sure she'd never been kissed like this before. Or perhaps the difference was the emotion behind the melding of lips.

When he stepped back, she wanted to protest. Until she realized they were in a busy hallway. Granted, they were out of the flow of traffic, but they were in full view of anyone passing by.

Still, she found herself seized with an almost overwhelming urge to wrap her arms around his neck and give him a ferocious kiss. Or two. Or three.

Instead, she smiled, and when he moved his arm so that her hand slid down to his, she gave his fingers a squeeze. "That was nice."

A startled look crossed his face.

"No, I mean it was more than nice." Stella stumbled over the words in her haste to get them out. "The kiss was fabulous."

He grinned now, full out. "I can do better."

"I can, too." She didn't take her eyes off his face. "If you want a rematch—"

Stella stopped herself before she continued with the rematch theme. "I seem to be having difficulty expressing myself today. It's that blasted cologne of yours."

She loved the way he smelled, a woodsy mixture of cologne and soap and maleness that brought a tingle to her lips and had heat percolating low in her belly.

"You don't like it?"

"I like it too much," she admitted.

"I like the way you smell, too. It—"

"What are you doing out here?"

Sam turned toward the feminine voice.

Lucy gazed at them, her brows pulled together.

"We're talking." Sam studied Lucy as if trying to figure out the point. "What are you doing?"

"Several of my catering employees are working the booths. I

was going to check on them." Lucy fixed sharp blue eyes on Stella. "I'd have thought you'd be in the ballroom taking pictures."

Stella hesitated. Granted, Lucy had a lot of clout in the community, but Stella didn't report to her. However, she didn't want the woman as an enemy.

"I was immersing myself in the feel of Holly Pointe." Stella shifted her gaze and smiled up at Sam. "A friend told me it's something I need to do more often."

If there had been a fireplace in Stella's tiny living room, the space would have been perfect. As it was, with the table lamp casting a golden glow and the smell of coffee and chocolate in the air, it was practically perfect.

"I can't believe you beat out a five-year-old in the cakewalk." Stella laughed and dipped her fork into the piece of devil's food.

"The kid already won a whole stash of Christmas goodies." Sam gave a shrug and leaned back in his chair. "I was saving him and his family from complete sugar overload."

"Your story is that you were helping him out."

"Exactly."

After she and Sam had completed their walk around the ballroom—and Stella had taken an obscene number of pictures—she'd been ready to call it a night.

Almost.

Instead of saying good-night when Sam had walked her to her door, she invited him—and the cake he won—inside for dessert and coffee.

It seemed a fair trade.

He provided the dessert.

She provided the coffee.

Now, fully relaxed, she sat on the sofa with her Uggs off and her feet tucked under her. "I'd never seen a Christmas cakewalk before. Heck, I can't recall the last time I've seen a regular cakewalk."

For standing on the winning number when the music ended, Sam had been able to choose from plates of decorated sugar cookies, Grinch cupcakes, and several cakes. It had been the devil's food decorated to look like a reindeer—complete with antlers—that caught his eye. "The cakewalk is always a big hit."

"Especially with the big kids. There were as many moms and dads as there were kids going around that circle."

"Kevin loved the Christmas cakewalk." Sam smiled. "But then, he loved anything and everything to do with Christmas."

Stella hadn't wanted to ask Sam much about his brother, but with that comment, he'd opened the door. "What was your brother like?"

When Sam hesitated, she raised a hand. "We don't need to talk about him if it's difficult. I know how—"

"No, it's okay." He settled back in the chair, his large fingers now wrapped around a red mug. "It's been four years since Kevin passed, and people don't mention him all that often anymore. But you know how it is when you lose someone close to you. They're never far from your thoughts."

Stella nodded. She did understand.

"Kevin and I were fraternal twins. I was the oldest." Sam flashed a smile. "By two minutes. We didn't look anything alike, and we were different on the inside, too. But he was my best friend."

"How were you different?" Stella kept her eyes on Sam's face as she sipped her coffee.

"I was the quiet, reserved one." A smile hovered on the corners of his lips. "Kevin was outgoing and gregarious, the life of every party. But never obnoxious or over the top. He loved people and life, and it showed."

"It was unfair for him to die so young."

"There was a lot of anger and shock with the initial diagnosis."

Sam's eyes grew distant as if he was looking back. "I think my parents and I took it harder than Kevin. He was the kind of guy who, corny as it sounds, made lemonade out of lemons."

"How did he do that?" Stella couldn't imagine how anyone could find the positive in a diagnosis that could eventually take your life.

"Well, he said he was glad he had time to put his affairs in order." Sam hesitated. "He—" he broke off.

Stella merely sipped her coffee and waited.

"He said if he'd died in a car accident, he wouldn't have had time to let all the people in his life know how much they mattered to him. The outpouring of affection from those he knew—or had known in the past—amazed and comforted him."

Stella felt the familiar tightening around her chest and forced herself to take a couple of calming breaths. "But surely he was angry. He was taken far too early, before his life had really begun. My parents were in their early fifties, and I felt they were gone way too soon. I was so angry."

"I think yours is a normal response. I certainly felt that way." His chuckle held no humor. "Kevin saw rage as counterproductive to making the fight back to health. Then, when that didn't happen, to enjoying what time he had left."

"He sounds like an amazing guy."

"He was one of the best men I've ever known. He showed me how to live. And how to die." Sam's gaze settled on the framed picture of her parents on the desk, the one taken on their twenty-fifth wedding anniversary.

Stella braced herself for questions, but instead Sam just sipped his coffee. They sat in comfortable silence for a minute before Sam continued.

"It was Kevin's shortened life expectancy that led him to buying the horses. Even back in high school, he had this dream of a whole herd but planned to wait until he and Lucy were married and settled. Instead of waiting, he took the money he'd saved and bought three."

Stella tried to hide her surprise. "He bought horses."

"Not just any horses, Icelandic horses." Sam laughed at her confused expression. "They're amazing. Very friendly, and they love people. I inherited them from Kevin. You'll have to come out to my place and see them. If you have time, I'll even take you skijoring."

"What is that?"

"Think of it as cross-country skiing with the horse pulling you."

"It sounds like fun." Stella set down her mug and picked up the plate with the cake. "Name the time. I'll be there."

"You'll have to dress warmly."

Stella rolled her eyes. "I'm in northern Vermont. In December. Of course I'll dress warmly."

"It needed to be said." Sam appeared to be trying to hide a smile. "You are, after all, a Florida girl."

"A former Florida girl."

His gaze sharpened. "You've decided not to go back?"

"I'm still weighing my options." Stella thought of her friends and the job that could be hers if she came through with this article. "I'm enjoying my time here, but I keep telling myself that my life is there."

"No job. No apartment. No boyfriend." Sam's tone remained light and conversational while his gaze had turned sharp and assessing.

Though it was a statement, she heard the question hidden in the comment. "Nope. No boyfriend."

Was it only her imagination, or did his shoulders relax?

"Good," he said.

"Why good?"

"Because." He stood, then sat beside her on the sofa, lifting the plate from her hand and placing it on the coffee table. "I want to kiss you again. If you had a boyfriend, I would keep my distance."

He sat so close that the heat from his body ignited a fire in her own. "You didn't ask me in the courthouse if I had a boyfriend."

"That kiss was spontaneous."

She lifted her face and shivered when he gently brushed back a lock of her hair with the tip of his finger. "And what is this?"

"This," he said as his mouth lowered to hers, "is deliberate."

CHAPTER TWELVE

Sam told himself to take this slow, but even the talk of Kevin over the past hour hadn't been enough to lessen the desire racing through his blood. The thought of kissing Stella again had been all he'd thought of during their time at the courthouse.

She tasted like chocolate cake, and when her hand wrapped around his neck, he could have danced a jig. But he was too busy pressing his mouth to hers again and again.

This melding of lips wasn't one-sided. She kissed him back, her mouth opening to his when he slid his tongue across her lips. When it slipped inside, his blood flowed like molten lava, and his pulse throbbed hard and thick.

His control nearly shattered when her fingers dipped inside the collar of his shirt.

"I want you," Sam groaned, his voice a gruff rasp.

They were no longer sitting up. She was on her back, and he was practically on top of her. And still they continued to kiss. Long, dreamy kisses interspersed with ones that had him wanting to tear off his clothes—and hers—so they were flesh to flesh.

His erection strained against his zipper, and she moved her

hips beneath him, her legs separating just enough for his hardness to rub her in the place that had her arching upward, her fingers digging into his shoulders.

Sam slid his hand beneath her bottom, bringing her even more fully against the length of his erection. He continued to kiss her, to murmur sweet words as she molded her body to his.

While fighting to retain control, Sam continued the grinding rhythm that had Stella moaning as if the pressure inside had suddenly become unbearable.

Still, he continued the hot, rhythmic stroking, letting her squirming set the pace while bringing her closer and closer to the edge.

He scattered kisses across her face, then took her mouth in a deep kiss that mimicked their lovemaking. She surged against him and cried out.

He continued the stroking until she sagged back. His body ached for completion, but tonight had been for Stella. He sensed that she wasn't ready to dive into a full-blown relationship that included sex.

Hopefully, tonight would help her see just how good it could be between them.

"I can't believe I—" Her hands dropped from his neck to lie limply at her side. The earlier patches of color on her cheeks were now fire-engine red. "I don't know what got into me."

"It sure wasn't me." He rolled off her, gesturing with one hand to his fully clothed body.

"You didn't—" She sat up and licked her lips. "I mean, you kind of got the short end of the stick."

He chuckled. "I'm not sure I like that description."

The red on her cheeks deepened even further if that were possible. "I meant—"

"I know what you meant." Sam couldn't help it. He kissed her again, reveling in the taste of her. "I should be heading home."

Her gaze fixed on his crotch as he stood. "It isn't fair that I—"

Leaning over, Sam tipped her chin up. If she kept looking at him there, he wasn't going to be able to control himself. "Another time perhaps."

Grabbing his coat from the coat tree, Sam paused, his hand on the knob. "Don't forget to deadbolt the lock once I leave. The town is safe, but you can't be too careful."

Stella reached him just as he opened the door. Her hand on his arm stopped him from stepping into the hall. "You're forgetting something."

He stepped to her. "A good-bye kiss?"

"That sounds wonderful." An impish gleam filled her eyes as she gestured with her head. "But I was referring to the cake."

"Ouch." Derek grimaced as he and Sam rode the horses on a road that flanked the edge of Sam's property. "It was all about the cake."

Sam had forgotten about his plans to go riding with Derek the next morning until his friend had banged on his front door at eight a.m. "Yeah, she didn't want me to forget it."

"Did you at least get a good-night kiss?" Derek slanted a sardonic grin in Sam's direction. "As a chaser for the one in the courthouse earlier in the evening?"

"You heard about that?"

Derek shot him a pitying look. "I don't believe there is a single person in the county who hasn't heard about Holly Pointe's city administrator locking lips with our new social media person."

Sam scowled. He didn't like the idea of Stella being the subject of public gossip. "We weren't that obvious."

"You haven't answered my question about the good-night kiss."

Derek, Sam realized, was like a dog with a bone. He was glad that he'd conveniently *forgotten* to mention everything that had gone on before the end of the evening. No matter how good his friendship with Derek was, there were some things best kept private.

When the silence lengthened, Sam realized Derek was waiting for an answer. "I got another kiss."

Actually, the attraction between him and Stella had exploded. Even when he told himself to take it slow, the connection only grew hotter and more intense.

"Mel likes her." Derek gave Vixen a pat.

"Your sister likes Vixen?"

"Not the horse. Stella." Derek made a sound of disgust. "Where's your head this morning?"

Back in Stella's apartment, Sam thought. On her sofa, feeling her soft curves against the hard planes of his body, hearing her soft, breathy moans as he stroked . . .

"Are you okay?"

Sam jerked his thoughts back to the present. "Stella and I talked about Kevin last night."

Derek smiled. "Did you tell her how he listened to Christmas music year round? Or how we had to watch *A Christmas Story* and *It's a Wonderful Life* every year?"

Sam chuckled. "Remember when he added *Elf* to the Christmas lineup?"

"I thought Zach was going to lose it that year." A smile of remembrance lifted Derek's lips. "Zach ended up loving *Elf*."

"I think about Kevin a lot at this time of year."

"I miss him, too, man." Derek cleared his throat. "You might want to, I don't know, touch base with Lucy sometime. This time of year is difficult for her, too."

"I thought she'd find someone else by now." The second after the words left his mouth, Sam realized how they sounded. "I didn't mean fall in love and get married. But to my knowledge, she hasn't even dated."

"Kevin is a tough act to follow." Derek lowered his voice,

though they were the only ones for miles. "I remember when he and Lucy started dating. I didn't see that coming."

"Because they seemed so different?"

"Yeah, even back in high school, I had her pegged for the big city. I thought once she finished high school, she'd go to some college, then settle in New York or Boston." Derek blew out a breath. "Instead, she and Kevin went to UV and returned to Holly Pointe."

"I see what you're saying about Lucy, but Kevin was the one I always thought would settle in New York City. He loved the lights, the fast-paced lifestyle, and the parties."

"Now that you say that, I agree." Derek's gaze grew thoughtful. "I wonder why he did stay here? The techy stuff he did as an independent contractor could have been done anywhere."

"I believe he stayed because of Lucy. Don't get me wrong." Sam lifted one hand. "If he'd wanted to move to the city, I think Lucy would have packed up and moved. But she liked it here, and he could work anywhere."

"He couldn't have had these beauties in the city." Derek gave the horse another pat. "I've never ridden a more surefooted horse that gives you such a comfortable ride."

"For over a year he was able to enjoy them." Sam wished it could have been decades.

"You have any plans for tonight?"

"Nope."

Derek cocked his head. "What? No plans with Ms. Carpenter?"

"No plans." Sam had already decided to text Stella this weekend, but that asking her out when they'd just spent the evening together might seem pushy. "What are you doing?"

"I'd hoped—" Derek paused.

Something told Sam he'd regret asking. "You hoped what?"

"That you and Stella . . ." Derek circled a hand in the air, appearing faintly embarrassed.

Sam grinned. "I have to say I find this sudden interest in my love life heartwarming."

"Shut up." Derek scowled. "I'm just happy to see you getting involved with someone on a more personal level. You've shut yourself off from people since Kevin died."

"Hardly." Sam tamped down a flicker of annoyance. "In case you've forgotten, I'm a city administrator. I see and interact with people all the time."

Derek shook his head. "Not the same thing. You don't open your heart to anyone. Not anymore."

Even as a part of him recognized the truth in his friend's statement, Sam forced a joking tone. "Aw, Derek, do you want more quality time with me to talk about feelings?"

"Yes, I do." Concern furrowed Derek's brow. "You and I have known each other practically our whole lives, and I've seen you grow colder in these last four years. It's been subtle, and maybe most people don't see it, but I do. So if Stella is the person who can thaw you back out, then I think you're a fool if you don't at least try."

"Point made." Sam clapped his friend on the shoulder and deliberately changed the subject. "What do you have on tap for tonight?"

"I'll be at the school holiday program. The kids are doing a skit, and Cam has a lead role. Why don't you come? You can watch your goddaughter perform."

Going to a school Christmas program was low on Sam's list of fun things to do on a Saturday night. Still, there was a special place in his heart for Derek's daughter, and he knew Cam would be thrilled if he attended.

Not to mention, by embracing the holiday season, he'd be showing Derek that his assessment was off base. Sam cocked his head. "Will there be cookies and punch afterward?"

"Would it be Christmas without them?"

∼

Stella sipped some very excellent cappuccino from the corner table in the Busy Bean and scrolled through her list of activities to cover. She nearly groaned aloud at the entry under today's date.

Holly Pointe school holiday concert.

Stella couldn't recall the last time she'd attended a school Christmas event, but she could already envision this one. Little boys and girls dressed in holiday finery singing loudly and slightly off key. The parents would smile proudly from uncomfortable auditorium seats while videoing every precious moment.

The older kids would likely appear bored.

If she was lucky, there might—just might—be a moment or two worth capturing for the town blog. Still, she reminded herself, attending and reporting on these functions came with the job.

"Krista."

Stella's head snapped up.

Krista Ankrom stood at the counter, looking ready for the runway in cream-colored wool pants and a pink cashmere sweater. Her coat appeared to be cashmere, too. The twins were with her, studying the selection of scones and muffins that Dough See Dough supplied daily to the coffee shop.

"Kenny." There was genuine gladness in Krista's tone, and the smile she offered the older man was wide. "How are you doing? How's Norma?"

Kenny's deep rumble of an answer was too low for Stella to hear. But the look of sympathy that crossed Krista's face told Stella there was a reason Norma wasn't behind the counter this morning.

"Give her my best," Krista told the man, then fixed a sharp-eyed gaze on the twins who'd started shoving each other. "Neither of you are getting a treat if you continue to act this way."

Stella thought she heard the word "muffin" from one of the boys while the response of the other sounded like "cinnamon."

"The three of us will split a scone." Krista turned to Kenny. "We'll take a lemon-blueberry scone, two cups of hot chocolate, and a short skinny vanilla latte."

Reetha, the girl behind the counter with the short pixie cut, went immediately to work on the order. As there were no other customers in line, Krista continued to visit with Kenny.

Unfortunately, the former model lowered her voice so much that Stella couldn't hear what either one of them was saying.

When Krista picked up the order and took a seat not far from the window, Stella realized her luck might have turned. Especially when she discovered that instead of scrolling through her phone the way many parents did when with their children, Krista actually focused her entire attention on her sons.

"I'm not sure we'll have time to take you sledding this afternoon. Your daddy said something about wanting to take you skating at the lake."

It almost sounded as if the couple was sharing custody of the boys. Or was Stella simply reading more into the statements than was actually there?

"Of course, we'll both be at the program tonight."

Program? Excitement coursed like an awakened river through Stella's blood. She'd forgotten that the twins were in kindergarten. Krista had to be referring to the program tonight at the school.

She and Dustin would be there. Which meant Stella would have another chance to observe them together.

"I don't know," Stella heard Krista tell one of the boys. "Let me ask him."

"Kenny," she called out. "The boys want to know if you and Norma will be at the program tonight."

Kenny slipped out from behind the counter and strolled over to their table.

"Norma isn't feeling up to par, so I'm afraid she won't be there."

The look of pain that skittered across Kenny's face was gone in an instant, but it had been there long enough to have Stella's heart clenching tight. She wondered whether there was anything she could do for the woman who'd been so kind to her.

Kenny shifted his gaze from Krista to her sons. "Did you know Santa Claus will be serving cookies in the gym after the program?"

"Yay!" One of the boys shot a clenched fist up in the air.

"We can't have cookies if they have red frosting," his brother said. "Mom says it makes us hyper."

Kenny shot Krista an understanding look. "The cookies are coming from Dough See Dough, and there will be a good assortment of ones with dye-free frosting. As well as gluten free."

"The boys just have issues with dye, but it's nice to know that those kids—and adults—who can't tolerate gluten will have options."

The comment made Stella realize that, despite being located far from any major metropolitan area, this small town was progressive. No wonder people loved living here. Because of the strong sense of community, this was the perfect place to raise a family and to grow old around people who cared.

It was easy for Stella to see herself living here. Spending time with friends and cuddled up in front of a roaring fire with Sam...

Stella shook her head, trying to banish the compelling image of her and Sam kissing on the couch, his fingers toying with the buttons on her shirt...

"Can I get you a refill?"

Stella didn't know what surprised her more. That Kenny had been able to cross to her table without her realizing it or that just the thought of Sam had need all but erupting in her.

She must have been staring blankly because the older man gestured to her cup.

"Thanks for asking, but I'm fine."

When he started to turn away, Stella reached out. "Kenny."

He turned, and his lips, tucked inside that white beard, lifted in a smile. "Changed your mind already?"

She shook her head. "It's about Norma. I didn't mean to eavesdrop, but I heard you mention to Krista she wasn't feeling well. Is there anything I can do?"

The sorrow that she'd only caught glimpses of before now filled his eyes.

Stella's gut clenched when the older man pulled out a chair and sat down as if he was too exhausted to stand for another second. It was obvious that whatever was going on with Norma wasn't as simple as a bad winter's cold.

"Norma has cancer." Just saying the word had Kenny's voice thickening with emotion. "The doctor says she has a good chance of beating it because we caught it early. He said it was low grade, whatever that means, and that it had stayed in the bladder."

"Cancer." Stella found herself repeating the word. A shiver of dread traveled up her spine. "Will she have to have chemotherapy?"

"Not the kind of chemo you're probably thinking of." Kenny's hands, resting on the tabletop began to shake, and he placed them in his lap. "Last month, Norma had surgery. The doctor cleaned the cancer out of her bladder, then washed it out with this chemo drug. I forget the name. She goes in once a week to get the drug."

"Does the drug make her sick?"

"No and her hair hasn't fallen out, not yet anyway. It does make her really tired. Right before Christmas, they'll do a scope again and check for new tumors. Then she'll have two or three months to rest. At least I think that's the plan."

Kenny scrubbed a hand across his face, looking ten years

older than he had only minutes before. This time, when he dropped the hand to the table, she covered it with his.

"She'll be okay."

"I hope so." He offered a wobbly smile. "I don't know how I can go on without her."

Stella met his gaze head on. "I worked with someone at the *Sun Times* who was diagnosed with bladder cancer fifteen years ago. Jim is still going strong."

"The doctor in Burlington at the cancer center told us most people with bladder cancer die of something else. And, like I said, we caught it early."

"So why is she not feeling well today?" Stella didn't mean to press, but she was sincere in her desire to help the couple. If there was anything she could do to lighten their load, she wanted to do it.

"She got a bladder infection, which they say isn't uncommon. Once the antibiotics kick in, she'll start feeling better." He offered a watery smile. "I hope so anyway."

Stella met his gaze. "What can I do to help?"

"There isn't anything—"

"While Norma is under the weather, I'd be happy to fill in behind the counter, either taking orders or filling them." When she saw the refusal poised on his lips, she raised a hand. "I worked as a barista in college. Though that was nearly ten years ago, I still remember."

His hesitation gave her the impetus to push.

"How about you orient me now?"

"You have your own work to do."

"True," she acknowledged. "But as long as I'm not at an event, I'm available."

"I couldn't pay you much—"

She held up a hand. "You won't pay me at all."

"But—"

"You and Norma have been so good to me." This time it was

Stella's voice that thickened with emotion. "I won't take a dime for helping you, so don't even offer."

"Thank you." His eyes filled with tears and her own followed suit. "You're a wonderful woman, Stella. I'm pleased to call you my friend."

Stella thought of the notes she'd placed in her work file about Kenny. When guilt wrapped its tentacles around her heart and squeezed, she told herself she hadn't written the article yet.

Research notes were just thoughts until they made their way into an article, then into print.

She wasn't a hack journalist out to bury anyone in innuendo and lies. That wasn't the kind of woman her parents had raised. And she wouldn't go down that path, even to regain her job.

CHAPTER THIRTEEN

"These are primo seats." Derek made the pronouncement as if he were in the front row at a major concert instead of in a seat five rows back from a high school stage.

As the auditorium was nearly full and they had another thirty minutes before the program started, Sam guessed Derek must have arrived at some ungodly early hour to snag these seats.

Thankfully, he'd saved one next to him for Sam.

Sam fought to find a comfortable position in the unyielding wooden seat. He quickly discovered that comfort was nearly impossible for someone of his height. He'd had more legroom flying coach. "Why didn't you pick the front row?"

At least there, Sam thought, no one would have been in front of them, and his knees wouldn't be up against his chest.

"Too close," Derek spoke with the assurance of a seasoned parent. "You don't have a good view of the stage from that location."

"Was Cam excited for tonight?"

"She's in middle school. It's not cool to be excited about something like this." Derek's lips quirked. "But she loves to sing, so yeah, I think she's excited."

"Do you ever wonder if Elin regrets her choice?"

"You mean her choice to walk away from her child?" Derek kept his voice even, but a hint of bitterness crept in. "Elin made it clear she didn't want me or the baby."

He blew out a breath. "It does no good to stay pissed about something that happened thirteen years ago. She could have had an abortion, and I couldn't have stopped her. Instead, she chose to have the baby. I'm grateful for that."

"She planned to give the baby up for adoption."

"Until I told her I wanted custody." Derek gave a humorless chuckle. "She didn't see that coming. She tried to say the baby would be better off with two parents. I told her this was my child, and he or she would be better off with me."

Sam vividly remembered that time. If not for Rosie stepping up to help her son, Derek might have had to quit school. As it was, he'd dropped the football team and the rest of his extracurriculars. Every spare minute he wasn't in school, he'd been caring for his child.

"I can't believe she left Holly Pointe and never came back."

"Her parents aren't here anymore." Derek shrugged. "Other than her grandmother, there's nothing here for her."

"Her daughter is here."

"Elin gave up all rights to Camryn when she walked away."

Sam let the subject drop, unsure why he'd brought it up in the first place. Unless maybe being with Stella had him thinking about what it would be like to have a family of his own.

"I heard she has some big, important job in Chicago. Or maybe it was in Denver." Derek opened his mouth to say more, then shut it. After a moment he spoke again. "Speaking of career women, I see your favorite reporter picked up a second job."

Sam narrowed his eyes. "Stella?"

"Do you know another reporter? Well, other than Kate, and she just does the reporting gig part time."

"Forget about Kate." Sam swiped a hand in the air. "Tell me about Stella."

"I like seeing that predatory gleam in your eyes when you say her name."

"Derek. If you don't tell me—"

"I saw her working behind the counter at the Busy Bean."

"Doing what?"

"Making drinks."

"Making her own drink?"

"No." Derek made an exasperated sound. "Making drinks for customers. It appeared she was helping Adriana and Reetha catch up, because while I was there, she switched back to helping Kenny work the counter."

"Where was Norma?"

"I don't know. I didn't see her. Maybe she was out shopping or something."

"That doesn't sound like Norma."

"Like I said, the Bean was super busy, so it wasn't like there was time to ask questions." Derek cast her a speculative look. "You could ask the woman herself."

"Norma?"

"No." Disgust filled Derek's voice. "Stella."

Sam turned in the direction where Derek had cast a careless hand and saw Stella standing in the far aisle to his left. She looked festive in a red tunic top with black thigh-high heeled boots. Her hair was twisted at her neck in some kind of messy knot.

The style was probably stylish, but his fingers itched to pull the strands loose so they tumbled around her shoulders as they had in her apartment last night.

As if she could feel his eyes on her, Stella glanced around, and her eyes locked on his. He didn't bother to pretend he hadn't been staring or attempt to look away.

The truth was, he didn't think he could look away. Their eye contact turned into something more, a tangible connection between the two of them.

He'd started to rise, to go to her, when the lights in the auditorium dimmed and the announcer gave the five-minute warning.

Sam sat back down.

"Later," he mouthed.

Her red lips curved into a smile, and she nodded.

Feeling satisfied, Sam sat back, unable to stop the grin.

"There's enough heat between the two of you to start a fire." Derek elbowed him. "Heck, if we were still in scouts, I'd say forget about rubbing two sticks together. All we'd need was you and Stella and that smoldering look to start the campfire."

Sam rolled his eyes. "Anyone ever tell you that you can be really lame?"

"You're going to need to do better than that," Derek told him. "I hear that all the time from Camryn."

The second Stella spotted Sam, she wished she could forget her assignment and simply sit beside him and watch the program. But then the performance began, and she fell into work mode.

Krista and Dustin sat together several rows behind Derek and Sam. She snapped a couple of shots of them.

She noticed they didn't touch. Was that what happened when you'd been married for a while? Did the smiles and little touches disappear? Then Stella thought of her parents and how her dad had held her mother's hand as they stood by the car to tell her good-bye.

The kindergarteners came on stage, with Jaxon and Jett Bellamy center stage. Stella slanted a glance at their parents and saw Krista lean close to Dustin to say something to him. He smiled at his wife and gave her that dazzling smile that had made him the biggest catch in the NHL.

Some of the tension in Stella's chest eased as she caught the moment on her camera. She wanted so much for Dustin and Krista's family-friendly image to be the real deal. Not only for them and for their son's sakes, but because she was a romantic at heart.

She loved movies where the couple ended up together as well as ones where good won out over evil. Each day she stayed in Holly Pointe had her hoping all her early speculations would be proven false.

Stella turned her attention back to the stage. The middle schoolers were doing a skit. Camryn Kelly had a lead role. She couldn't believe Derek had a daughter that age. The girl had to have been born when he was still in high school.

There was definitely a story there, but thankfully nothing that would interest Jane Meyers.

Derek clapped loudly at the end of the performance and whistled between his fingers. From where Stella stood, she could read his lips clearly. "That's my girl. Isn't she great?"

Her mom and dad had been that kind of parents, always so supportive and proud. Since their deaths, she'd been on her own. She'd learned to cheer herself on when life felt like it was too much to handle.

Was it wrong to wish there was someone in her life who would stand on the sidelines and cheer for her?

When she shifted her gaze to Sam and found him staring, she smiled, then refocused on the stage. But the tingling that spread through her body at the knowledge that his eyes were on hers didn't dissipate.

If anything, as the evening wore on, the tingling and the warmth only increased.

Stella liked Christmas songs, truly she did. And the skits were well done. But ninety minutes later, she was ready for the program to be over.

In order to get the best shots, she stood the entire time, moving closer to the stage and crouching down to get shots from a low vantage point, then going to the balcony and shooting downward.

Just like at the lake, it didn't take her long to discover that there were only so many pictures of those in the audience and on stage that one could take.

Stella slipped out into the hall when the show was nearing completion, or at least she hoped that having the entire group assembled on stage signaled that the end was near.

Once everyone descended on the gym for cookies and punch, she'd be taking pictures there. Which meant that if she wanted something to drink, she needed to grab it now.

The time wouldn't be wasted. While drinking a glass of punch, she'd update the town's social media sites.

Stella had just reached the corner that led to the gym when she stopped short.

Kenny, dressed in his Santa Claus outfit, stood all alone at the end of the hallway. The slump of his shoulders had her heart rising to her throat. Though she didn't want to intrude, she wanted to be there for him.

She opened her mouth to call out when she saw him pull out a mini bottle of alcohol that until now she'd only seen on airplanes. This bottle was colorless, so vodka would be her guess.

Good choice, Stella thought, *if you don't want liquor breath.*

One of the reporters she'd worked with at the *Sun Times* had put vodka in water bottles. If he had a meeting, the guy would pop a stick or two of tropical-fruit gum. Management never had a clue.

As if on autopilot, Stella pulled out her phone. When Kenny tossed back his head and downed the entire bottle in one gulp, she got the shot. Her hands trembled as she shoved the phone back into her bag.

Taking a couple of silent steps backward, she concentrated on making as much noise as possible as she rounded the corner.

She forced a big smile as she strode down the hall, a big smile plastered on her lips. "Kenny. It's good to see you."

Before she reached him, he popped a stick of fruit-striped gum into his mouth. "I didn't expect to see anyone come down that hallway so soon. I need to get into position in the gym. Is the performance over?"

As she drew closer, Stella noticed the sadness in his eyes, and her heart lurched. "Almost over. I thought I'd get a couple of shots in the gym before the hordes descend."

"Good idea." He smiled. "We can walk together."

"How is Norma doing this evening?"

The smile that had never quite reached his eyes now disappeared from his lips as well. "Not well at all. Kate wanted to help out, but she's overseeing everything in the gym this evening. Faith is staying with Norma while I'm here."

"That's nice of her."

"Faith is a good woman." Kenny gave a decisive nod. "Norma calls her a kind soul."

A kind soul who would never secretly gather data on a friend.

"An apt description." Stella kept her voice light. "What smells so good? Are you chewing Fruit Stripe?"

Kenny's rouged cheeks turned even more red. "Yes."

"It's a favorite of mine. I've loved it since I was a kid."

"I—I'd give you a piece but I'm out."

A lie, Stella thought, as she'd seen the half-filled package before he stuffed it into his Santa suit. Obviously, Kenny felt he needed to keep the other pieces for himself.

They reached the cavernous gymnasium, and Kenny, always the gentleman, held the door open for her. Once she was inside, he opened the door wide so that it caught and stayed open, then did the same with the other door.

"It's show time," Kenny announced when Kate hurried over. He gestured with his head toward Stella. "Stella tells me the program is nearing the end."

Kate glanced at the large clock caged in on the wall. "They're getting through early, but we're ready for them."

"I'll get in the chair." Kenny squeezed his niece's shoulder, then crossed the room where a chair, or rather a green-and-red-tufted throne, sat on a large square of red carpet.

A decorated tree sat to the right of the throne with huge painted boxes made to look like presents.

"Did the high school stage crew do those?" Stella asked Kate, snapping a few pics.

"They did, and I think they did an excellent job."

"I agree." Stella hesitated just an instant then went for it. "Kenny seems worried about Norma."

When Kate shot her a questioning glance, Stella explained. "He told me about the cancer diagnosis."

"I would have told you myself," Kate assured Stella, "but Kenny asked me to keep it quiet."

"I understand." Stella understood the need to come to grips with bad news in your own way and in your own time. "I'm glad he's reaching out more. I think he needs the support."

"Kenny is devastated. He loves Norma so much and hates to see her going through all these tests and procedures. Right now, she's feeling pretty bad because of this infection, and that's been hard on him." Kate gave a decisive nod. "But he's strong, and so is she, and they have a lot of support."

Kate surprised Stella by taking her hands. "Speaking of friends. Thank you for caring about Kenny. I heard that you helped out at the Busy Bean. You'll never know how much that means to all of us who love him and Norma."

"I didn't do anything." Guilt rose like bile in her throat. Stella tried to pull back, but Kate held on for a moment longer.

"You stepped in, and you helped out. You were a friend in his hour of need." Kate released her hands. "I see I've embarrassed you. That wasn't my intention. I'm proud of you, Stella. Proud to call you my friend."

~

The night only careened downhill from there. Stella got a shot of Krista, her face flushed with anger, brushing off Dustin's hand.

Stella wasn't close enough to see—or hear—what prompted the heated exchange. By the time she drew close, the couple had on their happy faces again.

But she had the money shot. A photo that might sink any hopes they had of closing the deal on a family-friendly network show.

Just as she had the picture of Santa guzzling down nearly two ounces of vodka mere minutes before greeting schoolchildren.

The sick feeling in the pit of Stella's stomach had nothing to do with the fact that she'd skipped dinner. While she didn't know Dustin and Krista, the way Krista had showed such concern for Kenny said a lot.

And Kenny . . . well Kate was right. The man had a kind soul.

The month of December may have just started, but any day, Stella knew, she'd receive a text from Jane demanding an update. Not just an update, but one that included any dirt she'd been able to dig up.

What would Stella tell her?

That was the million-dollar question.

CHAPTER FOURTEEN

Sam wasn't sure how he'd lost track of Stella. One second she was taking shots of Santa with the kids, and the next she'd disappeared. Derek had disappeared, too, but Sam had known that would happen.

Tonight, his friend had more in common with the other parents than he did with his single, never-married friend.

If things had gone differently, if he'd been more open to the possibility, Sam knew he could have been married by now. After Kevin's death, he and Britt had grown even closer.

Sometimes he wondered how he could have gotten through those dark days after Kevin's death without her. Days when he'd been forced to face the fact that no matter what he did or how hard he pushed, he couldn't save his brother.

Britt had remained in Holly Pointe even after his parents returned to New York, giving up a chance at trying out for a musical revival where she was said to be a shoo-in for a leading role.

She hadn't pushed, but when she'd wanted to talk about the future—their future—he wasn't ready. When Britt finally left, he hadn't tried to stop her.

Sam had always thought that his father had later written the lead in his play especially for Britt as a way of thanking her for being there for him. Whatever the reason, her stellar performance in that pivotal role had her winning the Tony.

Shoving aside all thoughts of the past, Sam pulled out his phone to text Stella. It wasn't as if she couldn't go her way tonight, and he go his, but she *had* nodded when he's mouthed "later" in the auditorium.

At least that's what he thought.

Where are you? he keyed, then hit send.

The reply came immediately. *Home. Headache.*

Need anything? Sam was ready to leave now. Ready to bring her whatever she needed.

I'm good. Let's talk tomorrow.

He almost called her. Wanted to call her in the worst way. Wanted to know whether she was simply being stubbornly independent. Perhaps there *was* something he could do to help.

Then he realized that Stella was strong and more than capable of asking for help if she needed it.

She had a headache.

She was resting at home.

She didn't want him coming over.

It was that last part that was the most disappointing. Until this moment, he hadn't realized how much he was looking forward to speaking with her again. To simply being with her.

He started toward the exit doors. Instead of spending the rest of the evening with Stella, he'd go home to a dark house alone.

"Have you seen Stella?"

Kate's question stopped Sam in his tracks. He turned.

"I texted her. She's went home. She has a headache."

"She did look a little pale earlier." Kate's brows drew together, and her eyes filled with worry. "I wonder if she needs anything."

"I asked." Sam lifted a shoulder in a shrug. "She said no."

Kate removed her phone from her purse. "I'll text and ask anyway."

There was no reason for Sam to hang around. He'd given Kate the information she'd asked for, and she could take it from here. But he lingered, curious whether Stella would tell Kate she needed something.

A ping announcing a return text came seconds later.

Kate looked up after scanning the message. "She's going to bed."

Sam wondered what it said about him that he was happy to hear that Stella had turned down Kate's offer of assistance.

"Good job coordinating this event." Sam put his hand on Kate's arm. "Do you need any extra muscle?"

"We're covered." Kate cocked her head and studied Sam for a long moment. "You and Stella are close, aren't you?"

"I like her." Sam started to say more, then stopped himself. Kate was Stella's friend. In this case, the less said the better.

"Do you think she'll stay in Holly Pointe?"

"I don't know." Sam had mulled over the possibility several times but had come to no conclusion. "She's mentioned the possibility, but I believe she's still considering her options."

"Have you told her you'd like her to stay?"

Sam shook his head.

Kate offered him a knowing smile. "You and I are a lot alike. I'm not really into commitment either."

Sam wasn't sure why the comment rankled. Everyone in Holly Pointe was aware that Kate made sure her relationships never got too serious. Of course, if Sam had a mother like hers, he'd probably be a commitment-phobe, too. "Stella and I are still getting acquainted. If she decides to stay, it needs to be because this town feels right to her, not because of me."

"Makes sense." Kate lifted a hand, palm out. "And I don't mean any offense, but the way I see it, Stella shouldn't even consider settling down to one guy until she has time to see everything Holly Pointe has to offer."

This conversation, Sam thought, had run its course. "Again, great job coordinating all this. I'll see you in church tomorrow."

As he pushed through the doors and breathed in the crisp outside air, Sam wondered what cynical Kate would have said if he'd been honest and told her the truth.

The fact that he could so quickly care for someone he'd only recently met scared him. He liked Stella. He admired her. He found her incredibly sexy and appealing.

All this in a little over a week's time. Kate was right. If Stella did stay in Holly Pointe, and right now that was still up in the air, she *should* take the time to see what other guys were out there.

But the thought of her being with another guy was like a knife to his heart. Which told him he was a lot farther down the falling-in-love road than he could ever have believed possible less than two weeks earlier.

Three texts from three different people in less than ten minutes had to be some kind of record. The second text, this one from Sam had been followed minutes later by one from Kate.

Stella tossed her phone down on the table and leaned back against the sofa. She hadn't lied. She did have a headache. The kind that felt like someone had clamped a vise around the top of her head and was slowly squeezing.

She knew the cause. Tension. Stella had experienced plenty of tension headaches prior to the layoff announcements.

Funny, just like then, it was the newspaper industry at the bottom of this one. Stella had barely stepped over the threshold of her apartment when Jane had texted her.

Need update.

Short and sweet but with an undercurrent of impatience. Or

maybe Stella was reading too much into the words. She had yet to respond.

The last thing Stella wanted was for Jane to think she was some docile dog that came running whenever Jane called. Of course, Jane was her boss, and it was to be expected that she'd want to see how the story was progressing.

The trouble was, Stella wasn't sure how much to tell the managing editor. While it was true that Santa, er, Kenny, had been seen—and photographed—downing a small bottle of liquor wearing his Santa suit before a children's event, that was only part of the story.

Kenny's beloved wife of nearly fifty years had been diagnosed with cancer. Kenny hadn't been drunk around the children. Yes, it looked bad. No, he shouldn't do it. But to include such information in an article about Holly Pointe, purely for its salacious value, didn't sit well with Stella.

Perhaps Kenny had a drinking problem, in which case, that issue needed to be addressed. The fact that he drank before a children's event should also be addressed.

Blasting that information coast-to-coast and portraying him as a raging alcoholic, well, that seemed wrong.

Stella took a few minutes to upload the relevant pictures, including the ones of Kenny as well as Dustin and Krista arguing and smiling at each other. She made her notes. Knowing this file was for her eyes only, she included her impressions as well as the facts.

Then she went to get a cool washcloth to put on her head.

Her phone rang less than ten minutes later.

"Jane." Stella forced herself to smile, hoping that would make her sound as if she were pleased to hear from the woman. "I just got back from a Christmas event. I received your text and was getting ready to get an update drafted."

"I realize I didn't give you much time to respond." Jane's voice sounded positively giddy. "I'm so excited about this story. Tell me everything."

Stella hesitated. Had Jane been drinking? Was that what had brought on this bout of cheeriness?

"I wanted to get my facts down before moving forward."

"This isn't a story that's going to press tonight, Stella." The cheer meter on Jane's voice had taken a severe dip. Though still pleasant, a slight chill underscored the words. "I need to know what you've discovered."

"Well," Stella tried to figure out how to stall, but the pain in her head had turned her brain to mush, "I'm still checking out Santa—"

"Drunk Santa. A marvelous addition to the article." Jane trilled the last word.

"We don't know for certain he has a drinking problem."

"We don't know for sure he doesn't." Jane laughed when she made the comment, but Stella had the feeling she was serious.

"In terms of Dustin and Krista, sometimes they seem happy, and other times, well, stressed. But they do have two very active little boys, and the holidays—"

"The public loves marital discord." Jane expelled a happy breath. "Especially when two people are trying to pretend otherwise."

"It's the same situation we have with Kenny, I mean with Santa. I don't have enough information yet to either confirm or deny that they're experiencing problems in their marriage."

"Again, I say if you think they might be having problems, that's good enough for me." Jane spoke in a lilting tone that scraped against Stella's last nerve.

"It's not good enough for me," Stella blurted out. "These people have children. They are on the verge of starting new careers in television."

"That's their problem, not ours."

"I don't want," Stella held on to her temper with both hands, "I mean, I won't write the article until I have all the facts. I won't slant the article a certain way to appeal to a certain type of readership."

There was an interminable span of silence, so long that Stella held the phone away from her ear to make sure they were still connected. She'd learned that cell service in this area could be unreliable.

"Jane?" she asked. "Are you still there?"

"I am." Jane cleared her throat. "Of course I want you to be certain of your facts before you write anything. I hope I didn't say anything to imply otherwise."

What did she say to that? "I know you want to put out the best paper possible."

"I do." Jane's tone turned conciliatory. "Which is why I'm going to ask you to simply continue to gather information. All data available to you. That way, when it comes time to write the article, you can wade through everything you've collected, and we'll proceed from there."

"Thank you for understanding."

"Just continue to do what you've been doing," Jane told her. "That's all I ask."

Stella had skipped church the first week she'd been in Holly Pointe but decided that if Jane wanted her to continue to assess the situation, there was no better place to watch people than in church.

Since Holly Pointe Fellowship was only half a mile from the Busy Bean, Stella decided to walk. She'd already learned that scraping the windshield of a car that had sat out all night was a good way to ruin a morning.

It felt strange climbing the short flight of steps to the front door of the church. The building could have come out of a

Norman Rockwell painting with its white siding and tall, narrow windows, each with a pointed arch, as well as a single bell tower.

Even as Stella stepped into the building, the bells began to chime. The walk had taken longer than she anticipated, and the congregation was already standing for the opening hymn.

With everyone on their feet, it was nearly impossible to tell where there was a place to sit. Stella backed up, seriously considering replacing this morning's service with a scone and latte, when she met an immovable object.

She turned and looked up into Sam's warm brown eyes.

"Leaving so soon?" He kept his voice low, as if for her ears only.

Though, as loudly as everyone was singing, he could have shouted and likely not been heard.

"I'm late."

"Me too."

She gestured with one hand to the congregation. "It's difficult to see where to sit. I'll come back another time."

"I know where there's an empty pew." Before she realized what Sam planned to do, he'd taken her hand and was guiding—okay, pulling—her down the center aisle.

Resisting would only make it look as if he'd brought her kicking and screaming to church, so she increased her pace and smiled at those casting curious glances their way.

When Sam stopped and motioned for her to enter the polished wooden pew ahead of him, she understood how he'd known there would be space here.

After all, she didn't know too many people who liked sitting in the front row.

CHAPTER FIFTEEN

Sam hadn't attended church regularly after Kevin died and Britt and his parents returned to New York City. Oh, he still attended Sunday services, but it was different going alone.

It wasn't that he was angry with God for his brother getting sick and dying. He'd worked through that anger years ago. Sitting alone in a pew just reminded him of everything he'd lost.

Besides, the horses needed tending in the morning, and there were always other chores to do.

For some reason, this morning had been different. The moment he'd woken, he'd found himself wondering whether Stella's headache was better and when he would get to see her again.

The thought of stopping over at Dough See Dough after the service and picking up one of the cinnamon rolls she'd liked at the soup supper had propelled him out of bed.

Now, here she was, sitting beside him, her thigh pressed against his. He'd helped her take off her coat once they were seated. She wore a wool dress in a brown-and-green plaid that made her eyes look more green than hazel.

"Quit staring," she said under her breath, keeping her gaze focused on the minister in the pulpit right in front of them.

He couldn't help it, Sam had to smile.

This had been one of the most enjoyable church services he could remember. Light streamed in through the stained-glass windows. Pastor Mann's sermon on Jesus's Christmas wish list was entertaining.

Stella must have thought so, too. When the minister had quoted 1 Corinthians 10:24, saying, "None of you should be looking out for your own interests, but for the interests of others," she'd straightened beside Sam as if hanging on the pastor's every word.

Finally, the closing hymn and prayers were done, and the pastor gave his benediction.

Sam rose, and Stella stood beside him.

"Tell me they don't usher out from the front of the church," she muttered.

The words had barely left Stella's lips when Derek appeared at the end of the pew, a big smile on his face as he gestured for them to exit.

On the way down the aisle, Sam was conscious of all the speculative glances sent his way as he rested the palm of his hand against the small of Stella's back. Growing up in Holly Pointe had taught him that there was no reason to deny his interest in Stella.

Everyone likely already knew they were dating.

The smile that he'd gotten used to seeing on her face was missing as they reached the back of the church. They'd barely reached the entryway when she turned to him.

"Thanks for finding me a seat."

She turned and headed directly toward the doors.

"Wait." In several long strides, he was beside her. "Where are you headed in such a rush?"

She cocked her head. "I've got a date."

Sam froze.

Stella grinned. "That's payback for you dragging me down that aisle to the front row."

The tension in Sam's shoulders disappeared. He shook his head. "What am I going to do with you?"

"I have some ideas," Stella's voice was barely audible. "None appropriate for our current location."

He followed her outside, eager to hear more, but she just kept walking.

"Where are you going?" he asked in frustration when he caught up to her.

"To the Busy Bean." Her smile flashed. "I have a date. With Santa."

Stella went on autopilot as she made lattes and cappuccinos and all other manner of drinks. Once Adriana and Reetha were caught up, Stella rang up orders beside Kenny.

She hadn't realized how many people visited the Busy Bean on Sundays. She was thankful that Sam had given her a ride, because by the time she walked through the door, Kenny and his two baristas were struggling to keep up with the large crowd.

After washing her hands and pulling on an apron, she'd gone immediately to work. She'd lost track of Sam and assumed he'd left, but she spotted him now at a table in the far corner.

Their eyes met, and he smiled.

"It was nice seeing you and Sam in church this morning."

Stella shifted her gaze to see Derek standing before her.

"Sam and I happened to arrive at the same time. He helped me find a seat."

"In the front row," Derek pointed out. "I wouldn't do that to my worst enemy."

"I'll pay him back." Stella's comment, made in a matter-of-fact tone, had Derek chuckling.

"He's met his match in you."

Stella smiled. "What can I get you?"

"I'm sensing you don't want to discuss Sam."

"Right now, I'd rather take your order." Though Stella liked Mel's brother, he was right. She wasn't about to discuss her relationship with Sam with him.

"Coffee, black, and a blueberry muffin."

"Got it." Stella glanced at the tables, but Camryn was nowhere in sight. "What about your daughter?"

"What about her?"

"Does she want anything?"

"She's in Sunday sch—" Derek stopped himself. "Youth group."

Stella smiled, remembering those awkward middle school years. No longer a child, but not quite a teenager.

"Well, it was good to see you." She gestured to the other end of the counter. "Adriana will have your coffee and muffin in a second."

"I'll see you this weekend."

Stella inclined her head, not following. "I'm not sure I'll be working here then."

"I was talking about the movie marathon at Sam's place Friday." Derek flashed a smile. "It sounds really lame, but it's fun. Sam cancelled it last year, and everyone missed it."

Just that morning she'd reviewed the December events she was to cover. "I don't have a movie marathon on my list to cover."

"It wouldn't be there because it's a private party." Derek cocked his head. "Sam didn't say anything to you yet about it?"

"No."

"Well, I'm sure he will," he said hurriedly when Adrianna called his name.

Stella tucked the date away as well as the fact that Sam hadn't invited her. Not yet, anyway.

She told herself that was actually a good thing.

It wouldn't do for them to get too attached.

Instead of thinking about Sam, Stella thought about her strange conversation with Jane while she took another order. The managing editor had said all the right things, at least toward the end of the conversation. Still, Stella had the feeling that the closer it got to Christmas, the more Jane would push for an article that focused on the scandalous.

Stella cast a sideways glance at Kenny. The man continued to work as hard as his young baristas. He hadn't left the counter since she'd arrived.

Determining whether he had a drinking problem would be key.

Once she had the information, she'd decide what to do with it.

The next few hours flew by, until at one o'clock, Kenny put a hand on her arm. "The girls and I, we can handle it from here."

Stella had stepped from the counter to clear some tables. She was wiping down the last one. She gazed around her and realized the rush had indeed ended. "Are you sure?"

"Positive." His eyes were as warm as his smile. "Thank you again for your help. Norma was worried about today, but I'll be able to tell her that with you here, we didn't even miss her."

Stella widened her eyes. "Don't tell her that."

Kenny gave a ho-ho-ho belly laugh worthy of any Santa Claus.

Only then did Stella realize he was teasing her. She chuckled. "Okay, I'll go. But tell me when you need me next."

"I'll let you know."

"Ken-ny." She met his gaze as she drew out the syllables. "I want to help."

"I know you do. You've done so much already." He paused as if noticing the subtle lift of her chin. "Seriously, Norma is planning to be back tomorrow. She's feeling much better. Mondays are always much more manageable."

"Okay, but you know where to find me." Still holding the cleaning rag, she gestured with one hand toward the ceiling.

"Yes." His eyes softened. "I know where to find you."

Without warning, Stella found herself engulfed in what could only be described as a massive bear hug.

"Thank you so much, Stella," Kenny rasped. "You're a gem."

Tears stung the back of Stella's eyes as she stepped back. "I just hope if I ever need a reference for a job as a barista, I can count on you."

Her goal had been to inject some levity in the heart-tugging moment, but Kenny nodded solemnly and spoke as if making a pledge. "You can always count on me."

Sam observed the hug between Stella and Kenny from his spot in the corner. His friends had long since left the building, leaving him behind. He could have gone, too.

Stella had likely expected him to leave.

Instead he'd composed and answered work and personal emails, scrolled through the latest news on the chaos in the world, and observed Stella.

When she'd greeted customers, her smile had lit up her whole face. That was new since she'd come to Holly Pointe. Though it hadn't been that long ago, that first day, she'd been guarded both in her actions and her responses.

While Sam loved the people of New York, he'd noticed that they didn't readily smile at strangers as they walked down the street or sat beside them on a subway bench.

A smile and a greeting were the norm in Holly Pointe, and Stella had caught on quickly. She had a good, kind heart and a desire to be part of a community. She'd found a home in Holly Pointe.

The question was, would she want to make this place her home?

Tears shimmered in her eyes as she stepped out of Kenny's embrace.

Something Kenny said had shock lighting up her face, then Kenny threw back his head and laughed. Stella quickly joined in.

Sam found himself smiling, just watching her.

Then she handed Kenny the cleaning cloth and took off her apron.

Kenny slung the green apron over his arm, gave her a wink, and headed back to the counter.

Only then did Stella glance around the tables.

Sam knew the second she spotted him because her smile flashed, and she wove her way through the tables to him, pulling out a chair and sitting down.

"I bet it feels good to get off your feet."

"It does." She expelled a happy sigh. "But it was fun. Though much more work than I remembered from my college days."

"I'm sure Kenny appreciated it."

"I know he did." Stella hesitated. "You've known Kenny a long time."

"My whole life."

"I want to ask you something but as friend-to-friend, not as the Holly Pointe city administrator."

The serious look on her face put him on alert. "Okay."

"I need you to keep what I'm going to tell you confidential." Her gaze searched his. "I need you to promise me that."

"I can promise unless it's something I'm required by law or my position to report."

Her momentary hesitation only increased his unease.

"What is it, Stella? Has someone hurt you. Did—"

She placed her hand over his. "No. No. Nothing like that."

"Then, what?" Sam flipped his hand over and laced his fingers with hers.

He followed Stella's gaze as it shifted around the half-empty coffee shop. There was a couple seated at a table about ten feet away, a group of four men about the same distance in the opposite direction, and other tables even farther away.

Stella chewed on her lower lip. "Not here. Come up to my place. I don't want our conversation to be overheard."

As they climbed the steps to her apartment, Sam rapidly considered and discarded possibilities. By the time they crossed the threshold, Sam's nerves were as tightly strung as piano wire.

What could she have to say that was so . . . private?

Stella motioned him to the sofa, then took a seat on the other end, angling her body to face his.

Sam lifted his hands. "Just say it. Whatever it is, just spit it out. The suspense is killing me."

He kept his tone light, but he meant every word.

"Last night, in the school hallway, on my way to the auditorium, I saw Kenny drink one of the little airplane bottles of vodka."

Sam blinked. This hadn't been one of the possibilities he'd come up with on his trek up the steps. "Are you certain there was vodka in the bottle?"

"I can't be certain." Stella spread out her fingers. "The liquid was colorless. But if he wanted a drink of water, he could have gotten one from the fountain in the hall."

"It is suspicious."

"Then there's the fruit-striped gum."

Just when Sam thought this conversation couldn't get any stranger, it did. "Gum?"

"Fruit-striped gum."

Sam listened as Stella explained about a former coworker who was likely an alcoholic and his penchant for fruit-striped gum, which apparently masked any lingering odor of alcohol.

"What are you thinking of doing?" he asked when she finished with the story.

"I don't know." Stella surged to her feet and began to pace. "I thought maybe since you've known him, you could tell me if this is a common thing or if last night was an aberration. You know, because of his worry over Norma."

The pleading look in her eyes tugged at his heart. He wished he had answers for her, but like her, he only had questions.

"I don't recall ever seeing Kenny drunk." Sam furrowed his brows together. "But then, most of the parties I've attended with him are ones where he's there playing Santa Claus."

"At the first party I attended in Holly Pointe, the one at the Bromley mansion, there was an open bar." Stella expelled a breath and dropped down beside him. "I saw him toss back three or four shots of whiskey in twenty minutes."

"You're very observant."

Though Sam hadn't meant it as criticism, her cheeks took on a dusky color.

"I didn't know many people." She appeared to be trying—and failing—to temper the defense tone. "I was there to observe and take pictures."

"I didn't mean anything by that comment other than I hadn't noticed." He expelled a breath. "That makes me wonder just how many other things I don't notice that I should."

"Have you ever heard of Kenny having a drinking problem?" Stella returned her earlier question and pressed the point. "Was last night something we need to be concerned about?"

"Just to be clear, if a citizen, any citizen, had brought concerns of this nature to the mayor, I would know about them. Because we are copartners with the chamber of commerce on many of the holiday events, if Faith had known of any such instances, I truly believe we'd have heard about them."

"I understand that, but I know Norma said something about Kenny having a hard time when their daughter was diagnosed with diabetes. I don't know if alcohol was part of that time."

"Leslie is at least fifteen years older than I am. That had to have happened years ago." He shook his head. "I don't see how what happened then is relevant to this discussion."

"It's relevant if he's an alcoholic who's been on the wagon and has now fallen off." Stella tapped her fingers against her lips. "Have you seen him drink at other parties in the past few years?"

Sam thought back to the events he'd attended. "Yes, but never to excess."

"Good." Relief washed across Stella's face. "Maybe Kenny doesn't have a drinking problem, and last night was an isolated incident."

"Not quite so isolated," Sam reminded her. "There was his behavior at the Bromley mansion party."

Stella waved a dismissive hand. "He was there as a private citizen. It wasn't as if he got sloppy drunk or anything."

"Let's talk about last night. Would you like me to speak with him before or after you do?"

Her gaze met his. "Do you need to speak with him at all?"

"I do."

"Why?"

"Because I'm concerned." Sam reached over and took her hand. "I'm concerned about the liability of having a Santa who's drinking during the time he's contracted to perform his duties. I'm also concerned about Kenny. I like the guy, and I don't want to see him get into trouble."

"I didn't bring this up because I wanted to get him in trouble." She pulled her hand back and raked it through her hair. "I wish I hadn't said anything."

"Why did you say something?"

She flung out her hands. "Because I care for him. And I care about Norma. I don't want people calling him 'drunk Santa.'"

Sam gentled his tone. "No one around here is going to call him that . . . and do you know why?"

She shook her head, her gaze downcast.

He tipped her chin up with one finger so he could look

directly into her eyes. "Because you came to me. Out of concern, you brought this matter to my attention before it became an issue. You did Kenny a favor. You did the city of Holly Pointe a favor. You have nothing to feel bad about."

Tears welled in her eyes and slipped down her cheeks.

Sam brushed the moisture away with the pads of his thumbs, his gaze still locked on hers. "I don't need to bring up your name in my discussion with him. All he needs to know is that someone saw him drinking in the school."

"What if he denies it?"

"He won't. Kenny is a stand-up guy. I think he'll be relieved."

"Relieved?"

"Whatever pressure he's under that has caused him to go down this path needs to be addressed." Sam cupped her face with his hand. "Trust me. We've got some excellent psychologists in this community that can help him find more appropriate and better ways to deal with his stress than alcohol."

"If you need to tell him who saw him, you can say it was me." Stella swallowed convulsively. "If he hates me, that's how it will have to be. If he needs it, I want him to get help."

"I know you want to help him. Because that's the kind of woman you are." Sam could no longer resist. He leaned close and covered her mouth with his.

CHAPTER SIXTEEN

By the time Friday rolled around, Stella's head was spinning. According to Faith, the first week in December was one of the busiest of the year in Holly Pointe. It was Club Week, where each club in the community held a special Christmas open house.

These holiday events were open to the public and were part of what made Holly Pointe such a special place. Each day, Stella's calendar included at least one—often two—of these gatherings.

When Sam had called on Tuesday to ask her to the movie marathon at his house on Friday, she'd just left the community lunch group's Christmas extravaganza and was heading to the Bromley mansion, where she and garden club members were decorating the home for the holidays.

Stella had nearly said no to his offer. Though she enjoyed her social media role, she was feeling overwhelmed by the whirlwind of activities. But even as an excuse rose to her lips, she accepted the invitation.

One, because Sam had been in New York for his mother's birthday, and she'd missed him. And two, because she knew that all the stress she'd been feeling had little to do with Christmas events and everything to do with the article. Day by day, she was falling more in love with Holly Pointe.

As saccharinely sweet as it sounded, the community really *was* the capital of Christmas kindness. Members of the clubs that she visited were welcoming and, well, kind. They epitomized the type of people the minister had extolled his congregation to be. They looked out for each other. And for her.

Each time she attended a meeting and members told her how happy they were that she'd come to Holly Pointe, the sick feeling that had taken up permanent residence in the pit of her stomach flared.

Stella feared that no matter how fair she tried to be, Jane would push her to make the story more salacious. But if she told Jane right now that she wouldn't skew the story, the managing editor would likely fire her and send someone else up here. Or just have them write the story from Miami.

As she strode down the street toward the courthouse on this Friday afternoon, with Christmas less than three weeks away, she told herself that by the end of the weekend, she would deal with the Jane situation.

The temperature was reported to be in the midtwenties, but with the sun shining brightly, it felt almost balmy.

Of course, she was dressed for the weather with her coat, boots, and hat. The new mittens she'd ordered from L. L. Bean had arrived yesterday. The sky was clear, and despite the chill in the air, the sun warmed her face.

One more event to get through before she'd spend the evening with Sam. She hoped he'd had a chance to speak with Kenny. She was eager to learn what he'd discovered.

The courthouse steps were only a few feet away when Lucy descended the steps and stopped directly in front of her.

Striking in a royal-blue boiled-wool coat, she wore a plaid beret and leather gloves that were as sleek and elegant as the woman herself. Next to the stylish blonde, Stella suddenly felt as clunky as a bull in a china shop.

"Hi, Lucy." Stella would have started up the steps, but the blonde didn't move an inch.

"I thought you'd be at Lit-n-Latte." Lucy cocked her head, and her blue eyes narrowed. "I'm the facilitator of the discussion group this year. Faith informed me you were coming to participate and take pictures. Our members were looking forward to it."

"I'm headed there now." Stella gestured toward the Courthouse. "My event list says the meeting is in conference room 112."

Lucy started shaking her head even before Stella finished talking. "We met there last month because the Busy Bean was hosting a dominos tournament at our normal meeting time. Faith must have forgotten to change the location on your list."

"It's lucky I ran into you." Stella wanted to like Lucy, truly she did. But it felt as if Lucy had erected this invisible wall between herself and the world that never let anyone get too close.

Or it might simply be that Lucy didn't want to let *her* get too close.

Stella could empathize. She continually had to fight the urge to not lean, not depend on anyone else too much. It didn't take a shrink to tell her that she feared being hurt again. Perhaps, because of Kevin's death, it was the same for Lucy.

As she and Lucy strolled down the sidewalk crowded with shoppers, Lucy slanted a sideways glance in Stella's direction. "I hear you and Sam are dating."

"Sam is a wonderful guy." Knowing the relationship that existed between him and Lucy had Stella carefully choosing her next words. "I'm new in town, and he's helping me get acclimated."

"You're the first woman Sam has shown an interest in since Britt." Lucy offered a warm smile to two older women who were hurrying down the sidewalk in the opposite direction, then added, "The historical preservation society is having a meeting at the courthouse this afternoon."

Another club, er, organization. Stella had to smile. Her friends in Miami had warned her that life in a small town such as Holly Pointe would likely be tedious. But it had been anything but boring.

"The women—and men—in the group have done a fabulous job collecting and researching the town's history." Lucy's eyes blazed with surprising passion. "We got lucky when Olive Stanhope returned to Holly Pointe."

There were a dozen questions hovering on Stella's lips. The more she learned about Holly Pointe, the more she wanted to learn. It would be easy to be drawn into a discussion of what the members of the historical society actually did, but Stella couldn't let herself be distracted.

Other than Sam, Lucy was the first person to mention Britt, at least within her hearing. She wouldn't be a reporter if she didn't seize this opportunity.

"Sam told me a bit about him and Britt." Stella kept her tone conversational. "Did you have a chance to get to know her when they were dating?"

Lucy hesitated for a barely perceptible moment.

"Whenever Britt was in town, we often did activities as a foursome." Lucy's tone stayed equally casual. "Britt is a lovely person. I miss seeing her."

Now came the tricky part, Stella thought. These were murky waters she was negotiating. One wrong step could have her going under in seconds.

Stella kept her gaze focused ahead. "I don't know the particulars, but it seems odd that Britt could be all about Sam until an amazing role in a Broadway play opened up."

When only silence greeted the comment, Stella slanted a quick sideways glance and found Lucy staring at her through narrowed eyes. Her stomach somersaulted. Perhaps that comment wasn't as tactful as she'd hoped. "Of course, that could just be me, looking in from the outside."

The hurriedly added disclaimer didn't erase the frown that now furrowed Lucy's brow.

"If you're implying that Britt used Sam to cozy up to his parents, you're wrong." Lucy's tone could have frosted glass.

"That wasn't what—"

"If anyone did the using, it was Sam." Lucy clamped her lips shut and picked up the pace. "One thing you need to know about me, Stella. I don't gossip about my friends, especially to strangers."

The last part held a bite and had Stella's cheeks burning as if she'd been slapped. Then again, she'd known the dangers in pushing for information from a woman she barely knew.

What had she meant about Sam being the one who'd done the using? Stella couldn't imagine the man she was getting to know using anyone. Lucy had to be mistaken.

The second they stepped into the Busy Bean, Stella heaved a sigh of relief, knowing the tense silence filling the space between her and Lucy would end. She let her gaze scan the room, noticing two things right off. Norma was back behind the counter, her cheeks a healthy color. And the entire back of the shop was taken over by women, ribbons, and children's books.

"There she is." Faith wove her way in between tables to greet Stella with a warm hug. "I worried you'd forgotten."

"You gave her the wrong location." Lucy's tone was matter of fact, not at all censuring. "I found her wandering around the courthouse. She'd likely still be there if I hadn't seen her."

Stella shot Lucy a look as Faith made a sound of distress.

"I'm so sorry, Stella. I didn't mean—"

"No worries at all. I hadn't even gotten inside when I saw Lucy and she told me the meeting was here." Stella offered Faith a reassuring smile. "It was no big deal."

Without giving either woman a chance to say more, Stella

took off her coat and tossed it on a nearby table with everyone else's. "I see ribbon and books and a huge glass jar with money inside. Tell me what's going on so I can be part of the fun."

Lucy opened her mouth, but Faith gestured to the group. "We are the Lit-n-Lattes Book Club. There is also another book discussion club that has been active for over forty years, the Holly Pointe Bookies. As many of their members are elderly, the Bookies don't meet over the winter months."

"Bookies and Lit-n-Lattes." Stella smiled. "I love the names."

"Do you like to read?" Kate asked with barely concealed eagerness.

"I adore books. There's very little that compares to getting lost in a story. Unfortunately, once I graduated from college and went to work, there wasn't a lot of time."

Faith and Kate exchanged a pointed glance.

"If you end up staying in Holly Pointe, I think you'll find the lifestyle here is more relaxed and conducive to being in clubs. You may rediscover that joy of reading."

Kate's words had Faith nodding in agreement.

"If that happens, we'd love to have you join us," Kate said. "Mel is planning on joining us once her mother is back on her feet. She desperately wanted to come today, but the new cook flaked out, so she's working at the diner today."

"I don't know if—" Stella began, then realized she wasn't sure how to properly end the sentence.

I don't know if I'm going to stay.
I don't know if you'll still want me once you read the article.
I don't know what to do with my life, and I'm confused.

"Think about it." Faith placed a hand on her arm, and those soft brown eyes behind cherry-red eyeglasses met Stella's. "The offer remains open. There's no expiration date."

"I'll keep it in mind." Stella picked up a roll of candy-striped ribbon and gestured wide with one arm. "My inquiring mind wants to know what you're doing with all this stuff."

"The money in the glass jar is for donations to buy even more books." Lucy stepped forward and took control of the conversation. "Our goal is to provide every first grader in Holly Pointe with three books for Christmas. We have a couple of fundraisers during the year, and the community is very generous."

"Our December meeting is always dedicated to putting an assortment of three books together, then tying them with a pretty ribbon," Faith added.

"The rest of the year, it's about reading and discussing books. We see it as our club's mission to provide lifelong learning for our members as well as a place to build social connections." Lucy offered Stella the first authentic smile she'd seen since they'd ran into each other by the courthouse. "Not only do we share and discuss ideas regarding the book of the month, the meeting affords us a way to stay connected."

"And enjoy yummy lattes and scones," Krista Ankrom said, slipping off her cashmere coat and adding it to a pile.

Then the former model handed Lucy a shopping bag filled with books.

"Dustin and I heard you were short of books this year, and we wanted to help out." The warmth in Krista's voice when she said her husband's name had Stella's ears perking up.

"That's so kind of you." Lucy took the bag from Krista and set it on a nearby table. "I didn't think you were going to be able to make it. Wasn't today when you and Dustin were speaking with the television producers?"

"It was." Krista brushed a lock of hair back from her striking face, the large diamond on her left hand catching the light and sending rainbows of color scattering. "Our meeting got rescheduled. Jim, that's the producer, had a family emergency."

"Your family is so precious," Faith said with heartfelt sincerity. "I can't imagine that the producer will find anyone better than you and Dustin and the boys."

"Oh, Jim is certain we're the right couple." Krista gave a little laugh. "It's me who isn't convinced. Opening our home life to cameras is a big step."

"What does Dustin think?" Faith asked, her brows pulled together in concern.

"He was all for it initially. And he's still more on board than me, but we've had a lot of discussions these past few weeks, some of them heated—" Krista stopped abruptly, then smiled radiantly. "That's not important. What's important is getting these books wrapped for the children."

Lucy, Stella quickly discovered, had a vision and was determined to stay the course to bring it to completion. Each three-book package had to hold a variety of books that would appeal to any young reader. They couldn't all be about cars or dinosaurs or princesses. There had to be a variety in each pack.

Stella took pictures as Lucy instructed newer members in how to tie a perfect bow. When Norma came over with a tray of lattes in festive Christmas cups and plates of colorfully decorated sugar cookies, Stella got it all on camera. Including the tears that filled Norma's eyes when everyone applauded.

Kenny remained behind the counter, tending to customers and directing them to the large glass jar in the back of the room for donations.

Once Stella felt she had enough pictures, she settled down beside Faith at the long rectangular table. Lucy had set up an assembly line, some members tasked with putting books together, others tying the ribbons, and still others placing them in boxes ready to go to the elementary schools.

"I assume I'll see you at the movie marathon tonight." Faith kept her voice low as she tied a gingham ribbon in green, gold, and red around a stack of books.

"I am going, but I'm not sure what to expect." Stella had been pleased when Sam had called to invite her to the event at his house. "Sam told me there would be a group of friends there, but he was still in New York, and we didn't have much time to talk."

Faith grabbed another precut ribbon, this one with a snowman pattern on only one side. "It really is a movie marathon. It starts off with *A Christmas Story*."

"That's the one about the kid and the Red Ryder BB gun." Stella watched with interest as her friend gave the ribbon a double twist so the pattern faced up as she wrapped it around the other side.

Faith brought the ribbon up, rather than down as Stella often did, to make the bow. After it was tied prettily, Faith grabbed another ribbon and moved to the next stack of books. "After Ralphie gets his BB gun, *It's a Wonderful Life*—"

"Every time a bell rings an angel gets his wings." Stella's delivery of the classic line had Faith chuckling.

"You're going to fit right in." Faith turned to Kate, who had apparently been assigned the task of picking up empty latte cups and dumping them in the trash. "Stella is coming tonight."

Kate paused, a cup in each hand. "Do you need a ride? I've got four-wheel-drive and an empty seat. Snow is in the forecast."

"I really appreciate the offer." A thrill of excitement shot up her spine. "But Sam insisted on picking me up. We haven't seen each other since Sunday and—"

"Ooh-la-la. The man is hot for you." Kate's voice took on a deliberately sultry edge before she lightened it by laughing. "Is he also going to give you a ride home?"

"I suppose he is." Now that she thought about it, Stella couldn't recall him mentioning the drive home. "I hate the thought of him having to drive me all the way home then turn around and go all the way back."

"I'm sure he won't mind. I bet he wants the alone time with you." Faith's soft voice held a dreamy edge. "Completely understandable considering how long he's been away."

"It's only been five days," Stella demurred. While five days wasn't long in the grand scheme of things, it had felt like an eternity.

Stella couldn't recall the last time she'd missed a guy. But she missed Sam.

"If you end up needing a ride home, we can easily make room for you," Kate said.

"Who all is riding with you?" Stella asked.

"Faith, Mel, and—"

"Me," Lucy said. "Now less chatting. We need to be out of here in twenty minutes."

Stella thought of Kate's SUV. It was more of a mini SUV. While perfect for four, three in the back would be crowded. The thought of being thigh-to-thigh with Lucy in the back seat wasn't at all appealing.

She hoped having Sam drive her home wouldn't be too much of an imposition . . .

CHAPTER SEVENTEEN

Stella was glad Sam had picked her up early and brought her to his place. Not only because she wanted to help him get ready for the party, but because she'd never been to his farm, and there was much to see.

"My mother loves to cook, so she put in commercial-grade appliances when this was their home."

Even a nongourmet cook such as Stella could appreciate the double ovens, gas range, and humongous refrigerator. Not to mention the miles of counter space as well as the center island.

Somehow the kitchen managed to look both modern and inviting. She ran her hand along the granite countertop. "It's beautiful."

"Yes, you are." Sam's arms stole around her from behind, and he nuzzled her neck. "I missed you, Stella."

The sentiment brought a smile to her lips as she turned in Sam's arms to gaze up at him. On the drive to his house, they'd updated each other on their week. While he appeared truly interested in her daily routine, and she'd been fascinated by the events he'd attended with his parents, it had struck her as very impersonal.

Which was ridiculous. What had she expected him to do? Fling his arms around her and profess undying devotion? Well, okay, a tiny part of her had at least hoped for an I-missed-you kiss.

Of course, if that was really her hope, she shouldn't have told him she'd be waiting at the coffee shop, where a dozen eyes would be on them.

They were alone now, and she was in his arms. His tongue found the sensitive spot behind her ear, and all thoughts fled in the rush of sensation.

"Did you miss me?" he murmured as he scattered kisses down her neck.

"Yes, yes." She fought to say more, but thinking became impossible when his hand cupped her bottom and he pressed her against his hard length.

Desire, hot and intense, gushed through her, and she wondered what it would be like to make love on a kitchen floor.

The ringing of the doorbell had them springing apart and Sam muttering a curse under his breath.

"Who could that be?" Stella asked, her breath uneven as she fought for composure. She could still feel his lips on her neck and his hand on her breast.

"Someone who has incredibly bad timing." He blew out a breath, his smoldering dark eyes meeting hers. "Later."

"Will that later be before—or after—Ralphie gets his BB gun?"

Sam laughed. His irritation with the early guest appeared forgotten as he slung an arm companionably around her shoulder. "After both the BB gun and the angel getting his wings."

Stella liked it that Sam took her hand as they walked to the front door. As they strolled through the house, she turned her head from side to side as she tried to take it all in.

"I'll give you a personal tour." He bent to kiss her cheek, and she saw the promise in his eyes. "Later."

"You seem to like that word," she teased.

He chuckled as he opened the door.

Derek grinned at the two of them.

"Took you long enough." Derek pushed his way inside, then pointed to Stella. "You still haven't sent me pictures of Camryn sledding."

"That's because I don't have your email address. Let me get my purse. I left it in the kitchen. My phone is in it. We can do a quick AirDrop of the photos."

Moments later the task was complete.

"These are amazing, Stella." Derek glanced up and shifted his attention to Sam. "You should see the shots Stella got of Cam. Amazing."

Sam took a minute to study the pictures on the phone. "These are good."

Photography had been a hobby since Stella had been in grade school. She'd been told more times than she could count that she possessed the ability to capture what was important as well as a "creative" eye.

While Stella wasn't sure that was true, she enjoyed photography immensely. That's why the social media position had been such a great fit.

"This is it?" Sam held up the bag of chips that Derek had shoved at him while following Stella to the kitchen.

"What's wrong?" Derek pulled off his coat and tossed it over a bar stool. "You should have told me if you didn't like sour cream and onion. I could have picked up barbecue or even the plain ones with the ridges."

"I asked you to pick up snacks for this evening since I was getting into town so late." Sam let the bag dangle between his fingers. "Do you really think one bag of chips is enough to feed everyone?"

"The other guests will bring stuff." Derek waved a dismissive hand, appearing not at all concerned. "Even when you tell them not to, they do."

Stella realized with sudden horror that she should have brought something. Or at least *asked* if there was something she could contribute.

"I'm sorry." Stricken, Stella looked up at Sam. "I should have brought something."

Sam offered a reassuring smile that didn't reassure. "You didn't have to bring anything except yourself."

"I know I didn't have to, but I could have easily made up some stuffed pinwheels. Any time I've brought them to a party, they've gotten rave reviews. And trust me when I say that my salted caramel and chocolate stack bars are to die for."

"Pinwheels are a personal favorite." Derek casually removed the potato chip bag from Sam's hands and wandered to a cabinet. Pulling out a large glass bowl, he dumped in the chips. "Bring them next time."

"Okay." As she said the word, Stella felt a sharp pain in the area of her heart.

It was highly probable that the next time this group of friends got together, she'd be long gone.

The doorbell rang, and when Sam turned, Derek brushed past him. "I'll get it."

Once he'd left the room, Stella turned to Sam. "I didn't even think to bring anything."

As if sensing her distress, Sam stepped toward her and enfolded her in his strong arms. "Don't give it a second thought. You brought what was most important."

She cocked her head, not following.

"You." He kissed her softly on the lips. "You being here is what matters. Anything else is just . . . sour cream and onion chips."

Derek was right, Stella thought. Each woman had brought a dish. There was enough food to feed an army platoon. Lucy brought a bag of tortilla chips—which Stella discovered was Sam's favorite—along with a big bowl of something called "tequila-spiked queso fundido."

Stella wasn't certain of every ingredient in the dip, but it packed a punch.

Zach and Nate arrived with a six pack of Coronas and bottles of pale ale that were added to the Coors in Sam's refrigerator.

Somehow, when it was time for the movies to begin, Stella ended up on the sofa beside Sam. His arm was around her shoulders, and his fingers played with her hair as they talked and laughed their way through two complete movies.

They were nearly to the end of *Elf* when everyone started to get antsy.

"I hate to rush off." A regretful sigh escaped Kate's lips when she returned from her trek to the front door to check the weather outside. She turned to Sam. "The snow is really piling up out there. But it's the wind that has me worried. I'm afraid if we don't leave now, you're going to have a houseful of company tonight."

"We weren't supposed to get wind." Zach's comment earned him a pointed glance from Kate.

"Open that door and tell me what you think of the wind that we weren't supposed to get."

With an exaggerated breath, Zach clambered to his feet and headed for the door. He returned seconds later, a chagrined look on his face. "She's right. It's dumping snow, and the wind is bad."

Zach glanced at Nate, whose feet were comfortably perched on a hassock. "Since you're on call for pushing snow for the city, we better—"

His words were interrupted by a buzzing from Nate's phone. Pulling it out, Nate glanced down and pulled himself to his feet. "You called that one. George wants us out and clearing the parking lots by five a.m."

"What about the streets?" Stella frowned. "I would think the roads would be a higher priority than parking lots."

"There's a whole crew that deals with nothing but roads," Nate explained. "The head of public works is over that department, and they have the big plows. My department helps out by covering the off-street lots owned by the city. We use trucks with blades."

"Which is his long-winded way of saying," Zach clamped a hand on Nate's shoulder, "we won't be able to stay this year to see Buddy and Jovie get together."

"I understand if you feel you need to go, although you're all welcome to spend the night. This old house has enough beds." Sam was also on his feet now.

"We'll be fine," Faith shot him a smile that radiated warmth. "But I appreciate the offer."

After grabbing coats and other winter gear, everyone headed en masse for the front door.

"Drive safe." Sam's brows furrowed in a worried frown. "The roads out here get treacherous, especially when there's drifting."

Kate shot Stella a questioning look, making it clear that the offer of a ride home was still on the table. The fact was, if Stella planned on leaving, it made sense for her to ride with Kate and the others.

There was no reason to make Sam drive her into town, then have to drive back in an ever-worsening storm.

Stella gave Kate an imperceptible shake of her head, and the brunette's eyes took on a knowing gleam.

If Sam chose to drive her back to Holly Pointe, Stella would insist he spend the night. If he didn't want to spend it with her, she'd press him to stay with any number of friends he had in town. Heck, if he didn't want to impose on anyone, there was always his office.

But if he decided that he didn't want to navigate the treacherous roads at all, she'd take him up on his offer to stay here all night.

While it was comforting to know there were any number of beds available for her to choose from, there was only one bed Stella wanted to be in tonight.

"I'm going to help clean off vehicles." Sam gave her shoulder a squeeze and quickly pulled on his coat and boots.

Stella watched him and her other friends—yes, that's how she thought of them all now—step into the swirling whiteness, and a feeling of belonging settled over her.

It was suddenly clear what must be done. While Sam was cleaning off the vehicles, she needed to do her own cleaning and remove this heavy weight from her shoulders.

Her desperate straits had blinded her to moral implications of what she'd agreed to do. In her heart, she knew that sensationalizing a story to sell more papers was wrong. Not only that, writing the article would be a betrayal of the friendships that had been extended to her since arriving in Holly Pointe. Even if Stella tried to be objective, Jane would do whatever she could to skew the article toward the salacious.

Sensationalized news sells papers. That was Jane's mantra, and it was why Stella decided she didn't want to work for her.

Not on this project.

Not ever.

Stella picked up her phone and sent Jane a quick text pulling out of the project and promising to repay the money Jane had advanced her as soon as possible.

Once the message was sent, Stella shut off her phone. She didn't want to hear back from Jane tonight.

Tonight was all about following the path that was right for her, a path it felt as if her entire life had been leading her toward.

Stella wanted to get a job and stay in Holly Pointe.

She wanted to have lunch with friends and talk about books over lattes.

If Sam told her he wanted her to sleep in one of his many beds, that's where she would sleep. But she hoped, hoped, hoped he would want her in his bed with him.

Because now that her assignment no longer stood between them, Stella was ready to open her arms—and her heart—fully to Sam to see where it might lead.

∼

While Sam braved the wild and wintery outdoors, Stella sat and finished the movie. She loved a happy ending, and the conclusion to *Elf* left her with a smile on her face. Then Stella turned her attention to cleaning up the living room. In the pantry, she found some lovely storage containers—no doubt left over from his mother—and put what little food hadn't been devoured into containers, then popped them in the refrigerator.

The chips had disappeared with lightning speed, leaving nothing behind but empty sacks. Once the living room was back in order, Stella hand-washed the bowls and pans that the heartier food had come in.

She was drying the last bowl when the door leading from the garage opened and Sam tromped into the mudroom adjacent to the kitchen.

"You look like a snowman." She lifted her hands, one still holding the tea towel, wanting to help but not knowing how.

His hood was up, and he'd tied a scarf around the lower part of his face, leaving only the eyes uncovered. Snow and ice covered his coat and the insulated rubber boots that went to his knees. "It's really coming down now. But it's the wind that's making it so much worse."

"It took you all this time to clean off their cars?" It seemed like forever ago that Stella had heard the engines roar to life. When Sam hadn't come in, she'd kept busy and tried not to worry.

"I made sure the horses had everything they needed." Despite the scarf, his cheeks were reddened from the cold.

After pulling off the gloves, he pushed back the hood and removed the stocking cap, revealing hair standing in dark, spiky tufts.

The coat came off before Sam moved on to the rubber boots. He heaved a sigh when the second boot hit the floor. "I'm glad that's done. I don't want to go out in that weather anytime soon."

Stella felt a tingle of excitement. "Does that mean you won't be taking me back to Holly Pointe tonight?"

His fingers stilled on the boots he was moving to the side. He looked up at her. "Do you want to go home tonight?"

"Not particularly." She smiled, feeling cheerful. "I'd much rather stay here and spend time with you."

"Good." His lips lifted in a slow smile.

"In one of your many bedrooms."

The smile faded then reappeared. "That's okay. There's a lot to choose from."

"Unless you're the sharing type."

He inclined his head, a look of watchful waiting on his face.

"I mean, there's no need to mess up another bed if you're willing to share yours."

Light flared in his dark eyes.

"But first." She stepped to him and began to unbutton his shirt, her gaze never leaving his. "I think a hot shower would feel awfully good to someone who just spent the last forty-five minutes in a snowstorm."

"There's just one thing." His eyes never left hers as he pulled her to him.

Fighting a smile, Stella gazed up him through lowered lashes. "What is that?"

"I'd not only like to share my bed." He brushed her lips with his, a tantalizing promise in the touch. "I'd like to share my shower. With you."

CHAPTER EIGHTEEN

The time spent in the shower with Sam was a delicious appetizer that Stella thought had completely quenched her hunger. Until the shower ended and they moved to his bed.

A bed that was as big and massive as the man himself. The snow continued to fall outside, but Stella didn't care as Sam lay beside her and kissed her until the heat she had been convinced was sated in the shower began to stir again.

"Are you sure you have enough condoms?" she murmured as his lips moved down her neck.

When he stopped kissing her, Stella worried she'd killed the mood with her practical question.

But the pill had never agreed with her system, and she needed to know they were safe. Safe in the shower. Now safe here in bed.

He brushed a lock of hair back from her face. "Thanks to a Duane Reade near my parents' apartment—and my forethought—we don't need to worry about running out."

"If I'd been thinking ahead, I'd have brought along the package I purchased in Jay this week."

"You bought condoms?" Amusement laced his voice.

"After our, ah, close encounter last Saturday, I could see

where this train was headed." She met his gaze, feeling defensive. "I wanted to be prepared."

"I like that about you." He kissed the tip of her nose, and she relaxed back against the pillow.

"You like that I'm prepared."

"Actually, I like everything about you."

"You don't know everything."

When he looked at her with a puzzled expression, she backpedaled. "I mean, we've only known each other a couple of weeks. Not nearly enough time to know *everything*."

"I know the important stuff." His lips curved. "I feel closer to you in the short time we've been together than I do to people I've known for years."

"It's the same with me." Stella was doubly glad she'd told Jane earlier that she wouldn't be doing the story.

Now no one would know she'd once been set to destroy this wonderful town with an article touting a drunk Santa and . . .

Stella abruptly pushed to one elbow, nearly clipping Sam in the jaw. "I forgot to ask if you've had a chance to speak with Kenny."

Sam hesitated. "As it's a personnel matter, I really shouldn't be discussing the situation with anyone other than the head of human relations and perhaps the mayor."

"Personnel matter." A knot formed in the pit of Stella's stomach. "Did you fire him?"

"No. No." Sam spoke quickly. "Okay, I spoke with Kenny privately and mentioned that someone had observed him drinking alcohol while in his Santa suit."

Sam paused, as if unsure how much more to reveal.

"You don't have to tell me what he said." Stella rested her fingers on Sam's arms, finding the warmth of his skin comforting. "Just reassure me that everything is going to be okay for Kenny."

"Everything is going to be okay."

Stella closed her eyes and expelled a ragged breath. "I was so worried. I found myself second-guessing my decision to come to you all week."

"You did the right thing in coming to me before Kenny did something where we'd have no choice but to fire him." Sam's eyes were dark and intense. "I want you to know that there isn't anything you can't tell me. Whatever problem or concern you have, we'll work through it together. It's the secrets and lies that kill a relationship."

This would be the time, Stella decided, to tell Sam the real reason she'd come to Holly Pointe. She opened her mouth, but instead of a confession, she heard herself ask, "Is that what happened between you and Britt?"

A startled look crossed his face. "Why would you think that?"

She lifted a shoulder in a slight shrug.

"Britt is a wonderful woman; smart and charming and extremely talented."

Stella wished she'd kept her mouth shut. And wished he'd kept his shut, too. She couldn't imagine anything could be worse than lying naked in bed next to a guy and listening to him praise his ex-girlfriend.

"If she's so wonderful, why did the two of you break up?"

She heard the peevish note to her voice and was sure he had as well. Great, now she sounded supersensitive and insecure.

"The connection I was talking about a few minutes ago, the one I felt almost instantly with you, was never there."

"Never?" Stella shot him a skeptical look. "You dated her for nearly two years."

"We dated long-distance for much of that time." He reached over and pulled Stella to him as if needing the closeness.

Stella loved how they fit so perfectly together.

"For all Britt's wonderful qualities, something was missing in our relationship."

"Did you think she was using you to get to your parents?"

Once again, Stella wondered when her mouth had become detached from her brain.

He jerked back. "Where did you get that idea?"

"There were lots of articles hinting at that. Especially when your parents cast her in their new play."

"They cast her in the lead role because she was the perfect choice." There was a determined gleam in his eyes. "She did not use me, and I didn't use her. It was just one of those relationships not meant to go the distance. I'm sure you've had a few of those."

"I dated a guy who was married." Yep, her brain was detached.

Sam stilled.

"I didn't know Tony was married. He didn't wear a ring, and he said he was single." Stella's chuckle held little humor. The idea that she could have been so ignorant still rankled. "Even though, looking back, there were signs I missed—or ignored—I was seriously shocked when I discovered the truth."

"When you say you discovered the truth, I take it that he didn't come clean and be honest."

"No." She couldn't meet Sam's gaze. "It was last summer, and I was house-sitting for a coworker for a weekend. Tony was supposedly out of town on business. When I went to pick up a few necessities, I ran into him and his wife shopping at a nearby grocery store."

"I can't imagine how you must have felt." He reached down and took her hand, bringing it to his lips. "What did you do?"

"I thought about confronting him right then and there, but . . . I didn't." Stella found herself gripping Sam's hand. "I blocked his number, and when he knocked on my door, I didn't answer. We never spoke again."

"Never?"

She shook her head. "Which was a relief, but as I realized too late, that meant there was no closure, either. But I certainly wasn't about to contact him just to tell him that he was a creep and a cheat."

"He didn't deserve you." Sam tugged her even closer. "This might sound strange, but I'm glad he was married."

"Why? So I'd have firsthand knowledge of what it's like to play the fool?"

"Because otherwise you might not have come to Holly Pointe and wouldn't be here now with me."

She really did need to tell him the truth about her road to Vermont. This seemed the perfect opening. "About that—"

"I think you and I have done enough talking about Kenny and past relationships. Right now, I'd like to focus on us."

Stella swallowed past the sudden lump in her throat and choked out the word. *"Us?"*

"More specifically, on making the most of this warm, comfortable bed with a woman I can't seem to get enough of." He gave her a scorching kiss that reverberated all the way to her toes. When his lips left hers, he smiled. "How does that sound to you?"

She blinked and tried to corral her scrambled thoughts. "Ah, what was the question again?"

His laugh was full and robust and had everything inside her yearning. For him and for a life that now seemed within her reach.

"Is it any wonder I'm crazy about you?"

As their mouths found each other's once again, Stella found herself mentally replacing the words *crazy about* with *falling in love*.

Because that's what she was doing. As strange as it sounded, after only two weeks, she was falling in love with Sam Johnson.

The snow finally quit falling in the morning, and the plows came through midday, clearing drifts that were over her head. By the time the plows moved on down the road, Sam had already tended to the horses and cleared the lane leading to the road.

He'd asked her to stay, but Stella knew that as the city administrator of a town with a snow emergency in effect, there were duties demanding his attention. Especially with another round of snow forecast for late tonight.

"You have no idea how difficult it is for me to leave you here." Sam kissed her softly on the lips, lingering for several heartbeats.

"You have duties to attend to, and so do I." Instead of stepping away or turning to open the door, Stella kept her arms around his neck. "You can hear the hum of conversation and laughter all the way up here, which means the Busy Bean is hopping. Kenny and Norma will need my help."

"Probably," he agreed as his gaze searched her eyes. "I wanted more time alone with you."

"I'm not going anywhere." She found herself wishing she could add *forever*, but she knew that would be presumptuous.

Their relationship was new, and these were early days. While she'd learned that sleeping with someone wasn't a promise of forever, neither could she deny the connection.

"If you need a place to bunk tonight," Stella said as she slipped her fingers into his hair, *"mi casa es su casa."*

"If I didn't have the horses, I'd take you up on it." The regret in his voice matched the look in his eyes. "If we get the amount forecast, along with the wind, the roads will likely blow shut again tonight. I strongly suggest you hang around home."

"If the roads get that bad, I want you to knock on my door so I can return the hospitality you extended to me last night."

He tugged her closer, a grin broadening his mouth. "Is that what you call it?"

Stella couldn't help laughing but quickly sobered. "I'm serious, Sam. If it looks like you won't be able to make it home, I want you to stay here."

This worrying about someone else was new to her, and Stella

didn't like the image of Sam's truck in a ditch, covered in a foot of snow.

She gave his hair a yank.

"Hey, what was that for?"

"I want you to keep yourself safe." Her voice trembled for just a second before she brought it under control. "I don't want anything happening to you."

When Sam's eyes filled with understanding, Stella knew he understood the war that raged inside her. A part of her wanted to keep her heart safe so she wouldn't be hurt again. The other part, the part that had already fallen for him, worried for his safety on dangerous roads.

The memory of hugging her mom and dad good-bye that one last time and never seeing them again was never far from her thoughts.

Stella leaned her head forward so it rested against the front of his coat. "Don't take any chances."

"I won't." He kissed the top of her head. "I promise."

Stella listened to the sound of his boots on the creaky steps. When she couldn't hear him anymore, she unlocked her door and stepped inside.

She glanced around the small, cozy space as if seeing it for the first time. Had it really been less than twenty-four hours since she'd walked out the door and down the steps to meet Sam? It felt as if a lifetime had passed.

This afternoon she felt lighter and more at peace than she had in years. Perhaps it was because she no longer had Jane's assignment resting like a heavy weight on her shoulders.

Stella may have sent the text, but she knew she hadn't heard the last from Jane. She unwound the scarf from her neck, slipped off her coat and hat, and dropped to the sofa. Only then did she pull out her phone.

Of course she had new texts.

And new emails.

Not just from Jane but from her new friends, wanting to know whether she'd made it home safely.

Guilt had her answering those texts first, apologizing and assuring everyone she was safely back in Holly Pointe and in her apartment.

Then, she set out to read Jane's increasingly vitriolic communications. In one of the last ones, Jane cited wording in the contract that Stella had signed and threatened legal action if she didn't turn in the article.

Thankfully, because of the serious reservations she'd had going into this project, Stella had carefully reviewed the contract. She'd paid special attention to the section regarding article specifications.

Nowhere in that entire section was there any wording that would require Stella to skew the article in a certain direction. Which was the reason Stella had felt comfortable signing it.

She knew, of course, the kind of article that Jane wanted and was demanding. But legally, Stella was only required to give the newspaper an article on Christmas in Holly Pointe within the specified word count. If the article she submitted wasn't deemed satisfactory, she would be given the opportunity to rewrite. If she couldn't give the newspaper an article they deemed publishable, Stella wouldn't be paid.

At this point, she didn't care about the money or the job that had been dangled like a particularly juicy carrot in front of her. All she cared about was that she was now free of Jane.

Well, *nearly* free of Jane.

For a long five seconds, Stella was tempted to take the coward's way out and let her fingers—or her thumbs—respond. But she hadn't been raised to take the easy way out.

Her mother and father had taught her be responsible for her actions and do the right thing.

Agreeing to the article had been a mistake. Her decision to step away from it had been the right move. But doing it via a text was wrong. Stella owed Jane the courtesy of a phone conversation.

As she dialed the managing editor's cell number, Stella found herself wondering whether Jane would answer. It was, after all, a Saturday night, and Jane had a very active social life. Not necessarily with people she liked, but rather with those she felt she could use in some way.

Stella wondered whether that would have been her destiny if she'd stayed in Miami. Would she have become as jaded and cynical as Jane?

She couldn't see that happening here in Holly Pointe.

"Hello." There was a coolness to the greeting that had Stella's stomach churning.

"Jane. This is Stella." Her fingers felt suddenly slick around her phone. She shifted the phone to her other hand and wiped her sweaty palm against her shirt. "If this isn't a good time, I can—"

"This is an excellent time. Give me a minute." Instead of muting the call, Jane must have turned to her companion. "Tom, I need to take this call. It's business. Be a dear and get me a glass of champagne."

Then she was back, and her tone was all business. "I admit I was stunned when I received your text. It caught me completely off guard. I had to read it twice."

"I don't believe—" Stella stopped herself and rephrased. "I'm not able to write the article you want. I wanted to let you know that now and not wait until the last minute."

"I'm confused. You and I discussed the various issues you'd be including in your article, and I wholeheartedly concurred with the avenues you were exploring." Jane paused. "In fact, I was excited and couldn't wait to receive the article and pictures. I thought you were excited as well. Then, out of the blue, I get your text. What changed?"

Stella closed her eyes and realized she'd done Jane even more of a disservice than she imagined. Not only had she accepted the assignment, she'd led Jane on.

Never once, other than to reiterate that she would need to have facts to back up anything she wrote, had she mentioned just how uncomfortable she was slanting the article toward the sensational.

"I've never been comfortable with sensationalized journalism." Stella hurried on before Jane could jump in and defend the track that she had sent the paper down. "I realize it's a tough market for newspapers nowadays, and I also understand you were brought in to shore up the bottom line. Lots of people prefer sensationalized news, and many reporters love to do the spin. I've come to realize that I'm just not one of them."

"I see."

There was a wealth of feeling behind those two words, and Stella's heart rate took a jump, but she forced a calm that she didn't feel as she responded.

"I will fulfill the terms of the contract by submitting the article to you by the specified date. If there are changes that I feel comfortable making that will make the article more agreeable to you, I'll do that. But I will not be including anything about Drunk Santa, Dustin Bellamy and Krista Ankrom, or Britt Elliott."

"You're planning on giving me a fluff piece." A hard edge had crept into Jane's tone. If Stella were in Jane's office now, she knew the editor's eyes would hold a steely gleam.

"I'm planning on giving you a well-written piece about Holly Pointe and what makes it special." Stella fought to keep her tone matter of fact and professional. "I believe readers who are looking for uplifting articles around the holidays will love it."

"I'll expect to see it in on time. We'll go from there."

"Yes, I'll—" Stella paused, then held out her phone at the silence on the other end. She frowned.

Jane had hung up on her.

"Well, that could have gone better." Stella spoke to the empty apartment as she began to pace. Of course, it could have gone worse.

Had she really expected Jane to applaud her for standing up for her convictions?

Her father would have.

Stella stopped before the framed photo of her parents. She picked it up and held it at eye level, gazing at the smiling faces. "You didn't raise me to be the type of person to betray a friend. You raised me to care about others. Even if these people weren't my friends, I'm not a gossip columnist. I went into journalism to bring the truth to light, to make the world a better place."

For one crazy second, Stella swore she saw her father nod.

This wasn't about doing what her parents thought was right. Or what Sam or her other friends in Holly Pointe thought was right. This was about her following her own conscience.

She would give the managing editor the best article she could write and do justice to this community that had stolen her heart.

Only then would she be able to enjoy Christmas and the upcoming Mistletoe Ball with the man she loved without a dark cloud hanging overhead.

CHAPTER NINETEEN

The knock at her door an hour later had Stella's gaze jerking away from her computer screen. She'd started and restarted the article on Holly Pointe but couldn't seem to get the feel she was after. Shutting her laptop, she hurried to the door.

She was about to open it without looking, then chided herself. Despite the fact that this was Holly Pointe, where people left car keys dangling from vehicle ignitions and house keys under the front doormat, she'd lived in a big city.

Caution was always a good thing.

Stella glanced through the peephole, and her heart leaped. She eagerly unlocked the door, pulled it open, and smiled at Sam. "Couldn't stay away?"

He glanced at the pink flannel pajamas covered in penguins that she'd donned after he'd left and lifted his hands. "What can I say? I'm a sucker for a pretty woman in penguins."

She laughed and stepped aside, motioning him through the doorway. "I take it the roads are bad."

He nodded and lifted a questioning brow. "Does the offer of a place to stay still stand?"

"Absolutely." She held out her hands and took his hat and

scarf, watching him shrug out of the heavy winter coat. "Would you like some hot cocoa?"

Surprise skittered across his face. "You have some?"

"Actually, once you left, I had this craving for the real stuff, so I made some in the Crock-Pot."

"Sounds . . . fabulous."

She felt Sam's eyes on her as she moved to the tiny kitchenette and removed two cups from the cupboard.

"Is there anything I can do?"

Stella turned to smile at him. "You can have a seat on the sofa and tell me if you'd like a dash of peppermint schnapps added to your cup."

At his look of surprise, she continued.

"When I was at the store, I saw the bottle and thought of my grandpa." Stella set the mugs on the counter, her lips curving up at the memory of her somewhat stern German grandfather and his love of schnapps. "I had to buy it."

"I did the same recently with spearmint candy canes." Sam dropped down on the overstuffed couch. "Kevin loved them. Me, not so much. But when I saw a package at the market, I had to pick them up."

Their eyes met, and Stella savored the moment of shared understanding.

She lifted the festive red mug, now filled with cocoa. "It's decision time. Schnapps? Whipped cream? Both?"

"Both." He heaved an exaggerated breath. "This is much better than being stuck in some snow drift."

"That's a pretty low bar you've set, Mr. Johnson." Stella chuckled as she handed him the mug, then took a seat beside him on the sofa. "How bad were the roads?"

Sam took a sip of the hot cocoa and sighed. "This tastes amazing."

She sipped her own and had to agree.

"The roads are horrible. The snow is coming down at a good

clip, but it's the winds that make travel treacherous. There was no way I could make it."

"What about the horses?" Stella settled comfortably against the back of the sofa, her fingers wrapped around the warm cup. "Will they be okay?"

"I don't like the fact that they'll have to stay in their stalls, but the ones they're in are large enough for them to move and turn around and even lie down in."

Then, as if anticipating her next question, he added. "When I took over their care, I installed automatic feeders and waterers in their stalls. While I like to monitor their intake and let them out for periods of time—even in this type of weather—they'll be okay."

"That has to be load off your mind."

"As you've already observed, the weather here can be unpredictable. You have to be prepared for any eventuality." Sam slanted a sideways glance in her direction. "I'm sure it seems like a rugged existence to a big-city Florida gal."

"Not really."

At his skeptical look, she smiled and continued. "It's different, but I've discovered I prefer this to the muggy heat of Miami. As long as I'm dressed properly, the cold doesn't bother me." She shifted in her seat to more fully face him, slipping a leg under herself on the sofa. "When it's stifling hot, there's only so many clothes you can take off. Here, if you feel chilled, you just add another layer."

His gaze traveled lazily over her, and her entire body began to vibrate. "Do you expect me to believe you could actually see yourself living in Holly Pointe?"

Her lips curved over the rim of her mug. "What, is that so difficult?"

"Well, aside from the climate, it's not exactly the mecca of culture."

Stella bolted upright, her cocoa sloshing precariously close to the rim of her cup. "Don't talk about your community that way."

Surprise flickered in his brown eyes. "What do you mean?"

The intensity of the emotion coursing through her shocked Stella. It was as if someone had called her baby ugly. "Holly Pointe is a wonderful town. When that publication called it the capital of Christmas kindness, they were on target. I've never been in a community where people so readily accept a stranger. Not only accept, they go out of their way to help and make that person feel welcome. As far as culture, there's more to do here than in most larger towns. And if a person wants to listen to a symphony or watch a touring Broadway show, you can drive an hour and a half to Burlington and make a night of it."

By the time Stella paused for breath, her voice shaking with conviction, Sam was grinning.

"What are you smiling about?" she snapped.

"I think you'd be a fabulous PR person for Holly Pointe." A softness settled over his expression. "You convinced me."

"You didn't need much convincing." Stella felt her cheeks warm, embarrassed by her spirited defense of a town that wasn't even her own. "Let's just say I'm enjoying my time here."

Like a hunting dog that has spotted a bird, Sam's gaze turned razor sharp. "When you say 'your time here,' it makes it sound like this is a stopover and you're planning to leave."

Stella supposed she could return to Miami, but other than a handful of casual friends, there was nothing there for her anymore. And since the incident with Jane, not even the possibility of a job.

She could go to Minnesota and perhaps find something near the retirement community where her grandparents lived. But she knew they already had a very active life. While she was certain they would be excited to have her close, she would in essence be starting a new life from scratch there.

But in Holly Pointe, she already had a place to stay. She had friends. And she had Sam.

"Stella?"

She blinked as a yearning washed over her. "What?"

"You didn't answer my question. Are you planning to leave?"

"At this moment, I don't have any plans one way or the other." She smiled. "Besides, you promised to take me skijoring. I'm not leaving until that happens."

He laughed. "Then I can tell you right now, a skijoring date is off the table."

The next week was one of the happiest of Stella's life. In addition to covering various holiday events, she filled in at the Busy Bean and helped Mel when she was short-staffed at Rosie's Diner. On Thursday, she spent a whole day helping Faith prepare signs she'd sold for mailing.

When Stella called Tasha to wish her a Merry Christmas, her friend couldn't understand why Stella was working so many hours for no pay. Try as she might, Stella couldn't make her Miami friend understand that in Holly Pointe, she'd rediscovered the spirit of giving that her parents had instilled in her.

It wasn't as if it was all work and no play. She saw Sam several nights that week and on the weekend. Like this afternoon.

They were attending the Dickens Village Festival. In addition to a craft show complete with food booths in the courthouse and a performance this evening at the local playhouse of *A Christmas Carol*, there would be a fruitcake relay.

"I thought you said National Fruitcake Day is December 27." Stella paused in front of Memory Lane on their way to the courthouse. "So why is the toss part of today's events?"

"Lots of people in the area come to town for the Dickens festival. Having the competition at the same time bolsters attendance for both events." Sam's gaze traveled over her. "You look nice."

"The plaid trapper hat is new." She kept her expression serious. "Isn't it lovely?"

He touched the ear flaps, deliberately brushing his knuckles against her cheeks. "Very stylish."

"It's also very warm."

"I like having a practical girlfriend." Sam brushed his lips against hers, paying no attention to those passing by.

His public displays of affection—holding her hand, placing an arm around her shoulders, and light kisses—had increased over the past week.

Each time he touched her, Stella found herself wondering whether his feelings for her were as deep as hers for him. She didn't ask. She knew it was too early to get serious, but she couldn't stop herself from wondering . . . and hoping.

"I have some good news."

Though something in his tone put her on alert, she smiled and inclined her head. "What news?"

"My parents are flying in this week for the Mistletoe Ball."

Eagerly anticipated by everyone, the ball would be held next Saturday, December 23. Faith had already asked Stella to help with decorations.

"That's wonderful. I bet you can't wait to see them." A knot formed in the pit of Stella's stomach. When Sam had said he was spending the holidays in Holly Pointe, she hadn't considered that his parents would come here.

"I want you to meet them." He took her arm, and they continued their stroll past cheerfully decorated windows. "I want them to meet you."

"I'd love to meet them." Stella hid her disappointment behind a bright smile. She'd been looking forward to enjoying the holidays with Sam. "Two more new friends to add to my growing list."

Sam smiled. "Actually, three new friends."

Stella inclined her head.

"They're bringing Britt with them."

~

Sam watched Stella across the giant ballroom, laughing with Mel, Kate, and Faith. Her three friends had convinced her to join their fruitcake relay team. He assumed by their gestures that they were utilizing the time before their event began to instruct her in how to toss a fruitcake through a basketball hoop.

From watching many of these relays through the years, Sam knew the basketball hoop toss was one of the most difficult obstacles that a team member needed to conquer on the way to the finish line.

"We should have signed up." Derek stood beside Sam, his eyes on Zach as the man army crawled under a rope stretched between two chairs with a fruitcake balanced on his back.

It was the last obstacle in the course. When Zach made it through, he scrambled to his feet, tucked the fruitcake under his arm like a football, and sprinted across the finish line.

Onlookers, including Derek and Sam cheered and whistled.

"Maybe next year." Sam's gaze returned to Stella.

"Did you tell her?"

Sam nodded.

"How'd she take the news?"

Pulling his gaze from Stella, he faced Derek. "She didn't have a chance to say much. We ran into your sister on the street when we were coming here, and she asked Stella to join their team. Apparently, there was some last-minute catering crisis that Lucy had to handle."

"But you did tell her Britt was coming."

Sam frowned. "I just told you I did."

"Most women would be jealous."

"Stella isn't most women." Though she'd done a good job of hiding any reservations, the hint of uncertainty that had flickered in her eye for just a second troubled him.

Sam wasn't going to worry about that now. He had all evening to pull out all the stops and convince her she was the only woman he wanted.

CHAPTER TWENTY

Stella considered the Thursday morning coffee klatch with friends to be a private celebration of sorts. Last night, she'd turned in the draft of her article on Holly Pointe, advising Jane in her email that she'd send pictures of the Mistletoe Ball on Sunday.

Although Jane had yet to respond, Stella considered the assignment completed. Or it would be once she sent the final photos. Now the only thing she had to worry about was meeting Sam's parents. And Britt.

"Being with all of you like this is oh-so-lovely." Mel lifted the cup of frothy cappuccino to her lips. "I didn't realize until I moved back just how much I missed living in Holly Pointe."

"You've decided to stay." Pleasure rippled through Faith's words like a pretty Christmas ribbon.

Like Kate and Faith, Stella held her breath awaiting Mel's reply. The four women had decided to meet at the Busy Bean for coffee and scones before heading out to Grace Hollow.

Stella had been informed by her new friends that assisting Lucy's crew with the decorations for the Mistletoe Ball was an annual tradition. Would she be here next year to continue the tradition, Stella wondered? She hoped so.

"I *am* going to stay," Mel announced.

"I'm so glad." Faith reached across the table and gave Mel's freckled hand a squeeze.

"Yay!" Kate lifted her cup of plain black coffee in a mock salute.

"I totally get it," Stella heard herself say, then flushed as three pairs of eyes shifted to her.

"Ah, another fan of this wonderful community." Kate spoke in a teasing tone, but Stella saw the spark of pleasure in her eyes.

"Are you going to stay, too?" Mel asked with an eagerness that she didn't bother to conceal.

"If Sam has anything to say about it, she will." Kate shot Stella a wink.

Faith only gazed at Stella, her eyes warm and accepting of whatever decision Stella had reached.

"I'd like to stay." Taking another bite of the delicious blueberry scone proved to be a mistake. The light and buttery quick bread turned to dust in her mouth as she thought of Britt. She gulped her coffee then cleared her throat. "I'm just not sure yet."

"Is your hesitation because of Britt?" Sympathy skittered across Mel's face. "Derek told me she and Sam's parents got into town late last night."

Stella started to say no, but then stopped herself. When she'd gotten up the courage to tell Jane that she wouldn't be skewing the article, Stella had made a vow to be as honest as possible going forward.

Resting her hands on the table in front of her, Stella searched for the right words. When Kate opened her mouth to speak, Stella held up one of her hands. "I love it here. I can see myself making a home in Holly Pointe, building a life here."

The women's eyes never left her face. They remained silent, giving her time to say whatever she wanted to say without interruption. In the accepting silence, she felt surrounded by their love.

It was difficult to believe that it had been less than a month since she'd arrived in Holly Pointe not knowing a soul. She recalled how she'd watched with envy as the three sat at a nearby table laughing and talking.

Now she was part of this wonderful group. She glanced briefly at the counter and saw Norma snap Kenny with a tea towel. And part of this caring community.

The capital of Christmas kindness.

Stella turned back to her friends. "I hope that things work out between me and Sam. I really care for him."

Total honesty, Stella reminded herself.

"The truth is, I love Sam." She'd said the words to herself, acknowledged them in her own mind, but had never voiced her feelings to anyone. Until now.

"Oh, Stella." Faith's expression turned dreamy. "That's wonderful."

"Maybe." Stella couldn't stop the sigh.

"You're worried about Britt." Kate's direct gaze met hers. "What does Sam say?"

"Not to worry. That I'm the one he's with, the one he wants to be with." Stella slumped back against her chair. "But he was with her for nearly two years. That's a long time."

"I was with someone in Burlington for three." Mel expelled a shaky breath. "There were times I convinced myself that we were meant to be together. Deep down, I knew it wasn't meant to be. It's probably like that between Sam and Britt."

Stella nodded, recalling what Sam had told her about never having a deep connection with the Broadway star. "Possibly. I just don't want to get hurt. After my parents died, I promised I wouldn't care about anyone that deeply ever again."

"If you don't love, you don't hurt," Mel said almost to herself.

"If you don't love, you miss out on the best life has to offer." Faith spoke in a soft, firm tone. "Love makes life worth living."

Stella wondered whether that saying was from a sign, then chided herself. There was no one more sincere than Faith.

"Is the thought of staying in Holly Pointe but not being with Sam what's troubling you?" Kate, the most analytical of the three, appeared to be trying to get to the bottom line.

Stella considered, then shrugged. "It would be difficult for me to be here and see him every day but not be in his life."

"Maybe," Mel conceded in a tone that was surprisingly matter of fact. "But right now you *are* with him. And if the time comes and you do eventually part ways, it seems like you could decide then."

Baffled, Stella stared. "Decide what?"

"If the town and the friends you've made are enough to keep you here." Mel met her gaze. "I can tell you, I'd be very sad if you left. And I wouldn't be the only one."

"Each time I look at these barns, I'm amazed all over again that such a small community has this fabulous space." Britt Elliott, looking stylish in all black, tilted her head to gaze up at the massive barn that was Holly Pointe's premier venue.

Constructed of reclaimed lumber, stone, and steel, the barn had been modeled after the Big Sky Barn in Texas. Like that venue, the Barns at Grace Hollow were two barns. One was a chapel where wedding ceremonies were held, and the larger one was an event barn where receptions and other events were held year-round.

Sam didn't know why the comment rankled, especially since there was only admiration in the pretty blonde's tone. Maybe it was the use of the word "amazed," as if they were in the boonies and she was shocked that something so nice could be found here.

He knew he wasn't being fair to Britt. It *was* unusual to have such a first-class structure in a rural part of Vermont. Lucy's mother had had the barns built using money she'd gotten from the dissolution of her fourth marriage.

After a year or so, Paula Franks had lost interest in Holly Pointe and turned the operations of the venue over to Lucy. That changeover had occurred shortly before Kevin's death.

Lucy had thrown herself into the business after Kevin's death and hadn't come up for air since.

"I'm so happy we could make it to the ball this year." His mother slipped her arm through Sam's and smiled up at him.

Emily Danforth was a slim, petite woman, barely five foot two. Sam's father affectionately called her his little firecracker. Her hair was blonde, like Britt's, only his mom's strands were more gold than platinum.

Sam always thought his mother's eyes were her best feature. Not only because they were such a vivid blue but because of the intelligence and good humor always lurking there. Seeing her brought back memories of Kevin.

Same light coloring.

Same laughing blue eyes.

"Sam." His father's voice held an insistent edge.

Sam focused on his father and found the man's gaze fixed firmly on him.

If looking at his mother was like seeing his brother, for Sam, gazing at Geoff Johnson, talented playwright and all-around good-guy, was like looking at himself in twenty-five years.

Tall with dark hair and brown eyes, his father's face might hold a few more lines and his hair some strands of gray, but it was still like looking in a mirror.

Sam inclined his head.

"I asked if your new girlfriend will be able to join us tonight for dinner."

His mother and Britt turned curious eyes in his direction.

If this was what it felt like to be center stage with the spotlight on you, it was no wonder he'd never pursued a career in the theatre.

"I haven't been able to reach Stella since I let her know last night that you had arrived." Sam kept his voice free of the irritation he'd felt over his texts being ignored and his calls going straight to voice mail.

He wasn't worried, knowing she often turned off her phone when she was involved with something, but he'd really wanted to nail down plans for tonight.

"Dinner at Rosie's Diner isn't much of an incentive." Britt flashed him a teasing smile.

"I happen to like the food at the diner." Stella's voice came from behind them.

Sam turned, a smile already on his lips.

Her arms were wrapped around a box marked "table linens."

She'd been working today, he realized.

"Rosie's hamburgers are to die for. I've never had better," Emily confided. "Whenever we're in Holly Pointe, Geoff knows we need to have at least one meal there."

"Let me help you with that." Without waiting for a response, Sam lifted the box from Stella's arms. "Stella Carpenter, these are my parents, Emily Danforth and Geoff Johnson. And, our family friend, Britt Elliott."

For all her initial hesitation about meeting his parents, Stella appeared surprisingly relaxed, shooting the group a warm smile.

"It's a pleasure to meet you all." She turned to Sam. "I'm so sorry. I just realized five minutes ago that I had my phone turned off. I saw your messages, and I was planning to call once I finished bringing these boxes in."

"I understand." Sam wished he could touch her, even just a hand on the arm, to reassure himself that all was indeed okay between them.

Unfortunately, right now, his hands were full. But that could be easily remedied. "Where should I put these?"

Stella pointed to a work table against a wall to the right, where several more boxes had been placed.

"Is there anything else you need to bring in?" Geoff asked Stella.

"There are two more, about the same size as these." She gestured to his cashmere topcoat. "But you have a nice coat on, and the outsides of the boxes are dusty."

"A little dust never hurt anyone." His father flashed a smile. "Where can I find these dusty boxes?"

"They're in the back of a white maxivan. The vehicle is unlocked, and there's only two boxes left, so you can't miss them."

"I'll see you in a few." Geoff took off whistling.

"I'll hold the door open for Geoff." Britt scurried after him, appearing oblivious to the wind whipping at her blonde strands as she pushed open the door.

Once Sam set the box down, he glanced around the cavernous hall. He'd been to a lot of Mistletoe Balls, and to his critical eyes, it appeared the setup was nearly complete.

"It's beautiful, isn't it?" Stella dropped her coat on a chair. She stood, hands on slender hips, surveying the large chandeliers decorated with evergreen, ribbon, and holly.

"Lucy outdid herself again." Emily's expression softened when she turned to Sam. "How is she doing? I forgot to ask if she's dating anyone."

"Work keeps her very busy." Sam kept the answer deliberately vague.

His mother worried about Lucy and wanted her to be happy. The two women had grown close during the time when Lucy and Kevin were together and had shared a special bond during Kevin's illness.

Emily's brows puckered in a worried frown. "I hope she and I can find some time to talk while I'm in Holly Pointe. Text and email just aren't the same."

Sam slid an arm around his mother's shoulders. "If she can possibly swing it, I know she'll make time for you."

Emily gave a nod, then focused on Stella. "I understand you're new to Holly Pointe. Have you been enjoying your time here?"

Stella smiled. "I have. Very much."

"Will you be staying?" Emily cocked her head. "Or returning to Miami?"

Sam nearly groaned aloud. His mother made it sound as if he'd told her everything about Stella's background.

Before Stella could reply, Lucy strolled up, hands outstretched. "Emily. It's wonderful to see you."

His mother and Lucy hugged for several long moments, as if drawing strength from each other. While the pain had lessened after four years, this time of year remained difficult for everyone who'd loved Kevin.

Britt appeared just as his mother released her hold on Lucy. Britt and Lucy squealed their welcome and hugged.

Over their embrace, Sam saw Stella eying them with a pleasant but inscrutable expression. Though he couldn't be absolutely positive what she was thinking, he worried that she felt like an outsider.

Sam slipped around the women to stand at Stella's side. "Hey you."

Something in his voice had a smile lifting those luscious red lips. "Hey you back."

At that moment, Sam wanted nothing more than to take her in his arms and spirit her away. They'd both been busy this past week, and even though they'd texted every day and spoken on the phone every night, it wasn't the same as being with her.

"Come to dinner with us tonight." He lowered his voice for her ears only. "I want you to get to know my parents."

Stella's gaze turned watchful when his mother moved to them.

"You better be solidifying dinner plans," Emily said to Sam before her gaze shifted to Stella and turned pleading. "Please tell me you're joining us tonight."

Stella slanted a glance at him before refocusing on his mother. "I'd love to have dinner with you. Thank you for the invitation."

Sam smiled. It appeared he wasn't the only one who couldn't say no to his mother.

CHAPTER TWENTY-ONE

"I hope you don't mind that my mother invited Lucy to join us." Sam glanced at Stella as they descended the stairs from her apartment.

"Of course I don't mind." Stella was actually happy Lucy had been added to the group. The more people at the table, the less pressure there would be on her. "I'm surprised your parents and Britt were able to come to the ball."

"They'll fly back to New York on Monday. Britt's standby will be on stage tonight and tomorrow. Broadway is dark on Monday, so this is a perfect time for a getaway."

"They'll be here for Christmas?"

"Not this year." He shrugged. "They have an early flight out of Burlington, so they're staying the night there and flying out first thing Christmas morning. I'm just glad they could come for the ball. Besides, I was hoping you and I would spend Christmas together. Unless . . . you have other plans."

They'd reached the bottom of the stairs. Stella paused and turned to face him. "I'd love to spend the holidays with you."

Though they had spent some time kissing in her apartment

before heading out to meet his parents, he pulled her to him again. "Spending time with you is the only Christmas gift I want."

She laughed. "I guess that means I can take back your present."

There had been a sign at Faith's shop that had caught her eye. The words had spoken to her, and she had the feeling they would also speak to Sam. Or at least she hoped they would.

"Don't you dare." His arm was around her as they slipped through the Busy Bean, then crossed the street.

"Let me ask you something really quick," she said when they reached the door to Rosie's Diner. "Do you think your parents or Britt would mind if I took a couple of pictures tonight? If not, that's fine, but they are town celebrities."

"I don't think they'd mind. Just ask them to be sure."

"Okay." Taking a steadying breath, Stella stepped inside.

They were the last of the group to arrive. Emily and Geoff, along with Lucy and Britt, sat at a large round corner table.

Geoff rose to his feet when she approached the table and pulled out her chair.

"You're a gentleman, just like your son." Stella offered him a smile of thanks and took a seat as conversation at the table resumed.

The women were talking about some *hilarious* incident that had happened in the past.

As if realizing that the discussion left Stella totally in the dark, Britt paused and gave Stella a brief synopsis of what they were discussing.

"It was a Tony afterparty at the Plaza. Kevin couldn't have cared less about the directors and stars in attendance. All he wanted to talk about were the horses he'd just purchased." Britt's eyes grew soft. "He was like a little boy at Christmas."

Sam nodded his agreement, a smile tugging at the corners of his lips as if the memory brought him pleasure. "He couldn't stop talking about them."

"I had a calendar hanging on the wall in my office. Kevin had their arrival date circled in red." Lucy shook her head. "As if any of us could forget."

"Did you share his love of horses?" Stella asked.

"I did." Lucy glanced at Sam. "I was as excited as Kevin. After he—after he passed, I really wanted to keep them. But I didn't have the time or the facilities to care for them properly."

"I don't live on the other side of the country." Sam met her gaze. "You know you have an open invitation to come out and ride anytime you want."

"I know." She offered him a wan smile.

"Well, anyway, we're at this party." Britt jerked a thumb in Geoff and Emily's direction. "These two were schmoozing on the other side of the room. This older woman, who is considered the grande dame of the Broadway stage, strolls up just in time to hear Kevin say, 'Ask Lucy. She'll tell you. There's nothing like fifteen hands between your legs.'"

Britt held up her hands. "Oh. My. God. You should have seen Lucy's face. It turned bright red. I thought the older woman was going to bust a gut laughing."

Stella laughed, and the last of the tension gripping her disappeared. Britt's generosity in letting her be a part of this inside joke had her liking the woman. And while she smiled and included Sam in the conversation, if there had been an attraction between the two of them at one time, it was clear that was over.

No one objected to her taking pictures, although Lucy and Britt both insisted on freshening their lipstick first. Emily let Stella take a picture of her with her hands wrapped around a monster burger.

Stella waited for the interrogation, but it never came. By the end of the meal, Stella felt comfortable with everyone at the table, including Britt.

They were all sharing one giant piece of sour cream chocolate cake when Lucy brought up Britt's standby.

"I hear she's a bit of a conniver." Lucy's single bite of cake—all she would allow herself—had long ago disappeared. She leaned forward, resting her forearms on the table. "I hear she'd love to take the role away from you."

Stella glanced at Geoff and Emily, who appeared dismayed at the turn the conversation had taken. Yet something in their eyes told her that whatever gossip Lucy had heard was accurate.

"I believe," Britt spoke carefully, as if negotiating her way through a potential minefield, "that it's the dream of most standbys, alternates, or swings to perform in a principal role. It's difficult for them to wait in the wings for that opportunity."

"It seems to me that theater would be dog-eat-dog business." For some reason, Lucy didn't appear interested in letting the subject drop.

"Most in the industry learn that generosity and kindness go a long way." Britt glanced at Emily, who nodded. "Temperament and arrogance can sink a career."

"Thankfully, we don't have many people in Holly Pointe who think of themselves before others." Sam stabbed the last bite of cake then offered it to Stella.

She shook her head as a hard knot formed in the pit of her stomach. Was that what he'd think of her when he found out about the deal she'd made with Jane?

"Sometimes you have to think of yourself first," his father said, apparently unwilling to let his son's statement go unchallenged. "Putting yourself first is often necessary to achieve your goals."

Sam shook his head. "You've always been a team player."

"I pride myself on that fact," Geoff admitted, "but to succeed in almost any business, you can't always be the good guy."

"Do you really expect me to believe that you're a cutthroat, get-ahead-at-all-costs type of guy?" Sam chuckled. "When have you ever put yourself first?"

"Well, when I was young and making my way in the theater, I had a roommate that mentioned a theatre company was looking for the type of plays he and I both wrote." Geoff's eyes took on a distant look. "I submitted mine right away, but Nick wanted to fine-tune his a little more. He missed the submission window. They chose to produce mine."

"Okay, sure, but you didn't try and sink your roommate to get ahead. You let your work speak for itself. That's competition, not betrayal. There's nothing selfish or dishonest about that."

Stella sat back and sipped her coffee. She needed to tell Sam the real reason she'd come to Holly Pointe. It wasn't that she hadn't wanted to tell him, the time just never seemed right.

Stella glanced at him as he countered one of his father's points with an example of his own. Sam caught her looking, shot her a wink, then went back to the discussion.

Tonight. She would tell him tonight.

She only hoped he would understand and forgive her.

There was no opportunity to speak with Sam alone. Once the dinner ended, Sam's parents and Britt were eager to get back to the farm. They'd been up late at some function the night before and were clearly exhausted.

Sam asked Stella to come to the farm with them, even offered to drive her all the way home, but she begged off. His parents didn't get back to Holly Pointe as often as he'd like, and she wanted them to have as much time together as possible.

Besides, she would be spending tomorrow evening with Sam at the Mistletoe Ball. She reassured herself that there would be lots of opportunities for them to talk.

Unlocking the door to her apartment, Stella dropped down to the sofa, relieved that the evening was over. The evening hadn't been uncomfortable. She liked Sam's parents, liked them a lot. She was glad for that fact because she knew they and Sam were close.

Idly, she scrolled through the messages on her phone.

Jane Myers.

There was an attachment to the email.

She read the email first.

Stella,

The article you submitted is not acceptable. It is bland and boring.

Santa as well as Dustin and Krista are only given passing mentions. Britt Elliott is not even mentioned.

I'm very disappointed in this submission. I know you can do better.

Please send me the article we previously discussed by nine a.m. tomorrow.

Jane

Stella frowned, her gaze riveted to two words: *bland and boring*. While the article she'd submitted to Jane might not have a tabloid slant, it had a wonderful, heartwarming feel that Stella was sure would resonate with readers.

With all the strife and turmoil in the political arena lately, people were looking for stories that reaffirmed their faith in man's goodness.

With her lips pressed tightly together, Stella opened the article. Jane had slashed through it with a red pen, writing things like "Where's drunk Santa????" and "I don't care about kids sledding!!!"

Stella clicked out of the attachment without reading all the comments and responded to the email.

Dear Ms. Myers,

The article I submitted is factual and complete. My initial questions regarding Kenny and the state of the Bellamy-Ankrom marriage were proven to be mere speculation. That is why there is no mention of drunkenness or marital discord.

In terms of Britt Elliott, the possibility that she was using Sam Johnson to obtain a role on Broadway was also proven false.

I have fulfilled the terms of my contract. I will not be submitting an article filled with falsehoods and innuendos.

Sincerely,

Stella Carpenter

Hitting send had Stella expelling a breath and slumping against the back of the sofa.

It was done. Over.

The contract with Jane had been fulfilled. Stella knew Jane well enough to know that she wouldn't be hearing from the managing editor again.

Finally, blessedly, she was free to move on with her life.

She only hoped that her speculation that Sam would play a big part of this new journey would prove to be true.

Stella glanced up from the table she was wiping when Kenny crossed the room to her. The onslaught of customers had finally died down.

"Stella, honey, you need to get ready for the Mistletoe Ball." Kenny's kind eyes brimmed with gratitude. "I can't tell you how much I appreciated your help. If Norma had worked all day, I don't think she'd have had the energy to attend the ball with me tonight."

"It was my pleasure."

Kenny pointed to the back of the shop. "Go upstairs now. Make yourself even prettier than you already are, for your young man."

Stella hesitated. "Are you sure you don't need me? I have plenty of time to get ready."

Kenny lifted the damp cloth from her hands. "I'm positive."

"Okay then." Stella surprised herself, and him, by leaning over and brushing her lips against his cheek. "You're a wonderful husband. I hope when I marry that I find someone half as wonderful as you."

"Sam's a good man," she heard him call out as she strolled to the back of the shop.

Stella kept walking even as her lips curved into a smile.

Kenny was right. She'd been planning to spend the day with Sam and his parents. But when she'd hurried down the steps this morning and seen Norma so pale and unsteady behind the counter, she'd called Sam.

He'd understood the need for a change in plans.

But tonight, tonight was all her and Sam. They would dance, with the scent of evergreen surrounding them, to a band that had been brought in from Burlington. They would drink champagne and laugh and talk with friends.

Sam would call her beautiful, and she would feel beautiful when his eyes caressed her.

He'd already told his parents that he was taking her home after the dance. They wouldn't be expecting him back before morning.

Excitement surged as Stella dressed for the Mistletoe Ball.

She washed and curled her hair. Sam liked it loose, so instead of pulling it up or twisting it into a knot, she left it hanging to her shoulders. A couple of glittery pins added a little sparkle.

The dress was a black Alexander Wang crepe gown with a thigh-high back slit. She loved the asymmetrical one-shoulder neckline in the dress she'd purchased last year after selling a magazine article. Ankle-strap heeled sandals in gold and lipstick in cherry red completed the look.

Instead of the suit she'd expected, Sam wore a tux.

Her gaze lingered, and then she stepped close and fingered his lapel. "You're breathtaking."

His eyes never left hers. "You took the words right out of my mouth."

Instead of Sam's truck, the car parked in the back lot was a sleek Mercedes sedan. She smiled as he opened the door. "Two questions. Whose car is this? And does it turn into a pumpkin at midnight?"

He grinned and slipped behind the wheel. "Mine and no."

"I thought you had a truck." In the close confines of the car, she could smell the intoxicating scent of his cologne.

The man smelled every bit as good as he looked.

"I have a car, too. I just don't drive it much during the winter."

She cocked her head. "Are you rich?"

He laughed. "Would it make a difference?"

"I might have bought you a different Christmas gift." She held up the black-and-white-polka-dot-wrapped gift with the cherry-red ribbon.

At his questioning glance, she added. "I like the thought of it being under your tree."

He took it from her extended hand and leaned behind to put it in the back seat. "When I see it there, I'll think of you."

She gave him a cheeky smile. "That's the plan."

"My parents like you," he said when he pulled onto the highway leading to the Grace Hollow Barns.

"I like them, too." She hesitated, then added, "I like Britt, too."

She saw his hands tighten on the steering wheel.

"There isn't anything between us. Not anymore."

"I know."

He cast a sharp glance in her direction at her matter-of-fact tone.

"I trust you, Sam," she said simply. "You wouldn't be dating or sleeping with me if you had feelings for another woman."

His fingers relaxed their hold on the wheel. "No. I wouldn't."

"I hope you know me well enough to know the kind of person I am." Stella took a deep breath. This was it. The perfect opportunity to tell him. "When I was back in Miami, I was desperate to find a job. I—"

"That looks like Nate's truck." Sam swung the Mercedes behind the pickup on the side of the road. "Give me a minute."

After turning on his flashers, Sam pushed his door open.

Stella saw that there was a woman in the car, but only Nate got out to greet Sam. Minutes later, Nate and Adrianna—one of the baristas from the Busy Bean—were in the back seat and the four were on their way to the ball.

"What's wrong with the truck?" Stella twisted in her seat, directing her question to the two in the backseat.

"Flat." Nate rolled his eyes. "Second one this month. The last nail ruined the tire, so my spare is already on. I called Charley at the garage, and he'll come as soon as he can and put on a new one. I figure I can find someone to take us back to the truck after the ball."

"Thanks again, Sam, for picking us up." Adrianna looked older. Maybe it was the low-cut red velvet dress or the way she'd twisted her hair into a stylish knot that made her look older. "I've never been to the ball before, and I didn't want to miss a minute."

Stella couldn't hide her puzzlement. "Why is this your first time? From what I hear, everyone attends."

"Because of the alcohol, you have to be twenty-one," Nate explained. "Adrianna wasn't old enough last year. And, because it's a fundraiser, the tickets are pricey. But cost isn't an issue because I'm a gentleman. I invited her. I paid for the tickets."

Stella wondered whether there was a way to make it so that more Holly Pointe citizens could afford to go in the future. She made a mental note to look into various possibilities.

Adrianna, visibly nervous and excited, talked nonstop the rest of the way to the barn.

Then Sam pulled into the long driveway, and Adrianna inhaled sharply. "Ohmigoodness."

"It's gorgeous." When Stella had seen the barns, it had been during the day. But now, with the white Christmas lights strung and shining in the darkness, the sight took her breath away.

There was valet parking, so Stella and Adrianna didn't have to walk across the lot in their heels. After turning over his keys and a sizable tip, Sam held out his arm to her.

"Catch up with you later, man." Nate clapped him on the back.

"If you need a ride back to your truck, let me know," Sam called after him.

Nate just lifted a hand, then took Adrianna's arm and kept walking.

Stella thought fleetingly of the missed opportunity in the car but decided she wouldn't dwell on that now. Tomorrow was another day. By Christmas, one way or another, she would find a time to tell Sam the truth.

CHAPTER TWENTY-TWO

Instead of moving immediately to the dance floor, Sam showed Stella everything that made up the Mistletoe Ball. In a beautifully decorated side room of blue and silver were item after item up for bid in the silent auction.

There was everything from an autographed copy of a popular author's first novel to a week in Steamboat Springs complete with ski-lift tickets and airfare.

Sam smiled as he caught Stella studying a ruby necklace set in an elegant modern design. He put in a bid when she wasn't looking.

After leaving the silent auction items behind, they grabbed a glass of champagne from a passing waiter, then familiarized themselves with all the food stations.

"All of this is included in the ticket you purchased?" Stella stared wide-eyed at an artfully displayed mountain of shrimp surrounded by baked crab poppers.

"Everything is included." He cupped her elbow as they moved to another station that focused on desserts. "All the food is donated so that one hundred percent of the money raised goes to either cancer research or local health programs."

Stella reached for a chocolate-cranberry cluster but pulled her hand back before making contact.

"Eat later. I want to dance first." She gazed up at him, long dark lashes framing big brown eyes. "If that's okay with you."

"I've been wanting to take you in my arms since the second I saw you." Sam led her out, away from the food and toward the dance floor. "I don't know what kind of perfume you're wearing, but it smells amazing."

Her sexy red lips curved as they stepped onto the hardwood floor. He took her hand in his, then pulled her close.

Sam wasn't inclined to be fanciful, but tonight felt magical. The lights overhead, the laughter and hum of conversation around them, and the romantic melody drifting in the air. He was acutely aware of the giant mistletoe ball hanging over the center of the dance floor.

Yet Sam knew it wasn't any of those things that made this evening magical. He'd been coming to the ball since he'd turned twenty-one and had been old enough to buy a ticket, but the feelings it stirred had never been like this before.

Stella was the reason.

His arms tightened around her. Until he'd met her, Sam had scoffed at the idea of love at first sight. When he'd heard stories of guys marrying someone they'd met only six weeks earlier, he'd mentally thought them fools.

To his way of thinking, it took years to really know someone. Take Lucy and Kevin. They'd been friends and dated for years before falling in love.

Okay, so maybe his own parents had married quickly and were still happy. They were the exception to the rule.

But . . . Stella.

It was as if she was the woman he'd been waiting for his entire life. Now that he'd found her, he wasn't going to let anything—

Lucy appeared and jerked Stella from Sam's arms. Her blue eyes flashed fire.

"How could you betray us?" Lucy spat the words. "We trusted you."

Stella's eyes widened. She appeared as confused as he was by Lucy's rant. "What are you talking about?"

Sam put his hand on Lucy's arm, aware of the curious stares being cast their way. "Lucy. Calm down. What's got you so riled?"

The blonde shoved her phone at Sam. "Read for yourself."

"Let's get off the dance floor." Without glancing at the phone's display, Sam took it and ushered the two women to a quiet corner.

"Read it." Lucy insisted, tossing her head back and glaring at Stella. "See for yourself what your new girlfriend is really like."

Sam lifted the phone and began to read. For a second, he had to pause as a tightness squeezed his chest and his vision blurred.

"What does it say?" Stella asked, trying to read over his shoulder.

He ignored her. He didn't look at her. He couldn't.

The words swam before him for a second, but he bore down and forced himself to concentrate. This time he read until he got to the end.

His hand holding the phone dropped to his side.

He barely felt Lucy leaning over to pry it from his grasp.

Sam lifted his gaze to Lucy. "How did you see this?"

"I have an alert on my phone for anything to do with marriage or weddings in the area so I don't miss any reviews of my work." Lucy shifted her gaze to level those now-piercing blue eyes on Stella. "Because of Krista and Dustin, a link to the article popped up."

Stella held out her hand. "May I read it?"

Without a word, Lucy slapped the phone in Stella's hand.

"Is everything okay here?" Faith's worried gaze circled the threesome.

Sam didn't answer. He couldn't. And, even if he were able to find words amid the roaring in his brain, he wasn't sure what he'd say.

Stella quickly read the article. She closed her eyes briefly when she reached the end. Lucy snatched back her phone, her expression one of controlled fury.

By this time, the roar inside Sam's head had been replaced with a hurt that went bone deep. But it was the anger that resonated when he finally found his voice. "How could you do it, Stella? How could you betray all of us?"

"It wasn't my story. I swear." Stella held up her hands. "I didn't write it."

Lucy opened her mouth but shut it without speaking when Sam shot her a pointed glance.

"Your name is on the byline." Sam jabbed a finger at the phone now resting in Lucy's hand. "Are you going to deny those are pictures you took?"

"No, they are my pictures, but I didn't give Jane permission to run them."

"Jane?"

"The managing editor of the *Sun Times*." Stella swallowed convulsively, but her gaze remained firmly fixed on his. "She sent me here to do a story on Holly Pointe. I wanted it to be a heart-warming piece, but Jane was hoping for some dirt."

"You gave it to her." Sam shook her head in disgust. "Kenny. Dustin and Krista. Even Britt. You sold them out for thirty pieces of silver or however much you got for writing this trash."

"I didn't write that article." Stella took a step toward him, her tone pleading, but Sam held up a hand.

"Do you deny that you came here to dig up dirt?" His gaze pinned her.

"I told Jane I would not include anything in the article that I hadn't fully verified."

"I'll take that as a yes."

Stella blew out a frustrated breath, raking a hand through her hair and dislodging one of the glittery pins. It fell to the floor, but she paid it no mind. "I didn't write that story. I made private notes, wrote down speculations, but none of those things made it into the article I submitted."

"I don't believe you."

Her cheeks blazed red as if she'd been slapped.

"You never said a word to me about your real reason for being here." Sam clenched his jaw as emotion rose to clog his throat. "As close as we got, you never told me."

Guilt skittered across her face.

"I tried to tell you several times, but . . ." She took a deep breath. "Yes, I should have told you."

Sam didn't know what else there was to say. She'd lied and deceived him. It was over. The relationship they'd been building, the one he'd thought would last a lifetime, had been built on lies and deceit.

Stella pulled her phone from her bag. "Let me pull up the article I sent. You'll see it's nothing like—"

"I don't need to hear anymore."

Hurt and disbelief flashed in her eyes. "You'd condemn me without all the facts? Do I mean so little to you?"

Sam pushed down the stirrings of sympathy. He'd already played the fool. "I don't know who you are."

"You know who I am." Anger had her dark eyes turning to obsidian. "You're just too scared to take a chance. Too scared to put yourself out there."

"Don't turn this one me. You stabbed me—and everyone else in Holly Pointe—in the back."

"No. I did not! I've told you I didn't write that article. Jane may have put my name on it, but those are not my words." Stella drew a shuddering breath and paused as if needing a moment to collect herself.

Sam looked away, needing a moment himself. When he finally glanced back at her, he saw the slightest shift come over her.

"Perhaps it's good this happened. Good that I'm able to see the kind of man you really are." Stella drew herself up tall. "I don't want a man who won't fight for our love. Maybe I'm not that important, or maybe you're scared you might lose me just like you lost Kevin, so it's easier to cut your losses now."

"You're talking crazy."

"Am I?" A look of profound sadness filled her eyes. "You once told me there wasn't anything I couldn't tell you. Now you're not even willing to give me a chance to show you I'm innocent of betraying you and this town. Tell me, Sam, what am I supposed to think?"

Sam turned away from Stella then, her words hitting uncomfortably close to home. But he refused to feel guilty when she was the one in the wrong.

"Don't worry about taking me home." Her voice, filled with sudden weariness, still cut like a knife. "I'll find a ride."

With those words and her head held high, she turned and walked out of his life.

"It's for the best," Sam told Lucy when he caught her staring.

"We could have looked at the article she said she wrote." Lucy's tone held a questioning edge. "Just to be sure."

"I had all the information I needed."

"No. You didn't." Lucy ignored his pointed glare. "You reacted emotionally. I did the same. What would have been the harm in looking at the article she said she submitted? You love her, Sam. I saw that in your eyes last night. Why not give her the benefit of the doubt? Gather information, then make your decision."

"If I didn't know better, I'd think you were siding with Stella." Sam found he could barely say her name. "And I've never been afraid to fight for what's important."

Lucy merely continued to stare at him.

"But I won't fight for a woman who betrayed me and those I love."

∽

Faith offered Stella a ride home, and they left immediately. Only once they were inside the car and cruising down the highway toward Holly Pointe did Stella let the tears of frustration and anger fall.

Though Faith asked for no explanation, Stella explained everything, starting with the day Jane called her into the office.

"I was so excited. I wanted more than anything to get back on staff. When she offered this assignment, it seemed like the answer to my prayers." Stella clasped her hands together in her lap. "Since my parents' deaths, the holidays had been hard. I thought, well, this way I would be away from Miami and working. But I stressed to Jane that I wouldn't put anything in my article I hadn't fully verified."

Faith slowly nodded. "Were you at all concerned she might not accept an article that wasn't... tabloidesque?"

"That was the reason that when I submitted my article, and she rejected it wanting changes, I told her it was all she was getting from me. When she sent it back with her requested"— Stella made air quotes—"'changes,' I realized then, no matter what I sent, unless the truth was sensationalized, it wouldn't meet her standards." Stella frowned, thinking of the pictures of Kenny guzzling the bottle of vodka and Dustin and Krista arguing. "I only wish I knew how she got the pictures and my notes."

Faith slanted a glance in her direction. "Did you attach them by mistake?"

"No." Stella tapped her fingers against her leg. "I was very careful what I sent."

"Did you upload them to a shared drive?"

"They were stored on the newspaper's secured server. But I had the file set to private, for my eyes only."

"That's it." Faith softened her tone, as if sensing that Stella would be distressed. "There's nothing private on a company server. Undoubtedly you signed something when you began working for them that gave them the right to see—and likely use—anything you keyed in or uploaded."

Stella froze. Not from the cold—the air inside Faith's car was toasty warm—but from the realization that she'd been culpable. Her carelessness had played a part in what had occurred. It didn't matter that she hadn't intended for this to happen.

"Oh, Faith. Sam was right. This is really all my fault."

As tears threatened, Faith reached over and took her hand.

The love and acceptance in her friend's touch had tears slipping down her cheeks.

How could such a wonderful night have gone so horribly wrong?

CHAPTER TWENTY-THREE

The first thing Stella did when she got up on Sunday morning was to check her phone, hoping for a message from Sam. The article had caught him off guard, but she hoped that after a night's rest, he'd be willing to listen to her side of the story.

Even if he couldn't forgive her, she wanted him to know that she hadn't betrayed him.

She set down the phone with a heavy sigh. No texts. No emails. No voice mail.

Stella distracted herself by brewing coffee. She needed the jolt of caffeine before she made the trek downstairs to face Kenny and Norma.

As Stella watched coffee drip into the cup, tears slipped down her cheeks. Her heart coiled and uncoiled like a snake, squeezing so tightly that she could barely breathe. She'd hurt and lost those she loved. Not because of fate or a drunk driver. This mess was of her own making.

She closed her eyes against the pain, then opened them and drew a shuddering breath. Sure, she'd screwed up. Big time. But that didn't mean she couldn't do whatever possible to try and make amends. Maybe they'd understand and forgive, and maybe not. But Stella wouldn't let fear keep her from doing what she believed was right.

If being in Holly Pointe had taught her anything, it was the importance of letting the people you care for know it. Today, she'd let them know it by telling the truth.

First things first.

Squaring her shoulders, Stella called Jane. To her surprise, the managing editor answered on the third ring.

"That was quick," Jane said in lieu of greeting. "I take it you saw the article."

"My file was set to private. Those pictures and notes were for my eyes, not yours."

Jane emitted a gusty laugh. "Oh, you are naïve. I have total access to any file on the server. I've been monitoring your notes ever since you arrived in that Christmas town."

Stella closed her eyes for a second and took a breath. Jane was right. She had been naïve. "I'd determined that those suppositions were unsubstantiated, yet you published the article touting them as if they were fact. You need to print a retraction."

"Oh, Stella. You and I both know that isn't happening."

"If you don't," Stella spoke slowly and deliberately so there could be no misunderstanding, "I will make sure everyone knows I didn't write the story and—"

"Check your contract. We're within our rights to publish. If you read the article carefully, you'll see that it's worded in such a way to render legal action pointless." Jane's voice held a sly edge. "Ask Drunk Santa and the others if they want to keep this stirred up or if they'd prefer to let it die a natural death. I believe you'll find they'll pick the latter. Now, I have several important matters that need my attention."

The call disconnected.

Stella dropped her head into her hands.

Last night, when she'd told Sam she wasn't complicit, she'd lied.

To herself.

To Sam.

She wasn't some young college student. She'd been in the newspaper business since graduating from the University of Florida. How could she have made so many mistakes?

The biggest mistake was in not telling Sam the entire truth of why she was in Holly Pointe. If she had, he'd have understood that she hadn't sold out her friends. That she wouldn't.

Stella pulled to her feet. She couldn't put this off any longer. She had to apologize and make amends with those she'd hurt.

She would start now.

With Kenny and Norma.

The last thing Sam felt like doing on Sunday evening was celebrating an early Christmas with his parents and Britt. But the threesome planned to drive to Burlington tonight and fly back to New York City in the morning.

Sam wished they could just skip the presents. The scene with Stella last night had left his emotions too raw and close to the surface. But this time of year continued to be difficult for his parents, and he wouldn't spoil it for them.

It wasn't their fault he'd been taken in by a pretty face.

The doorbell rang as they were gathering in the living room.

"I'll get it," Britt jumped up.

"Who could that be?" Sam asked.

"Didn't I mention I invited Lucy to join us?" His mother shot him an apologetic smile. "After so many years celebrating with her, it doesn't feel like Christmas without her."

Lucy came into the room, her arms filled with presents, which she placed in the pile by the tree. Then Lucy turned to Sam, holding a small burgundy sack adorned with a silver ribbon.

"You won one of the silent auction bids." Lucy placed the sack on the side table rather than under the tree. "Since I was coming over, I thought I'd bring it along."

"What did you win?" Britt's eyes shone bright with curiosity.

"Nothing important." Sam waved a dismissive hand, thinking of the necklace Stella had admired. He fixed his eyes on Britt. With his parents hovering, it had been impossible to catch her alone. "Do you have a minute?"

"Sure, Sam." Britt offered a warm smile, and he was struck by how lovely she was, both inside and out.

He would never understand why the affection he felt for her had never progressed beyond friendship. "Walk with me to the kitchen."

The kitchen still carried the sweet aroma of the spiced apple cider his mother had made earlier on the stove.

Britt leaned her back against the counter. "What's on your mind?"

"I don't know if anyone mentioned the article in the *Sun Times* to you, but—"

"Your parents and I went to the Cookie Extravaganza this morning, and it was all anyone could talk about." Britt narrowed her gaze. "Don't tell me you care about what's said about us. You and I know the truth. That's what matters."

Sam stared, trying to make sense of her reaction. "Are you telling me having lies spread about you doesn't matter?"

"Well, I'd rather they print the truth." Britt moved close and placed a hand on his arm. "Most people, the smart ones anyway, know that kind of stuff is made up. I *was* surprised to see Stella's name on the byline."

A muscle in Sam's jaw twitched. "I was surprised, too. She says she didn't write it, but—"

"I know. That's what she told me, too."

"What?" Sam narrowed his gaze. "What do you mean that's what she told you?"

"I ran into her at the cookie festival." Britt paused and brought a finger to her lips. "I think she went there looking for me. She'd already visited with Kenny and with Dustin and Krista. Anyway, Stella apologized. Apparently, she'd speculated when she first arrived about our breakup, and those notes somehow made it into the final article."

"You believe her?"

"I do." Britt's tone was matter of fact. "She let me read the article, the one she actually wrote. I wasn't mentioned in this one. It was a lovely article about Christmas in Holly Pointe. Very warm and uplifting. What did you think of it?"

Sam shifted uncomfortably from one foot to the other. "I haven't read it."

Her gaze sharpened. "Why not?"

He looked away and shrugged. Did they really have to do this? He didn't want to talk about Stella. Right now, he didn't want to even *think* about her.

Though keeping her from his thoughts was proving impossible.

"I'm disappointed in you, Sam."

The admonishment fired his temper on all circuits. Britt was disappointed in *him*? "Me? I'm not the one who took advantage of friendships and the kindness of everyone in this town. Frankly, I'm surprised you'd want anything to do with Stella after what she pulled."

"The reason I love Holly Pointe is that people care about each other. They give each other the benefit of the doubt. They listen. They forgive." Britt touched his arm and met his gaze. "I know Stella hurt you, but by being so quick to believe the worst about her, you're not really living the Holly Pointe spirit. She may have unwittingly hurt you, but by not hearing her out, you're deliberately hurting her."

Sam shoved his hands into his pockets. Britt made forgiving sound so easy. It wasn't. Not for him.

"The article should be posted to the town's website by now." Britt smiled, her gaze never leaving his face. "Check it out."

Sam thought of the accusations Stella had flung at him last night.

"Stella told me I don't fight for what's important to me." His laugh sounded hollow, even to his own ears. "She thinks I'm scared to commit because I'm frightened of losing that person, just like I lost Kevin. Have you ever heard anything so ridiculous?"

For a long, uncomfortable moment, Britt didn't speak.

"You know what I think, Sam?" Britt cocked her head. "I think you never found a woman you cared about enough to fight for. Until now."

Sam mulled over her words as presents were unwrapped. Then his mother handed him the package that Stella had given him to put under the tree. "Where did you get this?"

His mom didn't bat an eye at his accusing tone. "It was in the back seat of the Mercedes. I brought it in."

Sam didn't want to open it, especially not with everyone looking at him. But he was beginning to feel like a jerk over how he'd handled things with Stella. He tore off the paper and stared at the painted piece of wood.

The piece had come from Faith Original. Sam immediately recognized Faith's artistic touch. The words—*So Many of My Smiles Begin with You*—started out in block lettering and ended with the *You* in a more stylish font. Woven strands of hemp crisscrossed the front. Tiny clothespins attached to the hemp held three photos.

The first he recognized from the event at the Bromley mansion, the day Stella first arrived in Holly Pointe. From her perch she'd captured a picture of him, right before he'd ordered her off the stairs. How she'd captivated him.

The second picture had been taken at Star Lake. It was one of the two of them skating across the ice, arm in arm. Stella was looking up at him while he gazed down at her. He recalled how much fun they'd had, and then he remembered something else. He'd told her he didn't give up on those he cared about.

With an increased heaviness in the vicinity of his heart, Sam shifted his gaze to the last clothespin. This shot was taken when they were on the blue toboggan headed down the hill. She was leaning back against him and laughing with sheer joy.

He lowered the board. "This, ah, this is from Stella."

"We figured." His father cleared his throat.

Though Sam hadn't mentioned what had happened last night, he'd seen his parents speaking with Lucy. He didn't doubt his parents and Britt had discussed the situation in detail with Lucy at the cookie exchange. "I need to speak with her."

"That'd probably be a good idea," his mother said, and his father nodded agreement. "When you do, be sure and give her our regards."

"I'll do that."

Later, after his parents and Britt were on the road, Sam pulled up the town's website and read Stella's article. Britt had nailed it. The piece was a heartwarming feature promoting the wonderful life that could be found in Holly Pointe.

Did Stella want to build a life here? Last night, he'd have said yes. Now he didn't know.

He pondered the question all the way into town. Striding into the coffee shop, he spotted Norma and Kenny behind the counter. While the tables were full, there was no one in line at the counter.

"I hope you know," Sam kept his voice low, not wanting to be overheard, "I didn't share any confidential information from our discussion."

Kenny surprised Sam by leaning forward and patting his hand. "Don't you worry none about that. Stella came to me and explained everything. She was worried about me. She never meant for those photos to get out."

"You believe her?"

Kenny jerked back as if he'd been struck.

"Course I believe her. My daddy used to say it's not people's words that tell you who they are, it's their actions." Kenny's broad hand swiped the air. "That article don't mean squat. That girl has been nothing but kind to me and my missus. Her actions showed us who she is, and who she is, is our friend. I don't want to hear you imply otherwise."

Sam raised his hands, palms out. "You won't get any argument from me."

"Good. Because it's all over town that you two had words at the Mistletoe Ball. Last I heard, you hadn't kissed and made up."

"Is she upstairs?" Sam glanced upward.

Kenny nodded.

"Take this." Norma reached into her pocket and pulled out a sprig of mistletoe. "It came off the big ball over the dance floor."

"Thanks, Norma." Sam tucked the mistletoe into his pocket. "Wish me luck."

"You won't need luck." Kenny slung an arm around his wife's shoulder. "Not if you've got love."

The unexpected knock at her door had Stella striding across the room to glance through the peephole. Her heart did a full somersault.

"Sam." Opening the door, she stepped aside to let him enter. "This is a surprise."

His dark eyes searched her face. "You were right. I was wrong."

"Well, that's an interesting way to start a conversation." She gestured to the couch. "Can I get you something to drink?"

She was pleased that her voice had come out steady when her entire insides felt like jelly.

"No. Thank you." Instead of immediately sitting, Sam paced to the window before dropping down on the sofa. "I was wrong not to give you an opportunity to explain."

She licked her lips. "Are you ready to listen now?"

"I am ready. But I think I've pretty much gotten it figured out already."

Stella took a seat in a nearby chair. Because the living area was so small, their legs nearly touched. As it was, she was forced to contend with the fresh scent of his shampoo teasing her nostrils.

Clasping her hands together, she went all the way back to the beginning. "After being off work for nearly two months, I was super excited when Jane Myers, the managing editor of the *Miami Sun Times*, called and asked if we could meet in her office."

Stella took him through everything, not leaving anything out, including her conversation with Jane this morning. "Attempting to pursue legal action appears pointless. Even if I won, which is doubtful, it would likely do more harm than good by keeping things stirred up."

"Kenny told me you apologized to him and Norma."

"I wanted them to know I didn't knowingly betray them." Stella dropped her gaze to her hands. She'd failed everyone she cared about. "I also apologized to Dustin and Krista. And, of course, to Britt and your parents."

The tightness in Stella's chest told her that this apology was going to be the most difficult one of all. "You were right. I should have told you all this before. You deserved better from me. I really am sorry."

"Apology accepted." His tone was terse, his voice as tightly strung as piano wire. His next words had her heart sinking to her feet. "Will you be staying in Holly Pointe?"

"Would it bother you if I did?"

He frowned. "Why would it bother me?"

"Well, it can be awkward to have a former girlfriend hanging around."

She watched those dark eyes go razor sharp.

"I don't think of you as a former girlfriend."

"You're right." Stella expelled a breath. "We really weren't together all that long and—"

He stopped her babbling by taking her hands in his. "You misunderstand. It's the *former* part I have issue with. I don't want to be your former lover or your former boyfriend. I want us to be together. The way we were before I made an ass of myself at the ball."

He tugged her from her chair until she was sitting beside him. "I'm sorry, too, Stella. I should have listened, I should have given you a chance to explain. I promise that won't happen again."

Stella didn't know what to say. After a long, sleepless night, she'd convinced herself there was no more Stella and Sam.

"You accused me of not being willing to fight for what's important." His hand cupped her cheek. "I will fight for you, Stella. I will fight for us. Whatever it takes to convince you I'm sincere. For however long it takes. That's how much you mean to me."

Tears slipped down her cheeks.

"I love you." The words flowed from his lips, seeming to surprise him as much as her. "I realize we haven't known each other long, but I hope, given time, you'll love me, too."

"I already love you," she heard herself whisper.

Sam closed his eyes and pulled her to him. She heard him murmur something that sounded like "thank you, God" against her hair.

Wrapping her arms around his neck, she rested her head against his chest and emitted a contented sigh.

"I opened your gift," he said.

She smiled against his shirtfront. "Do you like it?"

"A lot." He nuzzled her hair. "Do you know that so many of my smiles begin with you?"

"Hey." She lifted her head and feigned outrage. "That's my line."

He chuckled, and she went warm all over. It felt so good to be in his arms, teasing with him again.

"I've got a gift for you, but you can't open it until Christmas."

"You already opened mine," she pointed out.

"That's because my parents were leaving, and they insisted all the gifts be opened." His hand began to stroke her arm.

"I like your parents."

"They like you, too." Sam released his hold and sat back, his fingers pulling something from his pocket. "I believe it's time."

Stella studied the red berries surrounded by dark green leaves. "Time for what?"

"Time for us to officially kiss and make up." He studied her for a long moment, his gaze soft and caressing as he held the sprig aloft. "Under the mistletoe."

She smiled and leaned closer, never taking her eyes from his. "We already made up."

"Our first disagreement won't be officially over until we kiss."

She answered by wrapping her arms around him. Stella knew there would be other disagreements.

Other kiss-and-make-up sessions.

And, she thought, as his mouth settled possessively over hers, a lifetime of love with this man in the wonderful town of Holly Pointe.

From Cindy Kirk

I hoped you enjoyed this trip to the Capital of Christmas Kindness. Though Holly Pointe is a fictional town, I love the state of Vermont and couldn't imagine a better place to set a holiday romance

I've found that one trip to such a special town with so many wonderful people isn't enough. That's why I want to encourage you to check out Holly Pointe & Candy Canes. We met Faith in this first book but now in the second book in this heartwarming series we get to see her get her own Christmas miracle.

Dive into this second book in my Holly Pointe series and let this fabulous romance warm your heart today. **Holly Pointe & Candy Canes** *(Or keep reading for a sneak peek)*

SNEAK PEEK OF HOLLY POINTE & CANDY CANES

Faith Pierson had never played a contact sport. Which meant she'd never learned how to take a hit. That's why the body ramming into her at full speed had her stumbling.

She'd strolled into the Busy Bean Coffee & Tea Shop in downtown Holly Pointe, intent on grabbing a coffee and something sweet. The plan vanished as Faith swayed and fought to catch her breath.

"I'm so sorry." A firm grip settled on her arm, steadying her. "Are you okay?"

Faith looked up and found herself drowning in concerned hazel eyes.

"Wh-who are you?" Still reeling, she stammered the question.

"The father of the future linebacker who ran into you." The man cast a censuring look at the blonde girl with innocent blue eyes who stood before Faith.

Suddenly, where there had been one, there were now two. Faith blinked, but the mirror image remained.

She raised a hand to her head. Had the hit knocked something loose in her head?

"Please don't faint." The man spoke quickly and tightened his hold.

Faith blinked. She blinked again. When she spoke, her voice was reed-thin with barely contained panic. "I-I'm seeing double."

He offered a reassuring smile. "You're fine."

"I'm not," she insisted. "You don't understand. There's *two*."

"Twins." He kept hold of her with one hand and pointed with the other. "Charlotte and Hannah. Charlotte is the one who tackled you."

His gaze settled on the girl with a hint of mischief in her eyes. "What do you say to the lady, Charlotte?"

"I'm sorry." A dimple winked briefly at the corner of her mouth. "Me and Hannah were playing tag. I couldn't let her catch me."

"I've already told you this is a coffee shop, not a playground." The man's stern expression shifted from one girl to the other. "You both know better."

Hannah hopped from one foot to the other, appearing to take the rebuke in stride.

Charlotte didn't hop, but her blue eyes studied Faith with a thoroughness that had her wondering if there was something on her face.

She was ready to pull out a mirror when the child spoke. "You have dancing reindeers on your shirt."

"I like reindeers. Especially ones wearing ballet shoes." Hannah stepped closer and pointed at Faith's chest. "Does that bell ring?"

This morning, Faith had pulled on her favorite December outfit—a red plaid corduroy jumper with a turtleneck covered in dancing reindeer. A necklace with a large jingle bell completed the festive look.

Lifting the red braided cord, Faith held out the bell so it emitted a faint clang. "Want to give it a jingle?"

Hannah nodded even as Charlotte wedged herself between Faith and her twin.

"The lady asked me first." Hannah tried with both hands to push Charlotte to the side, but failed. "Daaad, make her move."

Faith wrapped her fingers around the bell. She loved children, no matter how young or old. This age—she'd guess the girls to be five or six—was a particular favorite. "Christmas is about love and goodwill. Right?"

The girls stopped shoving each other and exchanged a glance. Then they both nodded.

Relieved, Faith grinned, conscious that their father's scrutinizing gaze remained on her.

"You both want to ring the bell." Faith tapped a finger against her bright-red lips. "I believe I have a solution."

Lifting the necklace over her head, Faith shortened the cord before placing it around Hannah's neck. "Don't ring it just yet. Understand?"

With a wide-eyed gaze fixed on Faith, Hannah nodded. Her small hand curved around the bell the way Faith's fingers had only moments before.

Tears of frustration filled Charlotte's eyes, and her bottom lip quivered.

Diving deep into the cavernous depths of her quilted purse, Faith quickly pulled out another necklace, identical to the one she'd given Hannah.

When Faith slipped this one over Charlotte's neck, she was rewarded with a big smile that showed two missing teeth.

"Now we're ready." Faith lifted a hand. "On the count of three, you'll jingle."

"I don't think—" Their father shot a swift glance around the shop. "The noise will disturb the other customers."

"No worries." Faith flashed a reassuring smile. "This is Holly Pointe. We love all things Christmas. That includes jingling sleigh bells."

Returning her attention to the girls, Faith counted off. "One. Two. Three."

When the third finger went up, the girls rang the bells loudly.

The jingling caught the attention of those in the shop. Instead of grumbles, the sound prompted only indulgent smiles. Behind the counter, shop owners Kenny and Norma Douglas applauded.

"Thank you for the lovely concert, girls." Faith turned to their father. Now that she was steady again, she realized she'd forgotten her manners. She extended her hand. "I'm Faith Pierson."

The smile he offered as his hand closed over hers held warmth and apology. "Graham Westfall. It's a pleasure to meet you. I'm sorry it was under these circumstances."

Graham was a handsome man about her own age, with dark hair cut short and a firm jaw. Despite it being barely nine in the morning, lines of strain edged his eyes.

Faith had initially thought his eyes were hazel. Studying him now, she saw a shimmer of green with gold flecks. Attraction stirred. She'd always been a sucker for green eyes.

She wondered what had brought him to Holly Pointe. If he was visiting relatives, wouldn't they be with him? Of course, he could have come for the skiing. Jay Peak was just down the road. Many tourists, especially those with children, often chose to stay in Holly Pointe, even while on a ski vacation, because of the community's family-centered activities.

As those amazing green eyes had her wanting to flirt—though flirting wasn't her strength—Faith reminded herself that just because he wasn't wearing a wedding ring, didn't mean there wasn't a wife, perhaps in the restroom or even back at a hotel. "Are you visiting family in the area, Mr. Westfall?"

"I think being tackled by my daughter puts us on a first-name basis." His eyes crinkled at the corners. "Please, call me Graham."

She returned his smile. There was that tingle again. One she ruthlessly tamped down.

Possible wife in the restroom, she reminded herself.

Still, she couldn't stop herself from offering a teasing smile. "Only if you call me Faith."

"Well, Faith, in answer to your question, the girls and I arrived today." Graham shot a quick glance at a nearby table filled with coloring books and what appeared to be a jewelry-making kit. "My mother-in-law, Ginny Blain, lives in Holly Pointe."

Mother-in-law.

Suddenly, it struck Faith, a swift hammer blow to the heart. Ginny had had only one daughter, *Stephanie*.

This was Stephanie's husband. Though Faith hadn't grown up in Holly Pointe, she'd met Steph as a young girl. Steph had been pretty and vivacious, with an energy that drew you to her. As Ginny was Faith's grandmother's best friend, Faith knew all about the tragic accident that had claimed her life.

"I'm so sorry." The words tumbled out before she could stop them.

Surprise had his eyes widening for just a second. Then his expression became unreadable. He didn't ask why she was sorry. "Thank you. It's been a difficult three years."

Faith had been in Holly Pointe only a few months when Ginny had received a call that her only daughter had been badly injured in a car accident. At the time, the young woman had been living in Manhattan with her husband and twin toddlers. Before Ginny could get to New York, Steph passed away. The twins had survived the crash without a scratch.

"Won't you please join us? Give us a chance to make up for the trouble we caused."

Faith hesitated. She'd planned on this trip to the Busy Bean being a quick in-and-out. The holidays were a busy time at Faith Originals.

Still, Ginny was her grandmother's best friend. Graham was a visitor in her town. Making him feel welcome was the least she could do.

She needed only one thing first. *Caffeine.*

"Thank you. I'd love to get better acquainted. First, let me grab a cup of coffee."

"Tell me what you want, and I'll get it. My treat." He lifted a staying hand when she opened her mouth to protest. "Please. I owe you. My daughter upended you like a nose guard going for the quarterback."

"That's a bit of an exaggeration, don't you think?" The child might have made contact, but if Faith had been paying attention, she could have evaded her. By now, she'd be at the goalposts, er, counter, with a large coffee in hand.

Faith wished Graham would drop the idea of paying, but the determined gleam in those gorgeous green eyes told her that wasn't happening. "Just so we're clear—you don't owe me anything. However, since you insist, I'd love a cup of the Snickerdoodle-flavored coffee."

Graham cocked his head. "Cream? Sugar?"

"Black."

His grin flashed. "One coffee coming right up."

Faith felt the tingle again. Heck, maybe the impact with Charlotte *had* knocked something loose.

Two pairs of curious eyes settled on Faith as she took a seat at the cluttered table.

"Hi, girls. I'm Faith." With a sweep of one hand, Faith gestured to the tabletop. "Looks like you've got a lot to keep you busy."

A partially finished bracelet made of beads sat in front of Charlotte. A coloring book lay open in front of Hannah.

The pleasant rumble of Kenny's laughter had Faith shifting her focus to where Graham was conversing with the shop's owners.

"We're bored."

Faith pulled her attention from the counter and back to the twins. "Really?"

Hannah nodded. Her gaze lingered on a window decorated with snowflake decals. "I want to build a snowman."

Charlotte's mouth formed a pout. "I want to go sledding."

"I'm betting you'll be outside real soon." Though it was cozy-warm inside the Busy Bean, Faith couldn't imagine Graham intended to keep the girls inside all day.

"We were supposed to be at Gramma's house," Charlotte told her. "Uncle Shawn was there, so we had to leave."

Hannah nodded in agreement.

Faith decided the child must have misunderstood. Ginny would never turn away Graham. Or her grandchildren.

Graham returned with not only a cup of steaming coffee, but a freshly baked scone, complete with clotted cream and strawberry jam. "Norma thought you might like this. She said something about it being fresh out of the oven."

Faith caught Norma's eye and mouthed, "Thank you."

Charlotte zeroed in on the pastry like a heat-seeking missile. "Can I have some of it?"

Hannah's hand shot up as if in a classroom. "Me, too. Please."

"Please," Charlotte hurriedly added.

"There's enough here for everyone." Faith picked up a knife and waggled it at Graham. "That includes your dad."

Ignoring his protest, Faith cut the scone in fourths and gestured to the twins.

The girls needed no encouragement to grab a slice.

When she held out the plate to Graham, he shook his head. "The scone was for you. Now it's half gone."

"More than enough." Faith gestured with the knife. "Two pieces. One for me. One for you."

Graham appeared to be doing his best to suppress a smile as he chose the smallest piece. "Are you always this bossy?"

"Sometimes I'm worse."

"Good to know." He chuckled. "And thank you."

"You're welcome." Faith added a dab of clotted cream to the top of her piece, while the girls claimed the jam.

Moments later, Graham sat back and expelled a satisfied breath. "I have to say that was as good as anything I've had in the city."

Faith popped the last bit of scone into her mouth and let the taste roll around on her tongue. She considered the bakeries she'd frequented when she lived—and worked—in Manhattan. He was right.

"Truer words." She inclined her head. "Do you still live in Manhattan?"

Surprise flickered in his eyes as he took a long drink of coffee. Surely he didn't believe Ginny never spoke of him or the girls.

"Upper West Side. Across from the park." His gaze shifted once again to his daughters. "I'm amazed they have room in their stomachs after the breakfast they consumed."

Faith was glad to hear the girls had eaten something more substantial than a bite of scone for breakfast. "I'm not surprised. Ginny is an excellent cook."

"Actually, once we got into town, our first stop was Rosie's Diner." Graham's tone remained easy as his gaze slid to the twins, who were busy eating leftover jam with a spoon. "It seemed rude to arrive on Ginny's doorstep with two hungry girls expecting to be fed."

"I bet she was super excited to see you." Regardless of Charlotte's words, Faith knew Ginny wouldn't turn away family.

"Things were a bit hectic. Steph's brother, Shawn, and his family unexpectedly showed up last night. No notice, but none was needed. Ginny has an open-door policy when it comes to her kids."

Shawn and his wife, Morgan, had married right out of high school and now had three teenage boys. Though Ginny didn't gossip about her kids, Faith knew Shawn and Morgan lived in New Hampshire and struggled to make ends meet.

"Ginny made it clear they'd make room for us." Graham cradled the cup between his hands, and the lines around his eyes deepened. "Shawn was all for it. He's one of those 'the more, the merrier' kind of guys. Me, I gave up sleeping on sofas back in college."

"Air mattresses, Daddy, not the sofa." Charlotte look up from her coloring. "I think sleeping in Gramma's living room sounds like fun."

"If this wasn't a working vacation for me," Graham told Faith, "I might have tried to make it work. But I wouldn't be able to concentrate with the kids and the dog and—"

"Ginny doesn't have a dog," Faith interrupted.

"Shawn and his wife have a bearded collie," Graham informed her. "They brought him along."

Faith pulled her brows together. "I'm not sure I've ever seen that kind of collie."

"Think massive sheepdog. One that knocks over anything—and anyone—in its way."

Not even trying to suppress a smile, Faith grinned. "I take it you're not an animal lover."

"I like them fine, just not in a twelve-hundred-square-foot house that's already housing three adults and three adult-sized boys."

"Good point." Faith understood now why he and the girls weren't staying with Ginny. "Are any of Ginny's other kids coming home for Christmas?"

"From what Ginny said, Seth is spending the holidays with his wife's side of the family." Graham rubbed his chin. "Spence is still in Dubai. He won't come back for a visit until next year."

"They have camels where Uncle Spencer lives," Hannah informed Faith. "One day, I'm going to go there and ride one."

"Me, too," Charlotte told her sister before turning to Faith. "It's like riding a pony, only bumpier."

Faith smiled. "My brother and his friend once raced camels."

The girls' eyes turned as big as saucers before suspicion clouded Charlotte's baby blues. "Are you making that up?"

Graham's equally skeptical look had Faith chuckling.

"My brother once lived in Dubai. He and his friend worked for General Mills, their Middle East and Africa division, for a time." Seeing that the information had done nothing to convince the twins, Faith added, "I've got pictures."

"Do you remember when your uncle sent you pictures of him riding the camel?" Graham asked his daughters.

"Maybe my uncle knows your brother." Charlotte sat upright, and her eyes brightened. "What if they rode camels together?"

"Stranger things have happened." Though Faith knew in a city of three million, it was unlikely Evan and Spencer had met.

Charlotte picked up a crayon, leaving Faith able to focus on Graham. "When did Spencer move to Dubai? Last I knew, he was in San Francisco."

"He accepted a job there last May." He took a long drink of coffee. "Spence heads the marketing and communications division of a firm that deals in freight management and contract logistics on a global level."

"I'm not even sure what that means." Faith offered a little laugh. "It sounds impressive."

"Spence is a go-getter, that's for sure." Graham inclined his head. "What about you?"

Instead of telling him about her shop, Faith tapped a finger against her lips. "I'd say I'm more of a slow-getter than a go-getter."

An endless disappointment to my parents, she thought with a sigh.

The girls giggled.

"You're a slow-getter." Charlotte pointed to her sister.

"Nuh-uh." Hannah shook her head. "I'm a go-getter. You're the slow-getter."

"Girls." Graham's tone held a sharp edge, and the teasing instantly ceased.

When Graham refocused on Faith, he studied her with curious eyes. She braced herself for more questions about her "career," which would undoubtedly be followed by "encouraging words." While usually meant to be supportive, such encouragement always made her feel like she should be doing more.

Wasted potential. That's what her father had declared.

Faith lifted her chin. She didn't care what anyone thought. She loved her business and the life she was building in Holly Pointe.

She didn't have to justify the choices she'd made. Not to her parents. Not to this stranger. Not to anyone.

Graham shrugged. "The girls and I were disappointed with the change in plans."

For a second, Faith was confused. Then she realized he'd moved on in the conversation. He didn't intend to interrogate her or make judgments. Likely because how she lived her life was of little concern to him.

"I gave our nanny the month off for her sister's wedding." Graham's fingers curved around the ceramic coffee cup. "I have a project that absolutely must be completed by the end of December. I figured Ginny would get her twin-time. I could put in the hours on the project undisturbed. Win-win for all."

He shot another glance at the twins, who were now intently licking out the little silver cups that had once held jam and cream. Shaking his head, he continued. "We flew into Burlington this morning, then rented a car and drove the rest of the way here."

"What will you do now?"

"I've been calling around. Every place I've checked is either booked or the accommodations don't meet my needs."

Curious, Faith lifted her cup. "Which are?"

"A suite, rather than simply a hotel room." He glanced at the girls, now busily coloring, then back at Faith. "I need space to work. The girls need space to play."

Faith nodded.

"We may end up returning to the city. That would be unfortunate. I know Ginny was looking forward to spending this time with the girls. But—" Graham expelled a breath and shrugged. "Well, we'll see."

Faith thought of the second floor of her grandmother's home, an area that sat empty between Thanksgiving and New Year's.

The space would be perfect for Graham and the girls.

"There's a suite of rooms on the second floor of my grandmother's house that's available." Faith's tone turned persuasive. "There's a small kitchen and sitting area, as well as two bedrooms, each with their own bath. Trust me when I say you won't find anything nicer in the area."

Suspicion clouded Graham's assessing gaze. "If the space is so nice, why isn't it already rented?"

It was a valid question and one she'd have asked in his position. "My grandmother doesn't normally rent it out in December. With the main floor of the house turning into a Christmas wonderland, the downstairs becomes a noisy beehive. Your girls will likely love all the activity, but if you like to work in the quiet, I suggest noise-canceling headphones."

Interest flickered in his green depths. "How much?"

The rates normally went up during ski season, but because Graham was with Ginny's granddaughters, Faith gave him the summer monthly rate.

She wanted him to take it. For Ginny's sake, she wanted him to stay.

Faith offered him a bright smile. "Interested in a tour?"

Grab your copy of **_Holly Pointe & Candy Canes_** to see how this story ends.

HEARTWARMING STORIES TO KEEP YOU IN THE HOLIDAY SPIRIT

If you want to keep the holiday spirit going, may I recommend the following:

Christmas in Good Hope

Ami and Beck would rather forget the past, but this Christmas of love is one to remember.

It Started With Joy

When love blooms, with a little help from two pint-size matchmakers, Derek and Rachel find unexpected love at Christmas.

Holly Pointe and Candy Canes

If a romance between an artist and an ad executive can't bloom at Christmastime...then when?

Made in the USA
Monee, IL
03 October 2020